KEVIN PARTON

ANTEROS
ABSOLUTE BETRAYAL

Anteros
Absolute Betrayal
by Kevin Parton

Paperback ISBN: 978-1-7398233-0-6
Ebook ISBN: 978-1-7398233-1-3

Cover design by BespokeBookCovers.com

Find out more about the author at
www.KevinPartonBooks.com

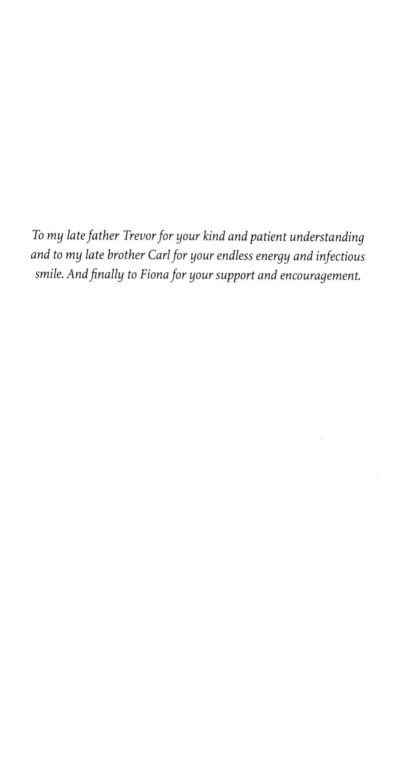

To my late father Trevor for your kind and patient understanding and to my late brother Carl for your endless energy and infectious smile. And finally to Fiona for your support and encouragement.

PROLOGUE

Amandine Faucher set the timer on the detonator and had less than ten minutes to get out of and away from the building. Standing in front of the mirror in the ladies' bathroom, she realised that her lipstick had worn off, so she carefully applied a fresh coat. The deep red shade, her favourite, complimented the fiery red locks of her hair which contrasted with her flawless, pale skin. The door opened, and she watched in the mirror as another dinner party guest entered. Amandine recognised her as the lady who had been laughing too loudly at a nearby table.

'Oh, I don't suppose that I could borrow that, could I?' the woman asked, eyeing the lipstick that Amandine was using.

'Of course, take it, I have another,' she said, smiling as she handed over the lipstick before leaving and making her way back into the main hall.

Her date for the night, Mr Li Jun, was engaged in conversation with another man and he had not noticed her return. She passed through the hall and slipped into a corridor that led to a fire escape where a car and driver would be waiting.

Suddenly, she heard hurried footsteps behind her and raised voices speaking in the local Cantonese tongue. Certain that they were searching for her, Amandine knew she had to create a diversion. Leaving the corridor, she entered a side room that was in darkness. Quietly closing the door behind her, she made her way to the far side of the room where she opened a large set of curtains. The outside security lights illuminated the room. It was a maintenance room filled with service cabinets and pipes ran up the walls and along the ceiling.

Amandine opened several of the cabinets, hoping to find something useful. She found the electrical fuse board and located the mains switch. The door of the room opened just as she flicked the switch. The outside lights were extinguished, along with those in the corridor. The building was now without power. In the main hall, guests were plunged into darkness. The door closed and Amandine heard footsteps running away. From the electrical system, she removed several fuses, which she discarded before making her way back into the corridor. She flung open the fire escape door and stepped in to the warm evening air. The noise of the hustle and bustle of downtown Hong Kong could be heard in the distance. The car was waiting, with the engine running and the lights dimmed.

'Stop!' a voice called out as she headed for the car.

Amandine froze momentarily, then turned slowly towards the voice. The woman from the bathroom, whom she had given the lipstick to, was pointing a gun at Amandine.

'Move now, away from the car,' she said, moving to block Amandine's path.

'I'm sorry, I got lost and...' Amandine replied.

'Shut up,' the woman said, and she flicked the gun sideways to hurry Amandine up.

Amandine watched with relief as the driver got out of the car behind the woman. Help was coming. He slowly crept closer and pulled a gun out of his jacket pocket.

He levelled the gun and fired. Amandine felt the impact on her chest and dropped to her knees, clutching at the stinging pain. Her hands turned red with her blood. She looked up in shock and confusion. Mark, her partner, was coming closer. Standing next to the woman, he raised his gun and aimed directly at Amandine.

'Get into the car Sarah. I'll finish this,' he said.

The woman walked away and got into the car, closing the door behind her.

'Mark, what are you doing? It's me,' Amandine choked out the words. Her blood was dripping through her fingers and running down her dress.

'Goodbye, Amandine,' he said. He pulled the trigger, leaving her for dead in the alley.

Accelerating hard around the corner, the car's engine roared, but the harsh sound was quickly obliterated by the sound of the explosion. The bomb decimated the building. Instantly, the area was turned into a burning mass of fire, destruction and death. Amandine had done her job; she had killed several members of the Zaiqi crime family. But in doing so, she had been betrayed by her own people.

1

ST MODWEN CHAMBERS, LONDON. JUNE 1993

In the reception area, a smartly dressed young woman attended to the occasional visitors and directed them to various rooms, usually for a meeting with a prospective legal representative. The two guests in the Chamberlain suite, on the third floor, were here for an entirely different reason: not to seek expensive legal advice or to be told damning news about a personal affair of theirs, but at the request of Mac Thomason. Mac was a fifty-four-year-old government official who had spent the last thirty-odd years of his career passing through the secretive corridors and passageways of Whitehall.

There wasn't a title for the role that Mac fulfilled and he was answerable only to a panel of three people. He didn't exist in any HR files or records and although he was recognised by most ministers, they simply had no idea exactly what he did, or who he did it for.

Colonel Malcolm Richardson walked towards his seat, carrying the coffee which he had just poured for himself. 'Are you sure that I can't get you anything?' he asked the woman sat at the table with Mac.

'No, thank you,' she replied with a smile.

This was a warm man, she thought as she watched Colonel Richardson sit down in his seat. He seemed honest and sincere, with the confidence that only comes with time and experience. She could tell that they were going to get along just fine.

'Allow me to do the introductions,' said Mac. 'Colonel, this is a friend of mine, who I have known for quite some time and I personally can vouch for her. Please meet Miss Sarah Rantsu. And Sarah, it couldn't give me greater pleasure than to introduce to you Colonel Malcolm Richardson.'

There was the polite shaking of hands between the two new acquaintances before they settled back into their chairs and gave their full attention back to Mac. Both were eager to discover the reason for his request to see them today. Mac rarely met people other than on a one-to-one basis, so today's unusual meeting must be for a good reason.

'You have both worked with me on other matters in the past,' said Mac. 'And I am quite sure that together, you will be able to help me with a job that I have recently been given. It's a home security matter, which requires the strictest confidentiality and skills that I believe only the two of you have.'

Sarah and the Colonel listened as Mac spoke, neither truly understanding how there could be a need for them to work together.

'I require you to find me a male recruit. One that will be used to infiltrate the lives of high-profile targets.'

'Why aren't you using someone from the regular channels?' asked the Colonel.

'Because we're looking for somebody young; someone who hasn't been influenced or corrupted by our ways yet. Someone who is still a regular everyday Joe who can be moulded into exactly what we need. Military or civilian, it doesn't matter,' Mac replied.

'What exactly will they be used for?' asked Sarah. 'Surely you can't expect to use a child for a deep cover task?'

'Not a child, a young adult. One that is eighteen or nineteen, maybe a little older. Young enough, but legal if we ever needed to show any accountability, which we wouldn't contemplate doing, of course. They are to become a weapon to infiltrate and remove our growing threats. And you two are going to be his trainer and handler over the next few years,' said Mac. 'The most important thing is that you find someone who can be moulded and is naturally likeable.'

'Do you have a target in mind?' asked Sarah.

'Yes. And if this works, whoever you find for me will remain operational and be used again and again,' Mac told her. 'All I can tell you for now is that the targets will be predominantly female.'

'Who will he work for, officially, Mac?' asked the Colonel.

'He won't, officially. This is going to be an experiment and the three of us will be the only ones with any knowledge of it, except for my sanctioning officers, of course. But this isn't 'officially' happening.'

Mac gave the Colonel and Sarah more details before asking them if they had any questions.

Neither of them had anything to ask of Mac, but Sarah asked the Colonel if he would be free to meet the following Monday to make plans. The Colonel confirmed he would, and they agreed upon meeting for a late breakfast at Sarah's favourite restaurant, Alicella, on Sicilian Avenue, Holborn.

'Well, it appears that you both have much to be getting on with, so I will show you out,' said Mac, as he shook hands with his guests and led them from the room. 'You both have my personal number if you need to speak with me urgently, but other than that, I shall await contact from you in due course.'

As Sarah and the Colonel left St Modwen Chambers, stepping onto the warm sunny street, just before lunchtime on Friday 25th June 1993, Mac watched them go. He paused for a while, contemplating the task ahead of them. He had an unnerving feeling inside, a coldness that contrasted with the sun's glare, which penetrated through the blinds screening the window he stood before.

'Lesley,' he said to the woman attending to the reception. She looked up from her work and he continued, 'Please ensure that CCTV and any audio recordings of the meeting are erased immediately.'

'Yes Sir, I'll see to it straight away,' Lesley replied.

Within an hour, a faxed message was received. 'MR AND SR TASKED. UPDATE TO FOLLOW ONCE SUBJECT SELECTED. SITUATION COLD.'

COLONEL MALCOM RICHARDSON had served in the British army for 36 years and was fifty-two years old. He had joined as a boy soldier and had served at every rank through to colonel. Originally, he had been with 1 Para, before successfully completing SAS selection, at the rank of sergeant. Here he had remained for 10 years, during which time he deployed on many military and humanitarian campaigns around the world. He was a soldier through and through and had sacrificed his personal life for his career. Although he'd had many lovers over the years, he had always felt that it would be selfish for him to ask another to be tolerant of his military commitments, ones that he was not willing to neglect. He had come close to marrying once, but it was not meant to be, and he was happy with his life choices and their consequences.

Since moving on from the Special Air Service, he had remained in Special Forces and the Secret Intelligence Service in various forms, at times operating as an undercover officer. He had eventually earned his commission as an officer and had remained in the services beyond the regular twenty-two-year military career. He currently held the position of Commanding Officer of Special Operations Northern Ireland, also known as S.O.N.I or the Unit.

This gave him access to all the military personnel records of the Army, Navy, and Royal Air Force. He had a network of contacts throughout these services that kept an eye out for him, identifying unique people. People who stood out from the regular service personnel; people who he could use for his work. His contacts worked in human resources, training departments, operational units, and even military prisons. By some strange coincidence, military prisons often provided his best candidates, who once put back on the right road, became ideal for conducting special duties.

THE COLONEL BEGAN by making several calls and sending out memos, detailing that he was looking for a particular recruit, younger than normal, and not yet institutionalised by the military. He asked his contacts to look for highly intelligent, free-thinking individuals who would be easily lost in a crowd.

It wasn't long before he got responses, which was expected, as his contacts were always keen to find someone for him. He read through the suggestions, dismissing them as he went along.

'This one could be good,' he eventually said to himself as he read through a personnel file. In fact, there were two which caught his attention more than any of the others, not because of any particular detail but because they were almost identical.

'Mmm, interesting,' he thought. 'I'll have a look at those two again later.'

IT WAS A BEAUTIFUL, summers evening, and her date for tonight was due to arrive in five minutes. Sarah Rantsu was almost ready and studying herself in the mirror, when she decided that there was no way she could have a visible panty line in this dress. She wriggled out of her knickers and admired herself again in the mirror. She pulled the figure-hugging dress back in to place and rubbed her hand across her backside, confirming that she had made the right decision. 'What girl needs underwear in temperatures like these?' she thought as she bent down to pick up the silky knickers from the floor. 'Although it is a shame to not wear such luxury,' she said to herself as she placed them back into the perfectly arranged underwear drawer in her dressing room.

Sarah was as confident as she was beautiful, and this added to her attraction. Her Mediterranean features were noticeable but not overpowering, her golden skin and dark eyes being the strongest clue to her partial heritage. She had silky long hair that was just a shade off being black and was a feature that she often wore up, emphasising the elegant lines of her neck and jaw. Her eyes drew attention from her perfectly shaped nose and thin but pert lips that were naturally red and enticing. She was quite tall at 5'10" and rather than muscular or athletic, she was slim yet feminine.

But of everything, it was the way in which Sarah carried herself that made her unique. She had a style and presence that was impossible to not admire; she oozed sex appeal with not so much as an ounce of effort.

She was thirty-one years old, and had been born in southern Italy, a short distance from Sorrento. Her mother had been English and her father a native Italian. They had both died when she was fifteen years old, which was when she had moved to London to live with her only living relative, her grandmother.

She had originally studied languages but had been spotted by MI5 when she had taken part-time work as a translator for a government aide who was under their protection. MI5 had sponsored her through university and then trained her as one of their field operatives. This was how Mac had come to know of her, and he had immediately envisioned how she could be best used for his needs. He had been struck by her beauty from the first time he had seen her. After speaking with her on only several occasions, he had known that he must have her at his disposal. A feeling inside told him she would be perfect for the line of work that he was involved in.

Sarah was immediately removed from MI5 service and all records of her time there were destroyed under the watchful eye of Mac. He had made sure that no one would ever know of any link between Sarah Rantsu and the British intelligence service.

She was an object of beauty, but that did not interest Mac. It was her magnetic personality coupled with her breath-taking looks, which made her a weapon that Mac could use on any enemy of the establishment whenever necessary.

'Right, let's see if Marcus is here,' she said to herself as she went to the window and looked down on to the street. Sure enough, he was there, with the roof down on his convertible Aston Martin. 'Oh, the poor thing, he's brought a cock extension along with him,' she muttered as she waved down at him. 'With you in two shakes,' she called out.

A table at the Dorchester wasn't easy to book at the last minute, you had to reserve at least two months in advance at this time of year - but not Marcus. He had booked the table only a few hours before.

'Would you care to choose the wine?' Marcus asked as he looked at Sarah, hoping that she would ask him to do so on their behalf.

Sarah had read the profile that she had been given on Marcus Antar and knew the answer that was expected of her.

'Oh, I'm not great at these things, won't you choose for us? I have no idea what to go for,' she said across the table with a shy, vulnerable look.

'Of course, let's have a Petrus Pomerol. French wine is by far my favourite.' For a man of Marcus' age, it could have been expected that he would have a young family, or at least a serious partner of some description. However, he had been born into one of the wealthiest families in Oman, and at thirty-two, he had never held down a serious relationship or done a single day's work. He was the quintessential playboy and had an unfortunate personality which made him a most unlikeable character.

Sarah smiled and nodded towards him, in agreement with his choice.

'So, how long are you in London for?' she asked, as the waiter handed menus to them.

'I'm not sure. I guess it depends on what comes up,' he replied. 'No plans at the moment, so I'm flexible.'

'Well, you have the weather on your side, so I'm sure that you will have lots to do, and there is so much going on around here right now,' she replied.

'Yes, yes, I think it would be a mistake to rush back to Muscat, especially when there is so much fun and beauty right here,' he said, looking across the table at Sarah. She gave him the most charming of smiles.

They chatted and laughed together throughout dinner, and Sarah flirted just enough to show interest in Marcus, but not so much as to make him think he had a guarantee of getting what he wanted so much. The evening passed quickly as they enjoyed dinner in the fine settings of the Dorchester Hotel.

'Maybe you could join me in my suite. It will be much more comfortable than it is down in the bar, much quieter,' Marcus suggested, as they walked from the dining room.

'Well, it is getting a little late,' she replied. 'I wonder if I should head off home?'

'Come on, Sarah, surely you have time for one small night cap?' Marcus pleaded.

She almost felt sorry for him with his sad puppy eyes. 'Yes, why not? Live for today,' she replied and gave him a mesmerising smile, flashing her perfect teeth, which lit up her face, making her even more radiant than usual.

'My God, this woman is delicious, I have to have her,' thought Marcus, as he felt himself stirring and becoming aroused. Watching her tongue moisten her lips, he had to look away for a second, in order to hide his thoughts.

'Fabulous, let's go,' he said, offering his arm to her. They rode the lift to the floor of his suite and were soon inside, away from the noise and bustle of the busy dining room.

'Make yourself comfortable. What would you like to drink?' he asked her.

'Oh, just a brandy for me please,' she replied, as she settled on to the large sofa facing where Marcus was preparing drinks.

'Would you like something a little extra?' he asked. From his expression, Sarah knew that this meant it was time for his evening lines of cocaine. His file had referred to his habitual recreational drug use, highlighting it as a vulnerability.

'I'm fine, but why don't you go ahead, I've heard that it can do wonders for...' She hesitated and smiled coyly at him before going on, 'You know, it's meant to make it sensational, isn't it?'

Marcus's face lit up as he turned to look at her and he felt his erection pushing against his trousers. 'I'm going to fuck your brains out,' he told her, overcome with excitement. 'Give me one minute,' he said, going through to the bedroom to retrieve the supply of cocaine that he always kept.

When he left, Sarah moved across the room to fetch her drink. She placed her handbag on the drinks cabinet so that it was pointing back at the sofa and activated the camera inside it to record. She heard Marcus opening a drawer in the bedroom and then snort, heavily, twice. She shouted through to him, 'Bring it in here, so that you definitely have enough. I don't want you running out of steam on me'. She took a small capsule out of her handbag and emptied its contents into the drink that Marcus had prepared for himself. She picked up both drinks and returned to the sofa, where she placed them on to the small table.

As she did so, Marcus came in to the room, completely naked, carrying a tray that was piled with cocaine.

'Put it here,' Sarah said, indicating to the table where she had placed their drinks.

Marcus placed the tray on to the table and came towards her, desperate to have her.

As he reached down to her on the sofa, Sarah twisted herself and pushed Marcus down into the spot where she had been sitting, now straddling him. He moved to sit up, but she challenged him and pushed him down again.

'No, sit where you can see me,' she ordered. Her voice was huskier than before, and Marcus could see an aroused look in her eyes that matched the horny smile on her face. 'I want you to see me as I undress,' she said.

She lifted his drink, which she passed to him, and then stepped back. His eyes were burning through her dress as he sat back with his legs stretched out in front of him. Sarah sipped her drink and placed the glass down on to a low table, bending over to emphasise the line of her legs and the curve of her backside. He saw the glow of her skin and the small blonde vellus hairs that grew at the tops of her legs. As she stood up straight, she began to lift her dress a little and dance slowly. He watched as more of her legs became visible. He could see that they were slender, but strong and toned. Her hips swayed from side to side and her pelvis gyrated in small rotations. Marcus knew soon she would be sitting on top of him with her pelvis circling around his hardness.

'Drink,' she commanded, pointing at his glass. 'Drink it quickly and then play with yourself for me'. As she spoke, she lowered one of her hands to the triangle between her legs and explored herself with her fingers. He could see the pleasure on her face as her eyes closed, her mouth opened, and she made the slightest of soft groans. Marcus gulped at his drink, finishing it in three swallows. He tossed the glass across the room and took hold of himself firmly with both hands.

Sarah slowly lowered the strap of her dress from one shoulder, revealing the tops of her full, firm breasts. Marcus wanted them in his hands. 'Take them out. Show me your breasts,' he said. She moved closer to him now, within touching distance. His senses were heightened and he could smell her. He reached out to take hold of her upper thighs. He looked up into her eyes, and she spoke.

'Twenty, twenty-one, twenty-two and I think you're ready,' she said, as she stood up straight. Marcus went to sit up, but he could feel nothing. He was paralysed. He tried to speak but could not, his body was burning and his breathing was suddenly strained. He looked at her and saw that she was moving into the bedroom. Again, he tried to get up, but could not even lift his head, no matter how hard he tried. He screamed in anger, but only managed a gargled sound.

'The bitch, what is she doing?' he thought, 'What is this and who is she, really?'

Sarah came back into the room to where Marcus was slumped on the sofa. She was carrying a briefcase in one hand and a pillow in the other. She knelt in front of him, placing the pillow and then the briefcase over his cock. She began to speak.

'We only have another four minutes before you are dead. If you don't tell me what I need to know, there is nothing I can do to help you. But if you help me, I will give you the antidote that will save you'. She spoke in a calm but authoritative voice. 'If you understand me, blink twice for yes.' It took a moment to sink in, but he blinked twice to acknowledge her.

'Good, is the memory stick in here?' Sarah asked, pointing at the briefcase on his lap. Marcus blinked twice and tried to shout out as he did, but no words left his mouth. Sarah opened the briefcase and looked through it quickly, seeing that there was no memory stick there.

'Three and a half minutes. Can you feel your heart burning? You are going to die if I don't help you, your choice,' she said to him. He blinked wildly, and Sarah could see the veins in his neck straining as Marcus fought to move.

Sarah closed the briefcase and walked over to her bag. From it, she removed a syringe and a small knife before returning to him and kneeling down again. She lifted the briefcase and the pillow and saw that he was still hard. She looked directly into his eyes and showed him the knife in her hand.

'I need the memory stick. I can give you one injection that will save your life, or I can cut this off and take it back to my boss to prove that I tried to negotiate with you. It's up to you, but we only have three minutes left,' Sarah said matter-of-factly.

Marcus knew she would never get out of the hotel alive. She may have not left alive, even before this, if he had used her how he usually used women. In his mind he pictured strangling her as he fucked her, just like he had many others before. The little bitch would pay for this, he would make sure she did.

'So, tell me, is it in the bedroom?' she asked, holding the knife against the base of his cock. 'You can still feel pain, Marcus, even though you can't move,' she said, pushing the knife against his cock, just enough for him to feel the blade.

His eyes widened in fury. No one had ever treated him

like this before and he would see her suffer for doing so. She pulled on the blade and he felt a stinging sensation. He blinked repeatedly, and Sarah smiled in response.

'Good, is it in the bedroom?' No response. 'In here?' He blinked twice and looked over to the drink's cabinet. Sarah followed his eyes and saw that he was looking at the cabinet.

She went to the drinks cabinet and searched through it. There it was, inside, right where she had been, only minutes before. She picked up the memory stick along with her bag and stopped the recorder. She then carefully placed the memory stick into her bag, which she snapped shut.

Sarah walked back over to Marcus and sat next to him. She held the syringe up so that he could see it, and then put her hand on to his chin, turning his face towards hers. She smiled at him and asked, 'Would you like me to give this to you now?' He blinked twice and strained to nod his head, but could not do so. He could feel the burning in his chest and wondered what she was waiting for.

'Fucking do it! Inject me quickly, you stupid bitch,' he thought. Sarah looked at him as she smiled. She was going to make him wait. He could see a sadistic glint in her eyes that he hadn't seen before.

'Tell me, how many girls have you killed?' she asked him. She was waiting for his answer, but he could not speak, no matter how much he tried. 'Over one hundred?' she suggested.

Marcus stared at her in disbelief. 'How the hell did she know about that. Who the fuck was she?' he wondered in horror.

'You have less than a minute now. Blink, if it's more than one hundred.' She was no longer smiling, and her voice had hardened.

He slowly blinked, first once and then again to confirm

that it was over one hundred. It was, in fact, one hundred and seventeen, and he remembered almost all of them by either name or some detail that he had clung on to for a sadistic memory.

'Thank you for being honest with me Marcus, I really appreciate honestly. And because you have been honest with me, I want to be honest with you. This isn't an antidote in here.' She looked at the syringe and depressed its plunger, emptying its contents. The fluid fell through the air and landed on to his legs and crotch. With all of his might, he strained to sit up, but his muscles were locked. It was hopeless. All that it did was to intensify the pain that was moving from his chest, down into his torso, and stomach.

'Just water,' she said. 'I told you a little lie before. You will soon feel your organs closing down and eventually your heart will stop. Before that you will find it difficult to breathe.' She could see the panic in his eyes. 'You'll experience one last, intense rush of pain and heat and then, poof, you'll be gone.' She smiled and watched his expression.

His eyes widened; tears formed in them, and then one fell down his cheek. 'Oh baby, don't cry,' she said as she wiped a tear away. 'I thought you liked this sort of thing. By the way, this will appear as a drug overdose, so no one will look for me. And it will take a few days before they realise that you've lost the information that you just gave away to me on the memory stick.' She stood up, collected all her belongings and returned to where Marcus was sitting.

'Not long now darling, thank you for dinner, ciao, ciao.' Sarah blew him a kiss, turned, and walked out of the suite, placing the "Do not disturb" sign on the door handle as she went.

Marcus was dead by the time the door closed behind Sarah. With the combination of the cocaine that he had taken himself, the 100 percent pure cocaine and accelerant mix Sarah had added to his drink, he was never going to survive. An autopsy would show the high levels of cocaine in his body, and no further investigation would be made. It would be an unfortunate death for an overindulgent play-boy, who had not known his own limits and had overdosed.

Rather than pass back through the hotel reception area, Sarah left through a side door and made one call, following which the CCTV was put back into operation. An engineer had been working on the hotel's CCTV for the last four hours, after it had suddenly stopped working. Once his job was done, the engineer also left and made a call to confirm that no recording of Sarah at the location existed.

2

S arah arrived early for her 10 am breakfast at Alicella
with the Colonel. She knew he would not be late
and although it was typical for her to never arrive on
time when meeting a gentleman; she had no intention of
keeping this one waiting. She knew he was someone who
she would in time both like and respect. She had felt it
when they had first met, just a few days ago. This was why
she had met him here in the restaurant that her grandma
had used to bring her to, a place that held happy memories
for her.

'Good morning Miss Rantsu,' said the Colonel, as he
stood to great her. He came around the table and pulled out
her chair.

'Hello Colonel, Ciao. You must call me Sarah by the way.
How are you today?' she replied, as she leaned towards him
and greeted him by touching cheeks in her customary way.

'I'm very well, thank you,' the Colonel replied, allowing
her to sit down, before making his way back to his seat.
'How about yourself? Did you have a good weekend?' As he
sat opposite her, he realised that she really was beautiful.

Even more than she was in the archive photographs he had looked through whilst checking out her credentials. He trusted Mac with his life, but he had still investigated Sarah's background for himself. Mac may have removed any record of Sarah's existence, but the Colonel had still found a way to research her credentials using his extensive resources.

'Yes, thank you,' Sarah replied. 'I had a spot of work to do but I went out for a lovely dinner, and of course, with this weather that we are having, it was excellent.'

'Excellent' the Colonel said. 'Let's get something to eat then, should we? I'm peckish this morning'. As he sat with Sarah, the Colonel realised he was genuinely happy to be in her company. What he had read about her was chillingly accurate: she was a wolf in sheep's clothing.

Over the next hour, they ate and discussed the task ahead of them, the roles they would assume and the good judgement of Mac for bringing them together on this task.

'I've been through MI5 and MI6 files and nobody really stands out for the role,' Sarah told the Colonel. 'I think that this project is going to become a fraction dirty and I'm not confident that one of their people will be right for it. Not only that, but there will always be an element of interference if they release someone to us, and we definitely don't want that.' Sarah had said what the Colonel had already concluded, which was why he hadn't made enquiries with his contacts at the security services in the home office.

'Yes, I agree,' he told her. 'I've actually found several possibilities. Two in particular stand out to me. But I fear it may be coincidence which makes them stand out.'

'How so?' Sarah asked him.

Her eyes flicked briefly to the scar on the Colonel's face. She had noticed it immediately when they had first met.

Running diagonally from his right eye, down his cheek to the corner of his mouth, it added to his rugged appeal. The colonel wore it well, and his innate self-confidence set him apart from other men. She made a note to herself that she would find out how he had come by the scar. She would normally have done a little investigating in to the Colonel's history before now, had she not been so preoccupied with several other tasks.

'Well,' the Colonel began, 'they are both from the Junior Infantry Battalion, the boy soldier training facility in Kent. They both did a year's training there, exactly one year apart, and both came top of their respective intakes, excelling in all areas. Richard Scholls is the civilian educational instructor down there and a friend of mine. He tells me he recommended one of them for officer training but he turned it down.'

The Colonel took two paper files from his satchel and handed them to Sarah. For security reasons, neither of the files contained the names of the men whose details were inside.

'Why did he turn down an opportunity like that? Isn't it every soldier's desire to become a commissioned officer?' Sarah asked as she began reading the first file.

'That's his file that you are reading now. Carl Parsons,' the Colonel said. 'He told Scholls he had only joined the army so that he could go to be with his older brother. His brother was deployed as an infantry soldier in the Gulf war. He told Scholls he didn't want to do anything that would interfere with or delay him in joining his brother out in Iraq.'

'His education results are exemplary. He achieved the highest possible scores. Why didn't somebody push him to go for the officer training assessment at least?' Sarah asked with a furrowed brow as she continued reading.

'They tried, but he eventually went AWOL.' The Colonel paused for a second and then added, 'One month before he was due to finish his training, he went absent without leave and spent a month living in London.'

'Why? And what did he do in London? Is that where he's from?' Sarah was now looking at a picture of the candidate in the file.

'That is a recent photograph,' the Colonel said. 'No, his family are from the Midlands. He went AWOL because his brother had returned from Iraq and as a result, he didn't want to be in the army any longer. He apparently thought that they were a bunch of idiots.'

'I bet they were pleased with his opinion of them!' she replied.

'He's from a regular, stable family: mother and father at home and a happy childhood. He's the youngest of three children, having an older sister and a brother, who I mentioned. He was a gentle, sensitive child, who was close to his family, none of whom ever imagined that he would join the military. Although described as bright and capable of achieving excellent results in his school reports, he has no qualifications. He left school as soon as he could, to join his brother; even forging his parents' signatures on his army applications forms so that he couldn't be stopped. He went to London because his family told him they were ashamed of him for going AWOL. His father told him he wasn't welcome at home and that he should hand himself back in to the army. Because of his own military background, serving in the Malayan war himself and his own father having been in the Military Police during World War 2, his father would not relent. The young man didn't want to, so he remained AWOL. Begging and sleeping rough, he spent a month in London just seeing the sights.'

'What happened after he handed himself in?' Sarah asked. 'I like his story so far; he seems a rebel.' Sarah looked up at the Colonel and smiled. 'Us women all love a rebel Colonel.' The Colonel chuckled in response.

'He completed the rest of his training at an adult facility and eventually joined his regiment, where he remains in service today. Ironically, his brother left the army straight after the Gulf war, and they never served together.'

'You are kidding me,' she replied, looking at the Colonel to see if he was.

'No. His brother was due to leave the army anyway, prior to the Gulf war starting. But like many others in the same boat, he wasn't released when it kicked off. So, as soon as it finished, he was gone.' The Colonel was smiling, but not at the misfortune, more out of pity.

'So, looking at these dates... he's now nineteen and he can leave in two years, which I presume he will want to,' Sarah stated, looking at the Colonel.

'Yes, to the timings, and probably yes again to him wanting to get the hell out of there as soon as he can,' he replied.

'Then why do you think he is a possibility for us?' Sarah asked.

'Richard Scholls remembers him well. Richard always thought that this one should have gone on to college or something rather than joining the military. Richard said that this Parsons lad didn't fit in naturally with the other soldiers. This was why he thought that he may have been more suited to being an officer. He described him to me as seeming to be lost. Unchallenged and at times uninterested in his training, but still always committed to completing the task and desperate to come first. I think Richard had taken a shine to him as he said that he felt disappointed that he hadn't been able to guide him more. In fact, Richard said that he hadn't met another student like him before or since. He asked me to let him know what has happened to him since he last saw him.' The Colonel stopped briefly, and Sarah looked up at him. 'I think we need to see him for ourselves,' he said.

'Ok, I agree, what about the other one?' Sarah asked as she opened the second file.

'Well, remember that these two were in the same training facility exactly one year apart from each other. Danny Lavin, whose file you have in your hand left and Parsons replaced him. One intake left at the end of their training and another came in to take their place. They had the same instructors, same facilities, resources and almost identical results in all that they did.'

'Only this one, Lavin finished his training and didn't go AWOL,' Sarah interjected.

'He didn't go AWOL until he got to his regiment, and then he went AWOL, within months of getting there'. As the Colonel finished speaking, Sarah looked up at him again. Her eyes showed disbelief, and she turned through the file to find the detail.

'My word,' she said. 'Did they ever meet, to give each other ideas?' It was there, in the file, AWOL for eleven weeks, sent to military gaol in Colchester afterwards.

'They never met. But if I told you they had actually slept in the same bed space, would you believe me?' the Colonel asked, looking at her with a grin on his face.

'Explain, I'm intrigued,' she replied.

'By coincidence, as Lavin finished his training and left, Parsons arrived, and was allocated that same bed space.'

'No, really? So, one year apart, they slept in the same dormitory and even the same bed?'

'Yes, that was what I meant, when I said that I fear it is coincidence which makes them stand out to me,' the Colonel said.

'What is Lavin's background?'

'Well, almost the opposite of Parsons. He lived with his mother for the first few years of his life until she couldn't cope with his abusive stepfather and gave Lavin up for adoption.'

'So, he was adopted?'

'Unfortunately, not straight away. He was passed from one foster carer to the next until he was twelve, when he was taken on by a German couple who were living in the UK. After living with them for a year, they returned to Berlin and took him with them. There was a bit of a social services blunder in that they never followed up on this. They just let him go and closed his file,' the Colonel explained.

'Was he ok, did this couple look after him?' Sarah asked.

'No idea. He was never registered with the German authorities. We have found no school information, no medical records, nothing. The next time he shows up is when he came back to the UK. He was sixteen years old, alone, and joined the Junior Army. Richard remembered him as being quick-tempered and fiery. He would fight anyone for anything and almost certainly win'.

'Does he have any siblings and what of his mother and father?'

'No siblings. His father was gone before he was born and his stepfather has spent more time in prison than out. His mother was murdered by the stepfather when Lavin would have been ten years old. He wasn't there when it happened, of course. It's a tragedy,' the Colonel said.

'Oh, it's awful. No wonder he is angry. The poor thing, he must be in emotional turmoil.'

'Yes, I'm sure. I imagine he has plenty of unresolved issues. Due to living in Berlin, he is totally fluent in German. One thing that stood out to Richard while Lavin was in training was his natural ability to adjust to military life. He said that rather than behave like a teenager, Lavin behaved like a war machine - an absolute monster when he switched his mind to it.'

'We have to see them both. It must be a coincidence, you are right. But it's a very interesting one. Let's find out more.' Sarah closed the files and handed them back to the Colonel.

Once Sarah and the Colonel had left, the lone man, sitting in a booth on the far side of restaurant also stood to leave. He was satisfied with what he had learnt. He was also confident that after many years of preparation, his plans were going to succeed. Dalton Gruber was an aloof character who seldomly socialised, or even conversed with others. He didn't feel any affection for other people and believed that a large-scale cull of the population was essential if the world had any chance of survival. He was an unsympathetic character who rarely felt any emotion, guilt in particular. As he passed the Colonel's table, he picked up Sarah's glass and placed it into a bag, carefully preserving her fingerprints. His mind circled as he tried to fathom who she was, but he could not find the answer, which frustrated him.

'Sir, that is not your glass,' the waiter called to him.

Gruber turned but did not speak. Instead, he looked at the waiter and allowed his eyes to convey his thoughts.

The waiter, only a young man, instantly knew that this was not an argument he wanted to have and nervously mumbled, 'Oh, I'm sorry Sir. My mistake.'

Gruber left with the glass; the interruption already forgotten. He had pressing business to take care of, so got into his car and made his way to the address he had been watching for several weeks, a high-end brothel. He felt a surge of pleasure in the knowledge that he was about to do something useful; something that would hurt an adversary.

Once there, Gruber parked around the corner and removed his glasses, which he had only worn for a disguise. As he locked the car and walked towards his target, he thought through his intentions and checked that he had made no oversights. Confident in his plan, he turned towards the front door on which he knocked four times in slow succession. After a moment, he heard a movement behind the door and sensed that he was being observed. The door opened, and a man regarded him in silence.

'I have a meeting with Charlene,' Gruber said. 'She is a relative.'

Hearing the prearranged entry requirement, the man stepped to one side to allow Gruber past and into an enclosed hallway. He closed the front door and moved past Gruber to the next door, which led from the hallway into the house. This door was made of solid steel and Gruber was satisfied with his plan. The man knocked on the door and looked up at a CCTV camera mounted on the ceiling.

Hearing the magnets in the locking device release the door, Gruber took a tiny can out of his pocket and sprayed in the camera's direction, covering its lens in grease, rendering it useless. The man was caught off guard and slow to react. By the time he realised what Gruber had done, it was too late. The blade severed his spinal cord at the base of his neck, causing him to collapse to the floor. Each of the following stabs were delivered precisely to ensure that he would not live.

Gruber placed the knife away and took a second to check himself before he went through the door and into the property. He pushed the door shut behind him and smiled at the idea of being in the fox's den.

'Yes, that's it. I'm inside the fox's den,' he thought. 'And Mr Fox is going to see just how fucking cross I am that he has been stealing chickens.'

A large staircase adorned with paintings ran up to the first floor and continued around to create a balcony. Gruber could see six rooms and calculated how long his task would take if each of them were occupied. From the left, he heard footsteps and saw a girl of perhaps seventeen wearing lingerie come through an archway. She smiled at him and held out her hand as she headed towards the staircase.

'Are you Charlene?' he asked, returning her smile as he took her hand.

'If you like. I can be anyone that you want me to be,' she told him with a voice that convinced him she was younger than seventeen.

'I would like you to be my assistant,' he replied.

She looked at Gruber and was about to reply when he tightened his grip on her hand. Her eyes widened when she saw his icy stare, and she nodded.

'Take me to the room from where they are watching us,' Gruber instructed her. 'And smile.'

The girl instantly understood and led him up the stairs to one of the doors off the balcony. She squeezed his hand tightly when they approached the door and allowed him to pass a step ahead of her. Gruber inclined his head towards the door and the girl nodded to confirm that this was the observation room.

In an instant, he was inside, having pushed the girl ahead of him as a shield. The two men staring at the screens were slow to react and initially only saw the girl. Their attention had been on the in-room camera views, showing the depraved acts demanded by the clients.

The first man saw nothing but felt a hand on his forehead just before his throat was cut so deeply that his head almost came loose. The second reached for the pistol on the table at his side, but never got that far. His hand was there one second and gone the next, leaving him stunned and looking at the severed limb. Gruber wanted to delay his death as things were moving far too quickly, as yet he had made no one suffer. But his priority now was to disable the cameras. He killed the man by pushing his head forwards to expose the back of his neck and cutting into his spine in several places. The man slumped in his seat and died as planned. Gruber checked the girl had not fled and was pleased to see that she had stayed and was watching him work.

'Are you going to kill me?' she asked.

'Not unless you have done anything bad,' Gruber replied, to which she shook her head. 'How many more of them are there?'

'Only Pavel. He is with Alyona in her room,' the girl said.

'Take me there.'

The girl led Gruber to one of the remaining five doors and stood in front of it. She put her hand out and gently pushed Gruber to the side of the door before she then opened it wide. The grunts from inside came to a stop and an angry male voice called out.

'What the fuck are you doing?'

'Would you like someone to come and join you?' the girl asked as she looked at Pavel, who was on top of a distressed Alyona.

'Yes, you little whore, get your ass in here,' Pavel replied.

'Please make this hurt.'

'You're fucking right I will,' Pavel said as he stood and made to grab the girl.

'I will,' Gruber replied as he shot past her in to the room and met Pavel.

His blade was not out yet, and he used his body to take Pavel off balance and toss him in to the air. The naked Russian was winded as he crashed to the floor, but quickly got up to fight. Three of his ribs were broken by the kick that Gruber landed on his chest and he again fell to the floor. Gruber removed his blade and used it to cut the longus tendon at the rear of both of Pavel's legs, making it unbearable for him to stand up.

Gruber flinched momentarily but realised that it was the girl entering the room to comfort Alyona, who was terrified. The girl quietened Alyona and assured her she was safe as she spoke in Estonian.

Gruber turned his attention back to Pavel. He circled him and looked into his eyes to watch his spirit dissolve as the realisation hit that death was coming. Gruber saw it and smiled.

'Do you want me to cut off an ear or your dick?' Gruber asked him.

Pavel began to cry and reached to protect his penis. With incredible precision and unbelievable speed, Gruber leapt past him and used the blade to remove an ear that promptly fell by his side. Pavel reached to his head and placed his hand where his ear had been a moment before. His cries grew and Gruber signalled for him to be silent by placing a finger to his own lips and making a shush sound.

'You,' Gruber said to the girl, 'Come here.'

She left Alyona and got off the bed. Standing next to him, she looked down at Pavel and the sorry mess he now was. She remembered all the times he had raped and beaten her, and she knew what she was meant to do. She held her hand out and felt the surprisingly light weight of the blade as Gruber handed it to her.

'No, please I beg you,' Pavel said as he saw the girl with the blade. 'I will do anything, please, no.'

'That is what I said to you each time you raped me, you bastard.'

Gruber held him down and covered his mouth to stifle his screams. He left space for her to work and knew when it was done. He took the blade back and slashed Pavel's throat to finish him off.

'As I enter each room, you are to round up the girls and leave with them. Here, take this,' Gruber said to the girl as he handed her a package.

'What is this?' she asked.

'Money. Share it between them and then go to the police.'

She nodded; he was impressed with her handling of the situation. One by one, Gruber went into each room and eliminated the client who was there, ensuring that they would commit no despicable acts again. After confirming that the girls had all gone and no one remained alive in the property, he himself left and headed for his car.

Unlocking the door, he glimpsed someone who must have followed him. He turned and went for his blade, but stopped when the girl cried out in fear.

'What are you doing?' he asked, startled.

'I can't go to the police,' she replied.

'Why? They will help you if you tell them what you have been through.'

'Not me, they won't,' the girl said sharply as the sound of police sirens wailed in the distance. She was panicking.

'What did you do?'

She looked at him for a second and he wasn't sure that she was going to answer.

'I killed my mother, but she deserved it.'

Gruber knew the police were only minutes away at the most. He had to make a decision.

'Get in,' he told her. 'Put your seat belt on and stopping looking like that.'

'Like what?' she asked him from the passenger seat of the car.

'Like you are guilty of something. Smile and relax in case they come past'. He slowly drove the car away and watched in his mirror as two police cars passed them, heading for the brothel.

'What is your name?' he asked the girl. 'Your real name?'

'Terhi Johanson.'

While Gruber drove in silence, he made his decision and visualised the future. Terhi Johanson was now his new understudy, and she would eventually fit perfectly into his plan. She just didn't know it yet.

3

AUGUST 1993

Chester had been home to the regiment for the last two and a half years, and was today the venue for the recruitment drive that Colonel Richardson and several of his staff members were carrying out.

A company of soldiers at a time sat in the parade hall to listen to the input on Special Operations Northern Ireland. After introductions, the S.O.N.I team gave a presentation that briefly described the type of work that they carried out. They emphasised that applications to join them were open to all serving military personnel, male and female from all the services, Army, RAF, Navy and Marines. All the soldiers present were listening intently, as it was known that the S.O.N.I staff worked in the highest levels of the intelligence world. The last person to speak at each presentation was Colonel Richardson.

'Thank you all for listening to my team of dedicated men and women,' he said to the audience. 'I would just like to add a couple of important details.'

He was wearing corduroy trousers, a tweed jacket, and smart tan-coloured leather shoes. 'What my staff do, is a dangerous job. They often work alone in scary places, with no support or backup at all. Sometimes they are killed. This isn't for the faint-hearted.' He was looking through the crowd, deliberately resting his gaze on individuals with each sentence that he spoke. 'I'm not looking for the best shot amongst you, or tough guys. I'm looking for people who can think for themselves. Think fast and act upon their own initiative.'

He looked around as he walked across the front of his audience. The Colonel made eye contact with the Private who was the intended target of the recruitment drive; the reason he had brought his team to Chester. He had made it his priority to locate where Private Carl Parsons had been seated shortly before the presentation had begun. He made sure that Parsons was looking back at him before he went on speaking. 'I'm not looking for people who only follow orders. I want the brightest and best amongst you. This will be far more mentally demanding than anything that any of you have ever done, more so than SAS selection. I can vouch for that, as I have done and passed both, selection and the training for S.O.N.I'.

He continued to look directly at Parsons and said, 'So, if you believe that you have what it takes, and you really want to be part of our unique family, get your applications filled in. If they are approved by your company commander, I will look forward to seeing you in the future'. He smiled, then turned to the Regimental Sergeant Major and said, 'All yours, RSM Green'.

As the soldiers filed out of the lecture hall, he saw Parsons look back over his shoulder. Just a quick glance, but he looked back for sure. 'He will apply,' the Colonel thought to himself.

'Regimental Sergeant Major,' he called over to WO1, RSM Green.

'Yes Sir,' replied Green, whilst bracing his body upright slightly, as a show of respect.

'Can you set up a little competition for me? A bit of fun really, but something to give your lads a challenge, if they are up to it.'

As a young corporal, many years ago, WO1 Green had himself been part of S.O.N.I. Although he and the Colonel had never been operational together, they had monitored the other's careers, and had nothing other than respect for each other.

'Fun and a challenge, Sir?' Green replied, as a knowing grin spread across his face. 'Anything in particular that you have in mind?'

'Well, I just so have the fittest lad you've ever seen, here in my team with me today. How about this? If any of this lot can beat him over 8 miles with weapons and twenty-five pounds of kit, I'll cover this weekend's beer tab for the Sergeants' Mess.' The Colonel knew that WO1 Green would accept the challenge and lifted his hand to shake on it.

'You're on, Sir,' Green said, shaking his hand to seal the deal.

'Make sure that every one of them takes part, Regimental Sergeant Major,' the Colonel added. 'It will improve your chances of winning and give me the chance to look at a few of them, if they are all there.' He had a smile on his face that told Green that he had seen someone of interest.

'Yes Sir,' he replied. 'Every one of them. I'll have it sorted for 1400 hours.'

With that, Green turned and headed off to make the

arrangements for the challenge, which was now only three hours away.

By 1345 hours, every soldier in C company was on parade and formed up in three ranks outside the company headquarters building. The three platoon sergeants had already spoken with their respective platoons and briefed them on the task ahead. Each soldier had their SA80 rifle to carry, and the required twenty-five pounds of weight in their webbing, which they wore on a belt around their waist. The sergeants were aware of the prize that was on offer to them, if one of their soldiers could beat the visitor.

As Sergeant Major WO2 Riley came out of the headquarter building, the soldiers were called to attention by Sergeant Lloyd.

'Company, company attention,' he bellowed at the top of his lungs. And in perfect timing, every soldier present stood smartly to attention.

'Right, you lot, stand at ease, relax,' Sergeant Major Riley ordered. 'Sergeant Lloyd, is everyone here?'

'Yes Sir, eighty-nine men, including NCO's present and correct,' said Sergeant Lloyd.

WO2 Riley addressed the company. 'Gents, I believe it has been explained to you what you have to do this afternoon. Does anyone think they can win it for me?'

None of the soldiers spoke, and Riley looked around, trying to find a few familiar faces. 'Scott, Burney, how about you two?' he said as he found them in amongst the ranks. Neither of them replied, but both knew that although they would be near the front of the race, if they came first, it would only be by chance. 'Parsons, where are you?' He found him at the far end of the parade. 'I'm expecting one of you three to sort this chap out, whoever he is, ok?' He walked over to Parsons and asked him, 'Is it in the bag then, can you beat this fella from S.O.N.I.?'

'Hopefully, Sir,' Parsons replied, with a cheerful smile on his face.

'Hopefully,' echoed WO2 Riley. 'Hopefully. Thank God you weren't leading the beach landings at Dunkirk. Hopefully? I want to hear a definitely, not a "hopefully"'. He had a grin on his face as he spoke to Parsons, mockingly, but it was in good humour. 'If I say that you can't beat him, you'll do it just to piss me off, won't you, Parsons?' he said, and several laughs could be heard from the soldiers.

'Silence,' shouted Sergeant Lloyd to bring them back in to line.

Riley knew Parsons well and that to set a personal challenge, or to give him a point to prove, was a sure way of provoking a response from him.

'Sir, if I don't win, I'll die trying,' Parsons said to WO2 Riley in a low voice, sincerely.

Riley feared Parsons might one day kill himself whilst trying to prove a point. In the year and a half since Parsons had joined the company, he had never seen him give anything other than 100 percent effort to everything. He liked this young man and could see that he had great potential: he was brighter than the average infantry soldier, far brighter.

'Well, there is far too much paperwork for a death in camp, so you had better just do the job and come first without behaving like a drama queen, don't you think?' WO2 Riley asked.

'Yes Sir,' Parsons agreed.

'Sir, he's certainly a queen,' another soldier said from amongst the ranks, and laughter exploded.

Before Sergeant Lloyd could shout, he saw that WO2 Riley was laughing also and let the interruption go.

'Queeny. Yes, that suits you, Parsons,' Riley chuckled.

OUTSIDE THE GYM, a sergeant outlined the route. The race would comprise of eight and a half laps of the perimeter road that ran along the inside of the camp boundaries. The last lap would finish outside the company headquarters.

Parsons made sure that he was towards the front, near to the start line when they were told to get in to place. He still hadn't seen this mystery man from S.O.N.I. and wondered if it was a hoax to make everyone run harder. He could, however, see the Colonel from S.O.N.I. stood talking with WO2 Riley, and for a second he thought they were looking at him, talking about him.

'Are you ready, set, go,' called out the sergeant, and they were off, all jostling against each other to get ahead.

Parsons looked to see where Scott and Burney were, just to check that they would not take an early lead. They were both running at his shoulder and gave him a nod when they saw he was looking for them. This was an 8 miler with heavy kit, so they were happy to sit back for a while and let the racing hares go off on their own.

At the front of the pack was a group of five soldiers, running one behind the other with DC in the lead. DC was an abbreviation of Death Child, as he was a morbid character who spoke of suicide and killings far more often than made people comfortable. Parsons was fifty metres behind this group with Scott and Burney. As they jogged, they discussed who the mystery runner from S.O.N.I. could be.

Burney suddenly asked who was running directly behind DC.

'It's Connor,' Scott replied.

'It can't be,' Burney told him, in between breaths.

'Why can't it be?' Parsons asked, now looking ahead to the leading pack.

'Connor is on compassionate leave for a funeral. He left last night,' Burney told him.

Their pace instantly increased, and they were now approaching the next pass of the company headquarters. Parsons stretched ahead of Scott and Burney and was the first to see WO2 Riley stood outside the building. Riley, who stood with the Colonel, waved his pace stick and shouted.

'What are you doing? Don't let him get a lead on you.'

As he got closer, Parsons asked with genuine interest and confusion, 'Who sir?'

'That fucker at the front that you are meant to be beating, you idiot, get a move on,' Riley bellowed out.

'Bollocks,' Parsons thought. 'Time to get a move on then'. He closed the gap between himself and the front runners over the next lap.

'Here he is. I told you he wouldn't be far away,' DC said to the runner at his shoulder. Parsons looked across at who he now knew was the runner from S.O.N.I. 'This is the one you've got to beat,' DC continued. As he spoke, DC nodded towards Parsons.

'Don't tell him this, you clown,' Parsons thought. 'There's the element of surprise gone. Well done, DC.'

'Anyway, I'm knackered. I'll leave it to you two now, see ya,' DC said as he reduced his running pace and let them go ahead.

After a minute or two, the S.O.N.I. guy said, 'I'm Gav mate, what's your name?'

'Carl,' replied Parsons.

'Long way to go still. You just stick at this pace and stay with me, then we can race for the win on the last lap,' Gav said.

'I can't stick with this pace,' said Parsons.

'Why not?' Gav asked, looking sideways at him.

'It's too slow,' Parsons replied and immediately increased the pace, taking the lead. Gav increased his own pace to match it, and they continued to run side by side in silence. The next time that they passed the company HQ, WO2 Riley had been joined by WO1 Green and several other members of the sergeant's mess. They all shouted out words of encouragement and advice for Parsons as the two runners passed.

Two more laps had passed when Gav said to Parsons, 'If you want to slow down a bit and save it for the last lap we can do, this pace isn't even touching me, but you look like you're struggling.'

Parsons didn't reply. The pace was hard going, and he knew that if it came to a sprint finish, he would struggle. In fact, he was struggling as it was. There was no way he would win in the event of it coming down to a sprint finish!

'I'm not struggling, and if this isn't even touching you, why not speed it up a bit?' Parsons said, increasing the pace a little by opening up the length of his stride.

'You are crazy,' Gav replied, increasing his pace to match.

As they came around to pass the company HQ again, Parsons saw that all the other runners had been taken out of the race and were standing, waiting for him and Gav to pass for the last time. They stood on the grassed areas on both sides of the road and as he approached; they shouted and cheered. Riley and the Colonel had smiles on their faces, as though they were sharing a private joke.

'Do you really think that he will beat my man?' the Colonel asked WO2 Riley.

'At this stage, absolutely, I'd bet my pension on it,' he replied.

'How can you be so certain?' the Colonel asked WO2 Riley.

'Because he wants to,' said Riley. 'I told him he wouldn't be able to beat your man. And trust me, he is as stubborn as they come, he will beat him.'

Colonel Richardson smiled outwardly at the thought of such a stubborn character. He remembered the criticism that he himself had faced in his early years, for being so stubborn. 'That attitude will get you in to trouble,' he had been told. And it may have done, had he not learnt to control it and use it to his advantage.

'Can this young man use it to his advantage?' he pondered. 'Let's see.'

Passing through the shouting and cheering crowd, and hearing his name being called out, gave Parsons a boost. He knew that it would have also done the reverse for Gav.

'Are you ready?' he asked.

'Ready for what?' Gav replied, looking across at him, puzzled.

'Sprint finish, I always save everything for the last mile,' and with that, Parsons kicked as hard as he could and broke ahead.

'You can't bloody sprint for a mile,' Gav shouted after him.

'I can, come on,' Parsons shouted back over the small lead that he was making.

They both kept the pace for another eight hundred metres before Gav eventually started dropping back.

Parsons did not know how far behind him Gav was, but

it didn't matter. He had to keep going. He felt lightheaded and his throat was painful and hot, as though it was on fire.

A member of the gym staff ran towards the crowd waiting at the finish line. 'He's in the lead, Sir. Parsons is in front,' he shouted across to WO2 Riley. 'They are coming around the corner and he's in the lead.'

'Yes, yessss,' called out Riley, his words followed by cheering and roaring from the other side of the road, where the crowd could now see the two remaining runners coming around the corner.

Gav was only ten metres behind Parsons, and upon seeing the crowd at the finish line, he dug deep and managed a final push.

The crowd went wild and were screaming at Parsons, 'Behind you, behind you, he's catching up,' pointing at Gav, who was closing in on him.

With legs like jelly, he glanced behind to see Gav narrowing the gap. Parsons looked ahead, gritted his teeth, and ran faster.

WO2 Riley came out into the road and stood on the finish line, jumping up and down. 'Run Parsons, he's right behind you, run,' he shouted at Parsons, whilst pointing at Gav just metres behind him.

Thirty metres, twenty metres. He looked behind him and saw Gav had dropped back. Not far, but enough. He was finished. Ten metres, Parsons could do it, even with his lungs on fire. Five metres to go. He was too parched to talk, but he felt the smile on his face as his cracked lips stretched across his dry teeth.

Staggering triumphantly across the finish line, he ran straight into WO2 Riley, who struggled to stay upright but took hold of Parsons in a bear hug and lifted him off the ground. Within seconds, they were surrounded, and he was being jostled from every angle.

'You did it, my old son, you bloody did it,' congratulated Riley, who was now minus his hat, which had been knocked off.

As Gav crossed the line, the crowd surrounded him, too, and cheered. The mood was jubilant, with everyone sharing pats on the back and high fives.

After taking the chance to get their breath back, Gav and Parsons congratulated each other. As they spoke, they were joined by the Colonel, who shook their hands and praised them for a fabulous effort.

'Well done, both of you,' he said. 'That last lap wasn't for the faint-hearted, but I had a feeling that you would both have what it takes!' As he said it, he gave Parsons the quickest of winks.

'Colonel, Sir,' WOI Green addressed him.

'Yes, Regimental Sergeant Major,' the Colonel replied.

'Sir, there is no need for you to cover the mess bill.' His words were cut off by the Colonel.

'Sergeant Major, I am true to my word and as agreed, I will pay for the sergeant's mess drinks bill.'

'Thank you very much Sir'. With that he called out, 'Company, company attention.' All present came to attention. He saluted the Colonel and then stood everyone down for the day.

The Colonel and Gav made their way back to the waiting transport. As they did, Gav asked, 'Sir, did you say that there is another potential candidate that you want to look at?'

'Yes, that's right Gavin, why?' he replied.

Glugging from a bottle of water, Gav asked, 'Can you try to not kill me with the next one, please, Sir?'

4

It was September when the Colonel held the next S.O.N.I. assessment centre at RAF Lyme. Upon arrival, each candidate was shown to a shared double room, where they would spend the following two nights. They assembled in a small lecture theatre for 1730 hours where Staff from the S.O.N.I. team and the Colonel welcomed them and wished them luck for the coming days. The applicants were given a brief description of the activities they would be expected to complete during the tests before being stood down for the evening.

Parsons briefly went to the camps bar, but soon returned to his room to get sleep to prepare for an early start.

An early start, it certainly was. At 0300 hours, the lights in the room came on and the shouting began.

'Out of your beds! Shorts, T-shirts and trainers on! Outside in two minutes, get a move on, you don't need to talk about it.' The member of the directive staff left the room only when he saw they were out of their beds and dressing.

Voices could be heard from the neighbouring rooms, where people were either struggling to get out of bed or racing to put their sports kit on. A sense of urgency vibrated through the building, as no one wanted to be the last person outside.

Parsons, although flustered and a little sleepy eyed, was relieved to be amongst the first of the applicants ready and waiting outside.

'Make a large circle around me now,' called out one of the staff. 'Down into the press up position, let's see a bit of urgency ladies and gentlemen,' he added, raising his voice as he did. 'Push back and make the circle bigger,' he shouted.

'Stop, everyone, just stop. This is looking like a fucking monkeys tea party in the park,' another of the staff yelled angrily. 'Space out and make the circle bigger, or you won't all fit in, will you? Now wake up, use your brain and think.' He paused, glanced searchingly and then said, 'Everyone to that building and back now'. He pointed at a tin building fifty metres away. 'Go, get a move on, there and back,' he bellowed.

All the applicants ran towards the building, and as they did so, one of them fell over. He lifted himself to his knees and hesitated, tiredly looking about at the other applicants. A member of the staff saw this and shouted, 'What are you doing? Who told you to lie down? Get up, you lazy piece of shit, now, get up,' they screamed. Staff were picking on the applicants and hounding them for any minor mistake they made. For the next 30 minutes, the applicants were made to run around the camp and made to feel uncomfortable. Eventually, they were formed up in a circle around the staff as before, only this time spaced out from one another.

'Ok ladies and gents. Who went to the clubhouse last night and tried to start a fight?' one of the staff asked in a calm voice. He paused and waited for one of them to answer, but no one did. The silence continued, and he said nothing, just waited as he looked around at their tired, confused faces. He waited for an entire minute before he said, 'Press up position, down'. As the applicants strained in the press up position, he slowly walked around the circle, passing inches away from their heads.

'I am WO1 Rogers', he introduced himself. 'A short time ago, I was woken up by the camp guard commander, so that they could inform me that one of you has threatened to plant somebody in the clubhouse.' He paused again and returned to the centre of the circle. 'Who was it?'

Silence. Except for the odd grunt of effort from the strain of maintaining the press up position. As applicants struggled and let their knees touch the floor or raised their backsides in the air, staff would order them to try harder.

'If you went to the clubhouse tonight, stand up,' WO1 Rogers said. Nine people, including Parsons, stood up. 'This is a start.'

A paratrooper Parsons had spoken to earlier at the bar was amongst those stood up, along with his friends. He was sweating profusely, having drunk eight pints of lager during the evening. He had left the bar just after midnight because the barman had refused to serve him anymore alcohol. Not happy in the slightest, he had become abusive. Only when he had been told to leave by another man in the bar had he done so. But not before threatening to plant him and kicking a bar stool over.

One of the directive staff approached WO1 Rogers and whispered something to him. Rogers nodded and then spoke.

'Everybody, stand up.' He paused while they stood, grinding his teeth together as he thought about what to do. In the good old days, he would have dealt with this by giving the offender a damn good hiding and knocking the attitude out of them. 'You will now all return to your rooms. No more incidents or God help you'. He looked at their faces and wondered how some of them could believe that they were worthy of a place here. 'At 0800 hours you will parade for breakfast in the canteen, dressed in whatever your regular day dress is. Do you all understand?'

In unison, the applicants nodded and said, 'Yes.'

'Good. The person who threatened the flight sergeant in the clubhouse, is to return to their room, pack their kit and be at the guardroom in ten minutes. You're out. Do you understand me, Corporal Taylor?' Rogers said, looking directly at the Para.

'Yes sir,' Taylor replied, lowering his gaze as his face burned with shame.

'Right, get away, all of you. And don't speak to that twat,' Rogers eyeballed Taylor. 'He's the reason you're all out here,' Rogers added as he walked away.

IT WAS 0830 hours when the class, minus Taylor, were again in the lecture room, ready for the day's activities.

'Good morning, ladies and gentlemen. How did you all sleep?' the Colonel enquired. He had a friendly smile on his face as he looked around the audience. 'Mr O'Dwyer,' he said, looking at one applicant seated close to him. 'How was your night's sleep?'

'Broken Sir, but fine thank you,' the applicant replied politely.

'Very good,' the Colonel said. 'You are all well rested. And the competition has already reduced by one, so if you are all ready, let's begin!'

The Colonel gave an outline of the sequence of the day's events and split them into three groups. He designated each of the groups a team leader and asked them to come and join him at the front of the room. He handed each of the team leaders ten coloured lanyards for their team members, each having a number on them, from one to ten.

As the team leaders walked back to their respective seats and began handing out the lanyards to their teams, he explained, 'As you can see, your team has its own colour, either red, blue or grey. And you each have a number. O'Dwyer you are now grey four, ok?'

Each of the applicants now knew their colour and number. 'You are not to use your names again whilst you are here. You will only refer to each other by your new given identities, this is important. Everything that you do from now on is being watched and assessed. Do you understand?'

They each nodded and replied that they understood.

'If at any point you feel you want to leave, simply approach a member of my staff and tell them so. Remember, you are here voluntarily. Good luck ladies and gentlemen,' he told them.

The three teams went off separately for the rest of the morning, rotating from one activity to another in a round robin system. Parsons was in the red team and was code-named red six. There were only nine applicants on the red team as the paratrooper had left because of his part in the club house disturbance.

After completing several other activities, red team arrived at a classroom for their next test.

'This is the map reading and navigation exercise,' they were told by WO1 Rogers once they were seated in the classroom. 'Some of you may have done very little map reading in the past. I know that it's not a skill often used on a submarine, so just do what you can.'

'Have you all got a map, a pencil and a blank piece of paper on your desk?' Rogers asked. All the applicants confirmed they had and were then asked if they could all see the enormous television screen at the front of the class, which they could.

'OK, your start grid is 0053,1126, find it on the map now.' Rogers paused long enough for everyone to find the point on the map that the coordinates referred to. As the TV screen came on, it showed a picture of a rural setting. It was a recording of a car journey along a route lasting approximately five minutes.

'You need to follow the route that the vehicle takes from your start grid until it ends. Let's begin.' He pressed play, and the video began.

'Is it going east or west?' Parsons tried to work out, as he watched the video playing and tried to compare it to the map. As the journey passed a red telephone kiosk, he located it on the map and circled the kiosk with his pencil, as well as writing its location on to his piece of paper. It was heading east. The vehicle in the video was accelerating down country lanes, and Parsons followed its route on the map, noting any turns that it took. The vehicle rounded a right-hand bend and approached a pub on the right side. He looked closely at the video, waiting to get the name of the pub. Surely that would be a detail that he would need later.

As he looked for a sign, an old lady with a walking stick walked out onto the road, causing the driver to make an emergency stop and skid to a halt. He scribbled down details of the old lady and her clothing as this happened, having given up on finding the name of the pub. Age, build, colour and so on, he wrote the lady's description as a list. The old lady waved at the driver and the journey begun as before, with the driver accelerating away until they had to slow for a tractor that it was now following. All the applicants were writing up any detail that they saw, having realised that a question paper requiring these details would be handed out afterwards.

Sure enough, after a few minutes, a woman came into the classroom from the door at the rear. She was carrying a bundle of papers and was acknowledged by WOI Rogers, as though being given permission to enter. She walked past where Parsons was seated, through the classroom to the front, and handed the bundle of papers to Rogers.

'I was right, they will be the question papers. That's what she's handing to him,' Parsons thought.

As she turned to walk back, Parsons made eye contact with her. She smiled and looked at him as she walked towards him. 'Christ, she is tasty,' he thought.

Parsons realised he was staring and became embarrassed. He couldn't help glancing up as she neared him. His throat dried up and his cheeks burned when he noticed she was returning his stare. Her intense blue eyes, which were framed by long, dark eyelashes, seemed to see right into his soul. She was gorgeous, breath-taking in fact. As she passed him, Carl glimpsed the curve of her backside. Knowing it was risky, he turned and drank in the sight. 'What I wouldn't give to see that again, preferably bare!' he thought.

As he looked back to the TV, he saw the vehicle had overtaken the tractor and was passing a bus stop. 'Shit!' he thought as he searched for it on the map. 'Got it, now pay attention!' He tried to concentrate on the video, but his mind wandered. 'What an ass she has' he thought, as he wrote down more details of the video journey.

Once the video had ended, WOI Rogers moved through

the class, handing out question papers. 'Right, start answering the questions when you get them and I will tell you when the time is up. No talking or cheating. Do you all understand that?'

'Yes Sir,' came the replies.

Question one: 'What was your start grid?'
Question two: 'At what grid was the telephone kiosk?'
Question three: 'How many people were there inside the telephone kiosk?'

'Missed that one,' Parsons thought. 'Zero, must have been'. As Parsons went through the questions, finding that he knew most of the answers, he felt confident.

Question eighteen: 'What was the name of the pub?'

'Shit' Carl thought, not having a clue. He assumed the footage had been filmed in England. 'Red Lion,' he guessed, jotting it down. He remembered it was the most common pub name.

He turned to the last page and read the final question.

'Describe in as much detail as you can any persons that entered the room whilst the video was playing.'

Carl stifled a grin as he read the question. He looked around and saw puzzled expressions from most of the applicants, who had been too preoccupied to have seen her. 'Oh my God, how long have we got left?' he thought as he happily envisioned the beautiful visitor who had completely bewitched him.

He filled a whole side of A4 paper with his description, scribbling furiously.

Age: 21 to 23
Build: Slim but athletic
Skin colour: White
Distinguishing marks: N/A
Elevation: 5'9" to 5'10" tall and stood upright
Face: Oval shaped; very blue eyes; small, straight nose; straight mouth; full very red lips, straight teeth, ears hidden by hair.
Gait: Elegant
Hair: Blonde (appeared natural), slightly wavy, shoulder length.

He went on to list her clothing in such detail that it would be almost impossible for anyone to not be able to identify her. He wanted so much to describe how he had felt lust from the moment that he saw her and describe the sex appeal that she called out.

He added one other word to his description, 'Tasty.' 'Well, she was tasty, so why not?' he thought; enjoying the memory of her perfect face and the curve of that fine ass.

'Pencils down,' announced Rogers. 'Are any of you having second thoughts?' he asked, as he was collecting in the answer sheets from each desk. He surveyed the faces before him.

'I'll bet that at least one of you is waiting for someone else to put their hand up, and then you'll join them.' He looked directly at Red five and asked, 'Five, do you still want to be here?'

The mortified woman couldn't speak. Her eyes shone

and her lips trembled. She summoned up the courage to answer when Rogers beat her to it.

'I watched you during the video and you seemed either lost or uninterested, Red five.'

She nodded her head with a hopeless expression on her face.

'Do you want to leave?' Rogers asked.

She nodded her head again, but this time with more vigour. She looked around to see if anyone was going to join her. 'Red five, there is no shame in admitting that it's not for you. There is more shame in pretending to be something that you are not.'

A relieved smile appeared on red five's face and she visibly exhaled.

~

AFTER A BUSY MORNING involving problem-solving activities, physical challenges and memory tasks, Parsons devoured his lunch.

Next came first aid, which was held in a mock office environment. Each member of the red team was supplied with a small first aid kit before they were given a briefing.

'Guys, my name is Johno and the briefing I'm going to give you is really important,' said a staff member that they had not seen before. 'I want you to imagine that you have deployed as part of a two-man team. Your partner has gone into a building to collect a package from a dead drop. They have been inside the building for too long and you must now go to check that they are safe.'

'You are to take your first aid kit, and administer first aid as you feel necessary. There is an extraction team on standby if you feel it necessary for them to be activated.

Your priority is to preserve life and not to retrieve the package. Do you all understand?' The applicants nodded, and he asked for the first volunteer.

The first to put their hand up was selected and left with a second member of staff. Five minutes later, the same staff member returned and took the next applicant. Johno was far more talkative than his colleagues and chatted with the applicants as they waited their turns.

'How are you finding it, guys?' he asked. The replies were all positive, and he responded with humour, making them feel comfortable enough to open up and be honest.

He then asked, 'So why are you here then? Why not stay where you are in your own units?' He looked around the room and nodded at the red one. 'What about you? Why did you apply to do this then?'

Red one gave a run-of-the-mill answer, 'I want a change staff, a challenge and to prove something to myself.'

'Where are you from? I mean what unit?' Johno asked, genuinely interested.

'Navy, submariner. I'm at sea for at least nine months of the year, so a change would be good,' he replied.

'Shit the bed mate, I don't blame you,' Johno replied, and they all laughed.

'How about you?' he said to Parsons.

'Mine's different to his. I just don't like it where I am staff.' Parsons felt uncomfortable once the words had left his mouth, but he had said it, it was too late now.

'How do you mean?'

'It's quite tedious and sometimes you're treated like kids; if someone does something stupid, we all get punished,' he explained to the staff.

'Well, that's no different from here. I mean, you were all

awake last night because of that arsehole playing the big man in the clubhouse, weren't you?'

Parsons thought about it for a second and then said, 'I don't think there will be people like him in your team. That's why he's gone. And it's not just that, I don't fit in back in my regiment, they're just different to me.'

'What if it's you who's different?' Johno asked.

Parsons shrugged and considered this. 'Well, there's more of them than me and they're all happy, so it probably is me that's weird. But either way, I don't fit in and it's shit. I hate it there.'

'I never said weird, I said different, that doesn't mean that you are weird mate.' He paused for just long enough before he went on, 'I mean you might be a right weirdo, but if you are, we'll soon find out.' He gave Parsons a grin, which made all the other applicants laugh.

Parsons laughed too, happy to have a brief chance to have fun. It was a welcome change from the claustrophobic atmosphere that had hung in the air since he had arrived at the camp.

As the staff member returned to collect the next applicant, Johno spoke, 'Come on weirdo, you're up next. Grab your first aid kit.' He smiled again and continued talking to the others as Parsons left the room.

As they approached the office block, the staff member escorting him gave him an update. 'Ok, since the last briefing, we have had further information come through to us. A few minutes ago, gunfire was heard from inside the building. Two men wearing balaclavas and carrying weapons were seen running from the building and getting into a vehicle, which they have now left in. Make your way through the building and react to anything that you find. The extraction team is standing by for a medical CASEVAC if you feel it

necessary. Think about your own safely and get in there, go.'
He motioned for Parsons to go in through an open door
leading down a corridor.

As Parsons entered, he could hear screaming coming
from a room twenty metres down the corridor and to the
right. He ran through his first aid training in his mind.

'Check that the scene is safe,' he thought. 'Then airway,
breathing, circulation.'

He had completed several of these scenarios in the last
few years, and the things that caught people out were always
the same. There could be something placed on top of the
door you had to pass through to get to the casualty, which
would fall and hit you when you moved the door. Or the
casualty would be found holding a live electrical cable that
would theoretically electrocute you when you touched
them. Most of the time, the first aid part was simple and the
safety element would be blown way out of proportion, just
to catch out as many people as possible.

He stopped at the door, about to enter the room. The
casualty was lying on the floor, screaming and appearing to
have been shot in the leg. 'Direct pressure on the injury,
entry and exit wounds, then elevate the limb,' he reminded
himself. He looked up to the top of the door and saw that
there was nothing there to fall on to him. He was about to
move into the room to treat the injured man when, from the
corner of his eye, he saw something through the gap
between the door and the door frame. He paused and
brought his head back just in time to see that it was a
masked figure holding a pistol.

The casualty on the floor screamed again and tried to sit
up, pleading with Parsons for help. He heard movement and
saw a shadow on the floor in front of him. The masked
figure was approaching.

Parsons experienced a flashback to a gunfight he had been caught up a little over a year ago, in south Armagh. He had been confronted by masked terrorists and had exchanged shots with them as they had fired upon an army patrol he was part of. The terror came back to him, causing him to relive the incident.

Fully immersed in the situation, his instincts kicked in. With all of his weight, he slammed himself into the door, pushing it towards the figure at the very moment the pistol appeared around the door's edge. He felt the door rebound with a thud and heard a moan from the other side. Catching the door, he pulled it back before using all of his strength to smash it forward again. He felt the impact as it crashed into something. The door was mostly shattered and hanging only by the hinges. He heard a clatter and saw that the pistol had dropped to the floor and bounced across the room. Still terrified, his body entered fight-or-flight mode. Wrenching the door out of his way, he kicked out at the masked figure.

The staff member blew a whistle and started shouting.

'Stop! End of exercise! Stop!' but Parsons could hear nothing. As the balaclava wearing man slid down the wall, Parsons punched him in the face, as hard as he could. The staff member stepped in, sensing danger because Parsons seemed detached from reality. For several seconds, Parsons could hear nothing and could only see the balaclava.

'Red Six, listen to me,' Parsons' hearing returned as the staff member shook both his shoulders. 'End of exercise! Do you understand?' He nodded but could not speak. Adrenaline still coursed through his body: his legs wobbled and his hands shook. A wave of nausea turned his face pale.

'Red six, take yourself outside and get some fresh air'. He was gently shaken again to ensure that he understood. 'Are you ok?' the staff member asked as he led him to the door and into the corridor. Parsons again nodded in confirmation, pushed his shoulders back and told himself to get a grip.

He walked down the corridor and into the open air. He hadn't realised at the time, but there had been no lights lit inside the building and his eyes now struggled with the bright light. He sat on a low wall, shielding his eyes from the sunlight, struggling to process what had just taken place. He had just tried to beat the living daylights out of a role player and had completely messed everything up. They had been telling him to stop, and he had ignored them. He put his head into his hands and knew that he had screwed up. 'Surely I will be the next one to be given a lift to the train station,' he thought.

He stood up and paced around. 'Shit, shit, shit,' he said, miserably. He noticed the staff member walking towards him. With him was the casualty role player and another man, who from his clothing, Parsons surmised, was the masked role player.

He turned to face them, and for no reason that he could explain, he stood to attention. As they approached Parsons, they looked at him, and the casualty started to laugh.

'What are you doing tiger?' he asked Parsons. 'You're not on parade now. Stand properly and chill out for a minute.'

Parsons relaxed his stance and looked at each of them, anticipating the bollocking of all time.

'You nearly chinned me in there, you little shit,' said the role player as he rubbed the side of his face where Parsons had punched him.'

'He did chin you,' the casualty said, laughing. 'Well done, mate. You're the only one today that he hasn't shot. He's just being mardy, so ignore him. Well done, that was a top, top effort.'

Shock was written all over his face. He went to speak and stopped himself. 'I do not know what the hell just happened, but if I speak, I'll spoil it,' Parsons thought.

'Right then, go back to the lecture hall and join Johno and the others. I'll catch you up. Tell them nothing, you're not supposed to discuss activities amongst yourselves, remember.'

Parsons nodded and walked away. Then he heard the role player say, 'Oi, Tiger. What was the weapon I had?'

He turned back and said, 'Pardon?'

'What weapon did I have in there?'

Parsons only had to think for a second before replying, 'Browning. A nine-millimetre browning.'

He looked at Parsons, smiled and then said, 'Fuck off before I give you a dig back, you cocky little shit.' Parsons didn't turn away soon enough to hide his grin.

'He's laughing at you, Buggy. He's just given you a good hiding and now he's laughing at you. That lad just had your pants down mate,' the casualty laughed.

'Fuck off,' Buggy muttered, as he rubbed at his tender jaw.

5

The day concluded with a standard military fitness test. After, it was announced that there would be a parade at 1900 hours, from which unsuccessful applicants would return to their units.

There was a tense atmosphere in the lecture room by the time 1900 hours came. All the directive staff were present, sitting on the edge of the small, raised stage that faced the seated applicants. They chatted quietly amongst themselves, as did the applicants. WOI Rogers and the Colonel entered the room. The Colonel quickly told everyone to relax to prevent them standing to attention. On behalf of himself and the applicants, the Colonel thanked the directive staff for their input during the day. He turned to address the audience.

'How is everybody?' he enquired, looking around at the remaining applicants. There were quiet replies of 'good' from several of them, but no one wanted to speak up. Tension filled the air.

'I bet you are all just wanting to know how you have done, am I right?' There was nervous nodding of heads, but the room remained quiet. 'Well, I'm afraid that you won't all be making it through to the training phase.' He paused and looked around again. 'But you all passed. You passed a personal challenge just by being here. I think that each of you knew from our road shows that less that one in ten would be selected to go on to the full S.O.N.I training course. Yet you still applied, still turned up and gave it everything that you had. How can that be viewed as anything other than success? Well done to every one of you,' he said sincerely, moving his eyes from one applicant to the next.

All eyes were glued to the Colonel's face. Hearts were pounding in anticipation.

'Ok, let's put you out of your misery,' he said, as he smiled at them. 'Sergeant Major Rogers, can you please call out the names of the people who will leave us this evening.' Rogers stepped forward, clipboard in hand, and read out aloud.

'Blue one, Red seven, Blue three, Grey six, Grey ten, Red three...,' Rogers continued to call out the numbers and as he did, Parsons had to close his eyes. His heart was in his throat. Until this very moment, he hadn't really considered how much he wanted this. Clenching his fists, he contemplated having to return to his unit. He realised how unhappy he was and the thought of being trapped there for over a year filled him with dread. Suddenly he was desperate - desperate to be good enough and find the place where he belonged.

'Blue ten, Grey four. The rest of you remain behind. If your number has been called out, please return to the accommodation block and prepare for departure. Transport will leave for the train station in ten minutes.'

'Shit, I missed it. Did he say Red six?' Parsons panicked, looking around the room. He saw another applicant was looking across at him. He was holding up the thumb of his right hand and smiling. 'Did he get through?' Parsons wondered. He silently mouthed the words, 'Are you through?' to the guy, who smiled and nodded.

'We both are,' he thought he saw him say.

Parsons pointed at his chest and whispered, 'Me?'

The nod came back from the smiling face and it dawned on him. In that moment, the weight of the world was lifted from Parsons' shoulders. The tension left his body as he exhaled: his hands unclenched, his neck relaxed, and he let out a shaky laugh. Parsons surveyed the other four people who had survived. They, too, were wondering what was to come next. It didn't take long before they found out once the unsuccessful applicants had left.

'Now, lady and gentlemen, please can you all move closer to the front for me?' The Colonel asked them to move to the front row of seats, so that they were not spread out around the room. Once they were all re-seated, he pulled up a chair and sat down to speak with them.

'You are all through to the interview phase, which will be held tomorrow morning. I can't tell you what will be involved, but if it helps, my advice is to spend the evening thinking about who you really are. Please don't feed us a load of bullshit that you think we want to hear. We are not looking for any stereotypes here. You cannot have the perfect answers. Just be yourself and be honest. Ok?' he said and waited for acknowledgement.

WO1 Rogers announced the times of their individual interviews and explained that they were to parade back in the lecture room at 0845 hours the following morning.

'Bring everything with you, as you won't be returning to your rooms after your interviews. Feel free to use the club-house this evening if you wish to. But please, be polite if you do,' he said with a smile and a raised brow. The applicants left for the evening and went to prepare for their interviews.

SEVERAL STAFF MEMBERS spent the morning with the applicants while they waited in the lecture room. They had been friendly and chatted, laughing at some of the events of the last few days. Everyone had now seen the bruise on Buggy's face and knew how he had come by it. This was proving to be by far the funniest and most talked about incident. Parsons felt slightly embarrassed about it but joined in with the good-natured banter.

'Just be honest and say what you think,' he kept telling himself. 'But don't be negative,' he added to his thoughts.

'Red six,' a voice called, and his heart sped up. It was time!

The escort knocked on the door of a room and Parsons heard the Colonel call out, 'Come in.' The escort wished Parsons good luck, opened the door for him and then closed it shut behind him.

There were three chairs in a line, facing a single chair in the otherwise empty room that appeared far too large for its current use.

Seated in the left-hand chair was the Colonel. 'Carl, come in and take a seat,' he said, gesturing with his hand towards the single seat. The Colonel had a friendly smile, which reassured Parsons.

'Thank you,' he replied.

'What should I do with my hands?' Parsons thought, conscious that the space between himself and the interviewers exposed his body language. He interlocked them on his lap.

'Carl, you are aware of who I am by now and you have met WO1 Rogers also,' the Colonel said, indicating to Rogers, who was sitting on the seat beside him. Rogers wore a blank expression. He looked directly at Parsons, but said nothing.

The Colonel had continued speaking and Parsons had to catch up with what he was saying, as he had been distracted by Rogers. 'So that leaves me to introduce you to a very experienced member of my team, Miss Rebecca Kelsall.'

Parsons looked to the right at the woman sat in the third chair, next to Rogers. He recognised her immediately. His jaw dropped as his face flushed. That beautiful face was imprinted in his mind. A jolt of attraction threatened his composure. Gazing at her smiling mouth and blue eyes, Parsons had to give himself a shake. It was her, the woman from the map reading test.

'Hello,' she said cheerfully.

'Er, hello,' he muttered hesitantly.

'The description, the description I put of her, I called her....,' he thought, in a state of panic.

'You can call me Tasty,' she replied, reading his thoughts.

The three of them watched as the horror of his predicament was written all over his face. Rebecca and the Colonel began to laugh. Taking pity on him, the Colonel helped Parsons.

'Carl, she is teasing you. Call Miss Kelsall "Staff". Well done on your description - it was very thorough indeed.'

'Thank you, sir,' Parsons replied, quite sure it wasn't the appropriate response.

'Let's go through how you have done,' the Colonel began. 'Map reading, excellent result. How did you get the name of the pub?'

'I didn't sir, I guessed it. I was distracted by the old lady in the video, but I thought that the Red Lion was the best guess.'

'Really?' the Colonel asked.

'Yes, Sir.'

'What a lucky guess, it was right,' the Colonel commented, looking across at the rest of the panel as he chuckled to himself. Looking back at Parsons, he continued, 'You got eighty-four percent in that test, so well done. We will skip the descriptive section, for the sake of everyone, if no one has any objection'. Parsons most definitely had no objection and deliberately avoided making eye contact with Rebecca for the moment.

'General math and English, how did you do in those two, do you think?' the Colonel asked.

'I enjoyed the math Sir, but I'm not brilliant at English so that might have let me down.'

Rebecca spoke now, 'It's not your strongest area, but it certainly isn't an issue.' As she spoke, she looked at the papers that she had on her lap to confirm what she was saying. Parsons nodded, acknowledging what she had said. He gave a smile to thank her for her kind words. She was too attractive for him to look at for longer than a few seconds, so he was pleased when the Colonel spoke again.

'And the first aid come situational awareness exercise. You did very well, didn't you?' the Colonel commented. 'The directive staff said that you saw the threat instantly and dealt with it so quickly that they barely had time to inter-vene.' He looked at Parsons, awaiting his reply.

'Sir, do you want me to be honest with you?' he replied.

'Yes, of course,' the Colonel said.

'I only saw him because I was looking for a bucket above the door.'

'You were doing what?' the Colonel asked, genuinely puzzled.

'Sir, in the first aid tests back at my regiment, they always set up traps for you, so that you fail before you even start. One of them is to balance a bucket on top of a half open door, so that when you open the door, it falls on top of you. They then say that you hadn't properly checked that the area was safe, and that's it. You've failed,' Parsons explained. 'I only saw him because I was looking for something ready to fall from above the door, Sir.'

'So why did you react to the assailant in the manner that you did?' Rebecca asked.

'I was scared. He had a balaclava on, and they terrify me. I saw he was moving around the door and it just seemed like the best thing to do.'

She was intrigued by his honesty and simple innocence. Not only had he admitted that seeing the threat to him was a total fluke, he also said that he was terrified by the sight of a balaclava, admitting fear. 'How the hell does this guy get by in an infantry regiment?' she thought.

'But you could have turned and run,' she replied. 'Why didn't you run away and get out of there?'

'If you run away, they'll just come after you, so you may as well just fight, even if you are going to lose, just fight,' Parsons said to her.

'When you say "they", who do you mean?' the Colonel cut in.

Considering the question, Parsons remembered bullies from his childhood. He had many to reflect upon, many who had been cruel and had troubled him. For a long time, he had allowed himself to be pushed around and beaten up, doing nothing to defend himself. In time, he had taken taekwondo lessons where the instructor had given him one-to-one coaching. He had taught Parsons that he was far better at attacking than defending himself. Eventually, he had learnt that if he couldn't get away from the bullies and they wouldn't leave him alone; it was better for him to give it his all and fight back as hard as he could.

Parsons sensed they were waiting for his answer and that his attention had drifted away for a moment.

'People who want to hurt you, Sir. If someone intends to hurt you, they won't stop because you ran away from them. They will just do it another time, so it's usually best to deal with it there and then.'

'There is logic in that if you ask me,' the Colonel agreed. Although he accepted Parson's answer, he sensed that there was something a little deeper, something in his history that had taught him to not run anymore. But that would be something to probe another time, not today. He talked through the rest of Parson's test results, with Rebecca asking questions from time to time.

'How old are you, Parsons?' Rogers asked, speaking for the first time. Parsons had almost forgotten that the Sergeant Major was there, but he now gave him his full attention.

'I'm nineteen Sir.'

'How long have you been in the forces?' Rogers asked.

'For three years, Sir,' Parsons told him.

'And how long have you been driving for?'

'For nearly two years, now Sir,' he told Rogers. He had been overjoyed when he passed his driving test. He had bought himself an old car and revelled in the freedom.

'Do you think you have enough experience to do this?' Rogers asked in a tone that made Parsons instantly feel inferior.

'I think so. I've already done a six-month tour of Northern Ireland and I've taken part in lots of...'

'The problem for me...,' Rogers said, deliberately interrupting Parsons. 'Is that you are only nineteen years old, and you've been in the Army for literally five minutes. You're not an experienced soldier Parsons, in fact, you've only had one posting since you left training.' He paused briefly and then added, 'If you were to get through to the next stage, you would have to undergo intensive driver training that you wouldn't be able to pass, with such little driving experience. I think you should go back to your unit and get some experience. Do a few more years of soldiering and come back when you are older. You just aren't ready for this; you're still too immature and you haven't lived enough yet.'

When Rogers stopped speaking, he looked to his side towards the Colonel and said, 'Do you agree?'

Before the Colonel could answer, Parsons spoke.

'What is the minimum age that you can apply to do this, Sir?' he said looking straight at Rogers.

Rebecca and the Colonel each turned to Rogers, waiting for him to respond.

'It's nineteen.'

'So, you have set that age limit? And if a nineteen-year-old applies to do this, they couldn't possibly have legally learnt to drive until they were seventeen?' Parsons looked at Rogers, waiting for his agreement.

'Yes, I suppose so,' Rogers conceded reluctantly.

'So, why have you set the age limit at nineteen if you think that it's too young?' Parsons was annoyed by Rogers. 'I learnt to drive a few weeks after my seventeenth birthday, so I couldn't have been driving for any longer than I have. And I joined the Army when I was sixteen, as young as is possible. If three years of service is not long enough, that's not my fault. How can you say that I've not got enough experience? You don't know what experience I have. I've studied Soviet tactics and military vehicle recognition in my own time. I've been on more courses, volunteered for more things and tried harder than anyone I know back in the regiment. What do you mean by doing a bit more soldiering? Sitting around for years, getting fat and unfit, avoiding work and eventually hating it like most of them back there do?'

Parsons witnessed this exact mentality all the time back in his regiment. Senior soldiers always being given opportunities, just because of their longer length of service, rather than their skills or ability. He had watched them waste those opportunities that he had been denied, and then they would make up excuses for their failure. Rogers was as bad as them and Parsons had just about had enough of this bullshit.

'Immature? I see soldiers ten years older than me setting off fire extinguishers and shitting in sinks for a laugh whenever they get drunk. I don't want to become like them. I don't want to be just another waster, waiting until I can leave.' He wasn't shouting, but being told that he had failed for these reasons that were beyond his control had set something off inside of him and his voice had risen. He decided he would leave the army as soon as he could - he hated it.

'Why have you let me apply for this if you already knew my age and the amount of time that I had been in the army? Why is your age limit not higher? I'm sorry, but with respect, I totally disagree with you,' Parsons aimed at Rogers.

'What about the description you gave of Miss Kelsall during your test? "Tasty". Don't you not think that was immature?' Rogers retorted, himself now becoming annoyed at being spoken to in the manner and tone that Parsons had used.

'No, I don't. That is what I thought when I saw her, and

that is how I would describe her. It's my opinion, an honest opinion,' Parsons told him.

The Colonel had remained silent, watching the exchange of words, but now felt that it was time to interrupt. 'You recently attended an NCO's cadre, didn't you Carl?' he asked. An NCOs cadre was the initial course on the infantry soldier's promotion ladder, to become a Lance Corporal.

Switching his attention to the Colonel, Parsons noticed he was addressing him by his Christian name, where Rogers had not. He had used his surname.

'Yes, I did Sir,' he said, feeling deflated and wanting to leave.

'I believe you passed it. Don't you want to remain in your unit and wait for promotion?' the Colonel asked him.

'Not really Sir, no. I only did it for something to do, to fill time and to get out of litter picking duty.'

'This is what I mean: that is an immature answer,' Rogers told Parsons.

'It isn't,' Parsons shot back at him. 'I had a choice of sitting around on my bed every day, waiting to go to pitch a marquee, paint the Land Rovers or some other boring tasks. Or to go on an NCO's cadre where I could get out and do something interesting.'

'I was referring to the getting out of litter picking duties, Parsons, you were being facetious,' Rogers said. Parsons didn't really know what facetious meant, but he understood it wasn't positive.

'I wasn't Sir, you just don't understand me.' He now realised that Rogers didn't understand him. He had never been understood at school or even when he had joined the army at Shorncliffe when he was sixteen. 'Why didn't people just say what they thought like he did? Why not say what you think in simple terms?'

'I don't smoke and I think it's disgusting that I have to pick up someone else's cigarette butts after they have thrown them on the floor. If I got promoted, I wouldn't have to do that anymore. So, if I have a choice between sitting around or doing an NCO's cadre, and the NCO's cadre might get me out of picking up cigarette butts, I'll do it. You've asked me to be honest with you, and I am.'

'Ok, I understand that,' the Colonel said. 'You are not concerned with promotion, that's fine. So, tell us, if you are unsuccessful here, what are your military ambitions?'

'I don't have any Sir. If I'm not successful today, I'll leave the army as soon as I can.'

Rogers sighed and rolled his eyes at the answer.

'You are a prick,' Parsons thought, looking at Rogers.

'Would you not want to take a shot at selection, go for the SAS?' the Colonel asked.

'No Sir, God no. To be honest, I can't stand all of that sort of stuff. Wearing cam cream, lying for days in ambushes, guns and all of those things, I'm not that type of person,' Parsons replied.

'Why are they dragging this out?' he thought, feeling completely deflated.

'What type of person are you then, Carl? Tell me,' the Colonel said encouragingly, trying to emphasise the word 'me'.

Parsons had spent the previous evening thinking of how to answer this question, but now his mind was blank.

'I don't know Sir.' He hesitated.. 'I'm just me.' He didn't know what that meant, not even to himself. 'I'm different, I think. I'm boring, quiet and I don't enjoy arguing like everyone else seems to.'

Parsons shifted uncomfortably in his chair and squeezed his hands together. 'I try hard and I like my own space. I want to do well and I think that I'm a good person. And I like animals, dogs mostly.'

All the words such as ambitious, achiever and determined had disappeared from his head. He had been thrown off balance by Rogers and he didn't really know what to say. Finally, he spoke.

'I want to be different though. I don't want to become like the rest of them. And I don't like people like you, sergeant major. I think you are ignorant and you're rude.'

There was silence as the Colonel waited, not wanting to stop Parsons. He had seen a glimmer of this boy's soul and he wanted to see more. He wanted to know if he had what the challenge ahead would require of him.

In the continuing silence, Rebecca feared that WO1 Rogers might retaliate. Rogers was impressed by Parsons blunt honesty.

'They are good qualities Carl - qualities that we are looking for,' Rebecca said. She felt a connection with him and wanted to dig deeper. 'Can I ask you a personal question?' she enquired.

'Yes, of course,' he replied calmly.

'Why did you go AWOL when you were in your initial training?'

He gently shook his head and said, 'I didn't want to be in the army anymore. So, I decided I wanted to live in Spain.'

'Spain, why Spain?' she asked, surprised.

'It's sunny in Spain'. He instinctively looked at Rogers, expecting a condescending reaction, certain that he would hit him if it came. There was no response from Rogers, and he felt guilty for his negative expectations of him.

'Why didn't you go to Spain then?' Rebecca replied.

'I didn't have my passport, so I was stuck.'

Rebecca nodded, 'So what did you do instead?'

'I went to London and stayed there.'

'Tell me about that,' she said.

'I got on the train in King's Lynn. That's where I was when I went AWOL. Well, I was at Stamford, but I walked to King's Lynn. From there I went to London and spent a month walking around, seeing all the tourist attractions and things. I knew it couldn't go on forever, so I went back and handed myself in.'

'How did you live for the month? Where did you sleep and get food from?' Rebecca asked, genuinely interested in how he had survived.

'I had no money, so when I first got on to the train in King's Lynn I told the conductor that I was a soldier on an escape and evasion exercise and that I had to get to London. He was kind, and let me travel without a ticket. He just took my details. Then when I got to London, I saw people begging. I'd never really been out of the area where I had grown up, so it was all new to me,' Parsons explained. 'Then I did it as well. Beg, I mean. If you stand outside Euston train station in the morning, in the doorway where people come out and you ask them for money, they give it to you. Sometimes I didn't even have to ask. I'd just put my hand out and they would hand me money. I'd get forty pounds in the first hour most of the time, and then I would go off for the day. I used to go to the shop just down from the station that sells military kit, not your basic kit, spy stuff. Pens with cameras in them and surveillance things. I used to love looking through the stuff in there. There is so much to see in London, so it was easy to fill each day. And at night, at Charing Cross train station, the Salvation Army gives away the sandwiches that haven't been sold in the shops. Even Marks and Spencer sandwiches. I'd eaten nothing from Marks and Spencer before that. Or since, actually,' Parsons told them. Even Rogers was listening with interest.

'They have warm soups as well, and they exchange blankets for you. A nurse examines your feet and checks that you are healthy all for free. Lots of homeless people have problems with their feet for some reason.' Parsons frowned as he said this, showing that he didn't understand why. Maybe it was the lack of cleaning facilities they had, or from too much walking. Although, he remembered that many of them would remain in the same place for a lot of their time. Maybe that was the reason, because they didn't walk far enough.

'Where did you sleep? Were you alone?' the Colonel asked.

'I slept with the other homeless people, mostly. I had my army sleeping bag with me. When you come out of Euston and turn left, there are some steps that lead down to the road. There is a big building to the side of the steps that has a venting system that blows out warm air underneath the steps. I'd sleep there a lot because it was warm. And there were usually a few other people sleeping there, so it was safer.'

'Did you ever have any problems? Anything bad ever happen?' the Colonel enquired.

'Some men tried to set us on fire one night. I think they were drunk,' Parsons said, surprising them. On seeing the shocked look on their faces, Parsons elaborated.

'When you sleep, you put cardboard on the floor as a mattress to stop the cold from coming through. And if it's windy, you build little walls around you with it, to block the draft. One night we woke up, and these guys had set the cardboard on fire. It took light and started to burn really quickly.'

'What did you do?' Rogers asked

'We jumped up and put the fire out. It had burned one of the sleeping bags, so we put that out too, but it was ruined.'

'Did anything happen to the men who had started the fire? Did you and the tramps fight back?' Rogers asked.

'They are homeless people sir; they don't like being called tramps. A lot of them have had good jobs, nice houses, families and have been successful. They've just not been able to cope with things and have had mental break downs and lost everything. I liked them and they were kind to me, protected me. But no, we didn't do anything to the drunks for starting the fire. They ran away.'

'That's quite a story, a bit of life experience,' the Colonel said seriously, as he considered what that must have been like for a young kid.

'Do either of you have anything further that you would like to know?' he asked of Rebecca and Rogers, to which they both confirmed that they did not. 'Well, I don't think that I've ever seen anyone stand up to Sergeant Major Rogers like that before and I'm sure that you have changed his mind in to giving you a chance here. What do you say, Colin?' he asked, using Roger's Christian name.

'Rogers shrugged and said, 'Why not? Let's give him a go at it.'

'Rebecca, what do you think? Has he impressed you enough?' the Colonel asked as he looked across to her.

'Absolutely. I'm looking forward to seeing how he does. Just don't let us down now that you have built up our expectations. I'll be keeping an eye on you.' She looked back at the Colonel as she finished.

'That's that then,' the Colonel announced with a smile. 'Your training will begin in November. Rebecca will speak with you before you leave today to give you further details. When you return to your unit, you are to tell anyone who asks that you have failed to get through this process. I will speak with the relevant people there to the notify them to the contrary and to make the necessary arrangements for your release to us. Congratulations Carl, we will see you in November.' To signify the end of the interview, the Colonel stood up and shook Parsons by the hand. WO1 Rogers also shook his hand and smiled for the first time since the interview had begun.

'Well done,' Rebecca told him as she shook his hand. 'If you return to the lecture room, I shall see you there in a short while.'

With that, Parsons was escorted out and led back to join the others in the lecture room.

In a room far away, a fax machine came alive, printing out dots to form the important words. Before the fax machine had fallen silent, a hand was waiting to retrieve the message.

'SECOND SUBJECT IDENTIFIED. DETAILS TO FOLLOW SECURELY.'

6

I t was Sunday 7th November when Parsons arrived at
Operation Hot Water to begin his S.O.N.I training. It
was a baptism of fire from the moment he arrived, like
nothing he had experienced before. The directive staff were
vile to the candidates, constantly applying psychological
pressure and trying to find their weaknesses. Having got this
far through the process, they had become candidates, rather
than applicants, and it felt like an achievement to be
addressed as one. Parsons had to sign the official secrets act
again and agree that if he was successful in completing the
training, he would take on a further three years of military
service.

Operation Hot Water had been running for six weeks,
and although Parsons had found aspects of it unbelievably
difficult, he felt he was doing well. He had learned both foot
and vehicle surveillance methods, photography, as well as
sharpening his weapon handling and unarmed combat abilities. Parsons had found the undercover techniques and
legend building particularly enjoyable. Passing the

advanced driving course with ease had made his day. That
would wipe the smug look off Roger's face.

The next phase of the training was a mock live deployment, where the candidates would spend several days
attempting to gain information about a target, referred to as
target one. This was the landlord of a public house in a
small town named Cowley. The location was in the Staffordshire Moorlands, near to the facility where they were now
based. Subject one, was oblivious to his part in the exercise
and was, in fact, a regular member of the public.

The candidates were to decide for themselves how they
would conduct their individual operational deployments.
Some chose to travel into Cowley each day and to look for
work to help with their legend and cover stories. They
would use the pub socially after work and find a way of
learning what they could in relation to the target subject.
Parsons was going to travel to a location several miles from
Cowley and hitchhike in. He was then going to try to stay
out overnight and spend all the time in the town, using dead
drops and telephone calls to feed information back to his
handler.

Before the candidates deployed, they were asked to sign
a document agreeing that in the event of them being taken
hostage, they could be interrogated. The document stated
that only if it was the opinion of a medically trained practi-
tioner that the treatment during interrogation was likely to
cause either permanent phycological or physical damage to
the candidate, that it should stop. The remaining twelve
candidates all signed the document and deployed in their
various guises.

Parsons eventually got a ride into the town and learnt
much about the guy, John, who had picked him up. It was
surprising how much John was happy to tell him. He had

two children from a previous relationship, but rarely saw them because of the less than an amicable relationship between him and his ex.

'Where are you from Carl?' John asked. Parsons had been advised that it was best practice to keep your Christian name as part of a pseudonym.

'All over mate, I grew up in care and I've lived in loads of places. Parsons had decided that he would build his legend around places he had actually visited and exaggerate the time that he had spent there. 'I've just come from King's Lynn though. I was stopping with a mate there, but he didn't pay the rent, so we were thrown out on our arses'. I fancied a change though, so I started hitching lifts and it looks like I'm heading for sunny Cowley.'

'Where are you stopping in Cowley? Where do you want dropping off?' John asked.

'I've not got anywhere yet mate, just drop me in the town and I'll get sorted. I don't suppose you could ask your gaffer if there's any work at your place, could you?' he replied.

'Yeh, of course I could. Take my number and I'll ask him in the morning. If you call me after five tomorrow night, I'll be home by then.' Parsons wrote down the telephone number and said goodbye to John as he was dropped off on Cowley's main street.

'Cheers mate. Speak to you tomorrow,' he told John and then went for a look around the town.

A FEW HOURS LATER, he was back in the debriefing room with Rebecca (his handler) and WO1 Rogers. Rebecca had been allocated two of the candidates to act as handler for, and one of them was Parsons. The Colonel had allocated candidates to handlers, and Rebecca had been surprised by how pleased she had been to discover that Parsons was one of hers. She had spent the last six weeks watching and training him and had decided that she liked him. He was a quick learner, and she was surprised by how level-headed he was for a guy of his age. She fancied him too, which made being around him very enjoyable.

Rebecca had been part of S.O.N.I. for three years now and was twenty-three years old. She had been born in Lincolnshire and had grown up there with both of her parents as an only child. She was close to her father and, as a child, had shared his interests in order to spend time with him.

Her first car, which she still owned, was a yellow VW Beetle. When she was fifteen, the car had been damaged and abandoned for months in a pub carpark. Each time Rebecca and her family had driven past the car, she told them she would have one just like it one day. Although it had been difficult, her father had traced the owner and purchased the car. It had been a labour of love as Rebecca and her father spent two years working on it until it was like new again. Rebecca's father had been her hero and role model as she had grown up and she had inherited many of his favourable personality traits.

Parsons gave Rebecca a full account of the day's events and asked for permission to find lodgings to improve his cover story. Rogers was present in the role of senior operations officer and had to make decisions on the entire operation, considering all undercover (UC) officer's deployments.

On this occasion, Rebecca and Rogers were of the same opinion that it was too risky for Parsons to take up lodgings at an unvalidated address. One of the other candidates had not reported back and was believed to be missing, possibly taken hostage having blown their cover. Considering the circumstances, Parsons was not permitted to take lodgings at this time, but that decision would be reviewed each day. For now, he would have to return to the camp each evening to be debriefed.

When the debrief ended, Rebecca followed him to the canteen where they ate together.

'Well done for today,' she told him. 'You've made a good contact and got your face seen, just don't become too well known too soon.'

'Do you really think I did ok?' he asked her, unsure whether he was doing things the right way.

'Yeh, I do. A lot of good ideas put into practice.'

'Brill,' he said, happy with Rebecca's approval. 'Can I ask you a question?'

'It depends what the question is,' she replied, smiling at him as she took another bite of her food.

'Is your name really Rebecca?' he asked.

'No' she said, as she shook her a head a little. Her lips twitched.

'What is it then?' he asked. She was chewing her food for longer than necessary, so he asked, 'What is your name, if it's not Rebecca?' She was grinning as she swallowed.

'Tasty.' They were eating the same meal (quiche Lorraine) and although it was tasty, he was surprised that she had commented on it. 'My name is Tasty, remember?' she said.

Remembering the relevance of the word, he became embarrassed. He was aware of a blush creeping up his face, but he didn't care. Rebecca's dazzling smile was all he could focus on.

'Do you know what a memory snap is?' he asked her.

'No.'

'It's when you remember something as it happens, take a snapshot, and put it away in to your memory.'

'Why would you do that?' she asked.

'I'll give you an example,' he told her. 'You know when you just said that your name was Tasty?' He looked at her and she nodded. 'Well, I am going to remember that and the smile on your face when you said it.' He paused again, and she waited for him to finish. 'And any time in the future when things get hard or... bad, I'll just look at that memory snap and it will all be fine.'

She smiled and felt herself flushing a little. 'Does it work?' she asked, as she looked into his eyes.

'That one definitely will. It was a good one.' He smiled back and noticed her cheeks were reddening.

She laughed, told him to eat his food and to stop being a creep. He held her gaze for a few more seconds and then went about finishing his dinner, as he was starving, having not eaten since breakfast.

THE FOLLOWING day was not as productive as the first, until in the evening, when Parsons made the call to John.

'John, is that you mate?' Parsons asked.

'Yes mate, it is. How you doing?' John enquired. He explained he had asked his boss at the slaughterhouse if there was any work for Carl, but that there wasn't any at the moment. He said that bits of work always came up there, so he would keep him in mind.

It was around mid-afternoon when Parsons deployed for the third day; his first stop was to visit the shopkeeper at the newsagents. He hung around in the shop, chatting for almost an hour, and then left to take another walk along the main street. He hadn't been walking for long when he heard a car horn beep. He turned to see that it was John pulling up at the side of the road in his car.

'Carl!' he called out. The passenger window was open and Parsons could hear trance music playing on the car stereo. He liked John and now credited him with good taste in music, too.

'Fancy helping me out for ten minutes mate?' John asked.

'Yeh, definitely,' Parsons replied.

'Jump in,' John told him, and they headed off. John wanted help in getting his mum's old sofa out of her house. He couldn't lift it on his own and had promised her he would sort it for her today, as he finished work early on Fridays.

'It will only take five minutes Carl, and then we can go grab a beer if you like,' John suggested.

'Sounds good to me,' Parsons replied, happy that he had caught a ride with John two days earlier, rather than anyone else. 'This guy is proving to be worth his weight in gold,' Parsons thought.

As they stopped outside a house on the edge of the village, John announced they were there and they both got out of the car.

'You'll love my mum mate, she an absolute angel. Do anything for anyone she would. Come on,' John said, and they walked around to the back of the house.

'Mum, you there?' he shouted, entering the kitchen followed by Parsons, 'Mum!'

Without warning, Parsons was knocked to the floor, and a sack was placed over his head. His hands were tied behind his back and his feet were bound. It happened fast and left him momentarily disorientated.

The next thing he heard was a voice telling someone to get the van backed up. Then the same voice spoke close to his ear.

'If you make one single sound, I will hurt you. Do you understand me?'

The authoritative voice was calm, controlled, and sent a chill straight through Parsons. He nodded his head with no hesitation. 'This is just an exercise, a role play,' he told himself. Fighting the urge to panic, he breathed in through his nose and out through his mouth. He had attended lectures on how to behave if taken hostage. Remaining calm and polite had been the key to survival. Suddenly, he was lifted and taken outside, where he was roughly bundled into a waiting van.

There were several prominent ridges on the van's floor. His chest took the force of the impact as he landed awkwardly on a ridge. Winded and in pain, Parsons struggled to breathe for a minute. Then he had to swallow down an urge to yell for help. 'Remember what he said,' Parsons thought., 'One single sound'. He closed his eyes and tried to remain calm. Every breath he took increased the pain in his lungs. This was scary even for an exercise.

Once the van pulled away from the driveway, he tried to work out in which direction it was heading by remembering the turns it made. After five or six changes of direction, it was hopeless, so Parsons gave up. Although he tried to visualise the route, he did not know where they were going. He was tempted to speak, but knew that it would end badly. 'Do what they say, but nothing more,' he remembered from his training. As the van jolted over bumps and potholes in the road, Parsons' sore ribs were smacked into the ridges of the floor. Slowly, an inch at a time, he shuffled onto his left side to help with his breathing. But a hand pushed him back, and he was hit hard on the back of his head with what felt like a clenched fist.

'Stay fucking still,' a fresh voice barked at him. There was anger in this voice. It differed from the first one, younger perhaps. After thirty or forty minutes, his body shook as the van drove over a cattle grid. He slid towards the back of the van as the gradient changed. One of the van's tyres spun for a second and Parsons guessed they were on uneven ground, not the main road. After five minutes, they stopped, and the engine went silent.

The van doors were flung open and Parsons was grabbed by the shoulders. Every movement caused a flare of pain in his ribs. The restraints were now cutting deeply into his wrists and ankles. He was propelled forwards so quickly that his feet dragged along the ground. His muscles strained as he tried to stay upright.

'Over there!' he heard.

'The first voice again,' he thought, 'he's in charge, he's their leader.'

He was dropped onto the ground, which was cold and hard, possibly concrete. Rope was looped through his arms and legs and then around his chest. He was pushed over on to his side and told to not move. He heard the rattling of doors closing, big doors like those in a barn or a garage. Time passed. Any sounds were muffled by the sack over his head.

Parsons tried to work out how long he'd been lying there. At least three hours, he guessed. The left side of his body had gone numb and a dull ache radiated out from his chest. The skin around the bonds on his hands and feet was raw and bleeding. He desperately wanted to roll over, but made himself wait. Eventually, he could not tolerate the pain any longer.

As he slowly moved, he strained his ears to check if he was alone. He straightened his legs first and felt the blood move through them. Once he could feel his feet again, he rolled over onto his back.

There was a sound followed by sudden movement. A vicious kick to the stomach, cruel hands on his body. They must have been right next to him all that time, waiting for him to move or speak. He was dragged and lifted to his feet. He tucked his chin into his chest and raised his shoulders for protection as blows rained down on his head and face. Five, six, seven times he was hit before hands circled his throat like a vice.

'Stay fucking still,' the angry voice said, tightening the grip on his throat. 'We told you to stay still,' was screamed into Parsons' face. The heat of the assailant's breath penetrated the cover over Parsons' head. He was forced backwards, landing heavily on a wooden chair. It felt like one of the old-fashioned kitchen chairs his grandmother had. His calves were tied to the legs and his forearms were lashed to the arms of the chair. Something wet dripped from his nose and tickled as it ran on to his top lip. The tang of metal in his mouth confirmed he had a nosebleed. It didn't hurt thanks to shock and adrenaline, but it was definitely bleeding.

There was silence again. A disconcerting silence. Parsons tried to count the time that passed. His senses were on high alert as he listened, desperate to hear anything. He could feel his limbs again and, although he certainly wasn't comfortable, he was thankful to be off the floor. He thought maybe another two hours had passed when he heard the calm voice again.

'What is your name?' It came from in front of him. He had been right - there was a seat there.

'Carl,' he replied.

'Carl what?'

'Carl Bramble,' Parsons replied in a submissive tone. He thought back to his interrogation training and remembered that he must behave in a nonthreatening manner. The longer he could remain alive, the higher his chances of being rescued.

'What is your name?' the voice repeated.

'My name is Carl Bramble,' he repeated.

No response. Chair legs scraped on the floor as the speaker stood up. There was the echo of footsteps, followed by the rattle of a door. Parsons was alone again.

Approximately eight hours later, the door opened again and the same voice called to him across the gap.

'What is your name?'

Parsons paused for a few seconds and then replied, 'Carl Bramble, that is my name.'

'Tell me what his name is.' the voice asked. Parsons repeated himself, but was cut off by another voice.

'His name is Carl Parsons,' came the quiet reply.

'Take her back, and don't fuck her before I do,' the leader said from across the room.

Parsons was exhausted. He hadn't drunk or eaten anything for over 24 hours. He was confused.

'Was that Rebecca? What was-'

A hard slap to the back of his head shocked him out of his thoughts.

'It's much more fun making her talk. I think she likes me. She's trying to keep on my good side in any way that she can.' He paused for effect. Parsons involuntarily sniffed, causing blood to enter his throat, which made him cough. 'I'm going to spend some time with her now. And when I come back, I want you to tell me everything that I need to know. If you don't... I will hurt you. I know you are from the training course. I know you are taking part in special operations training to prepare for being sent to Northern Ireland. You are not on a training course any longer. You have been captured by the IRA and this is real'. He was left on his own again.

Parsons thought this was too extreme for an interrogation scenario. If it was just a training exercise after all, this was over the top. The leader had said it wasn't training anymore, but that was surely just a tactic to make him panic. Using Rebecca was a clever touch. He thought that another few hours had passed, although he had little faith in his judgement of time.

'A noise! A car?' he thought. There it was again. He could hear it more clearly now, crunching over the gravel. He heard it rumble along the track and approach the building. It stopped and the noise of the engine died. Two doors opened and then closed. 'Two passengers,' he thought. From outside, he heard talking. He couldn't make out any of the words, but one voice stood out. The door of the barn opened, and he heard several sets of footsteps enter the room.

'I'll take it from here.' A man with an Irish accent spoke. 'Take that off his head.' The cover was roughly yanked from Parsons' head and the sudden light hurt his eyes, making him blink furiously. He did not know how long he had been there, but it was daylight once again. He could see three men stood in front of him, close to the doors. There were another two also, one on either side of him, so close that they were almost touching him.

All but one of them had balaclavas on their heads, so their faces were hidden. But one of them had done nothing to conceal his identity, the Irish man. He was a menacing mountain of a man, nearly twice the size of most men. The Irish man cast a long shadow, making him appear even larger than he was. He looked at Parsons for a few seconds and then spoke.

'Who are you?' he said in the strongest Irish accent Parsons had ever heard.

'Carl Brambles'.

For a man of his size, he was agile and fast. He covered the distance between himself and Parsons with lightning speed and punched him once to the side of the head. Parsons went flying. The chair landed on its side, trapping his right hand. His ears were ringing, and he felt sick. He couldn't feel any pain from his damaged hand, but his face felt like it had been struck with a hammer.

'Get him up,' the voice barked. Parsons and the chair were set upright again. 'Get him naked. I want his clothes off. I'll fucking show you this isn't a game.' The two guards next to him cut away at his clothes with knives.

'Her too. We will do them together,' the Irish man said as he paced in front of Parsons.

Rebecca was led into the barn and her clothes were removed by two of the masked men. They were rough and shouted at her to lift her arms and straighten her various limbs as her clothes were removed. She stood, shivering in her underwear, and Parsons looked at the bruises and scratches which covered her body.

'Fuck, what is going on?' he thought as he looked at her.

'Tell him. Tell him what this is about,' the Irishman shouted at Rebecca.

'He's nothing to do with this. He's a student,' she said. Her voice was broken and tears stained her cheeks.

'Tell him or I will cut his fucking fingers off,' he said calmly, taking a knife from one of the guards.

Rebecca began to cry and looked at Parsons. 'Carl, this isn't an exercise. You've been compromised. This is real. I don't know how it happened, just tell them what they want to know.' Her shoulders shook from sobbing as she turned away.

The Irishman pulled the chair up in front of Parsons and sat facing him, their knees almost touching.

'Every year you stupid bastards come here, to the same place to do your training, and you never thought that we would catch on. Do you think we're stupid?' he asked with an acidic smile on his face. He was breathing heavier and his agitation showed on his face. 'We've watched you. We've watched you train them here. And then we waited for them to arrive in the Provence. That confirmed what you were doing here. You were training the people who you were sending to come and fight us. Spies, covert spies.' His smile grew, and he continued, 'We know everything about the way you work, your bases in Lisburn, Bessbrook, and Holyrood. Yes, we know all about you.'

Rebecca spoke through her tears, 'He isn't one of us, he's just a student, please just let him go.'

Parsons suddenly understood what was happening. The camp had been watched, and this was real. Terror clenched at his guts. He had never experienced such fear. Shivering uncontrollably, Parsons struggled to breathe. This was it. He was going to die.

Rebecca was dragged from the barn. The doors were closed, but he could hear her screams as she was beaten. Tears ran down his face as the gravity of the situation hit him. He had to think clearly to buy time.

'Ok,' he said. 'I'll talk. He looked at the Irishman. 'What do you want to know?'

The Irish man sat back in his chair. 'I want to know everything,' he said, 'Let's start with your name.'

Parsons knew that the longer he could keep any conversation going, the longer it gave a rescue team to find them. The Colonel and Rogers must know that they were missing. He answered all the questions in the simplest terms, but politely and slowly. He asked for a drink of water and to stand up, but he was refused. He had to buy time, and he had to keep talking to do so.

'Tell me about her,' the Irish man asked, referring to Rebecca. 'Is she the boss?' he asked.

Parsons hesitated, not wanting to put Rebecca in any more danger than she already was. The Irishman saw the delay and warned him that if he tried to lie to them, there would be consequences for both Rebecca and himself.

'No, she isn't. I don't know what she does, but she's not in charge. It's a man in charge.'

'Tell me about him first,' the Irish man demanded.

'He is in his forties, late forties. His surname is Johnson, and he's an officer. I've only seen him a few times.' Parsons described his old Science teacher, Mr Johnson, in as much detail as he could. He described his appearance, the vehicle he used and even said that he was ignorant, which the actual Mr Johnson had been. Parsons thought that if he described a real person, it would seem more believable, and he would remember the details if he were questioned again later.

The Irishman asked more and more questions for what seemed like hours. Parsons continued to answer them, agreeing to what the Irishman already knew, but adding nothing more, and pretending to not know the answers where he could.

The Irishman got out of his chair and stood behind

Parsons. After a short time, he walked back into his view and spoke. 'I'm going to kill you both now. Is there anything else you can tell me to avoid that?'

Parsons couldn't find any words. The door opened, and Rebecca was led back in, still in just her underwear. A cover was placed over her head, and she was forced to kneel on the ground. She was crying and begging for them to not shoot her. The Irishman walked over to her, pausing only to allow one of his men to put a cover on Parsons' head too.

'You deserve this, you Brit bastards,' the Irishman said. A deafening gunshot rang out. Rebecca's crying stopped. Parsons felt sick as he heard Rebecca's body slump to the ground. He held his breath, waiting to hear her again. Silence. She didn't make a sound. He could smell the carbon from the shot and his senses were heightened to a level he had never experienced before.

Suddenly, there was a hot tingling sensation on his bare chest; he knew it was the gun that had killed Rebecca. This was it. They had been captured. This was the end.

'Even if you are going to lose, fight back,' the thought flashed through his head.

Summoning all of his strength, he pushed his body forward and dug his feet in to the ground as he fought against the ropes that tied him to the chair. The gun slid from his chest as he moved and thrust his head up and forwards. The top of his head struck what he guessed was a chin, and then he was falling, face down, on top of a body. He might have been about to die, but if he could hurt the bastard who killed Rebecca, he would stop at nothing. He smiled, then laughed wildly.

'You fucking coward!' His shouts became louder. 'Come on you fucking scum!' Louder even through his laughter,

'Come on!' He knew he had caught the Irishman, and it felt so good.

With a swift yank, he and the chair were hauled up. As the cover was removed from his head, he snorted blood from his nose and was about to spit, but stopped just in time. It was the Colonel.

'Carl, that is the end of the exercise. Carl, listen to me. The exercise is now over. Do you understand?'

He blinked. The guards, the Irishman, and Rebecca were all in front of him, staring.

'Carl, speak to me. It's finished now. Do you understand?' The Colonel shook his shoulders.

Parsons nodded but could not speak. Everyone clapped and smiled. He saw John, his friend who he had been with when he was kidnapped. John was part of the training team and had been in on the deception since his first meeting with Parsons.

'Well done,' the Irishman said, 'Well done, Carl.' The huge man's nose was swollen, and he wiped it with his hand. He showed Carl the blood and said, 'Great shot, you nearly took my head off'.

'Are you ok?' Rebecca said as she walked forward and crouched down to his level. He nodded, dazed and confused. 'You've passed, that's the end, you've done it.'

He was untied. The sensation was wonderful as he slowly rotated his ankles and wrists, relishing the feeling. His right hand was swollen and bleeding, but he didn't care. Gingerly, he stood up.

With shaky arms, he reached out to Rebecca and wrapped them around her. Muffling his sobs, he buried his head in her neck. It was over and he had passed.

7

Tomorrow would be Christmas Eve, and Sarah had only a few hours until she was to catch her flight to Naples. She sat in Alicella with the Colonel, having just listened to his account of how the last part of Parsons' training had gone.

'Are you sure that you are not exaggerating the interrogation scene? It sounds like the ending to a film,' she accused the Colonel.

He laughed at the suggestion and told her, 'My dear Sarah, if anything, it was more intense than I have described. They are looking forward to having him on their team. It is a shame that he won't be joining them, really.'

'Yes, it is awful that he thinks he is going to be one of them when he isn't, but it can't be helped.' Sarah sounded sympathetic, but hurried on. 'Do you think he is ready to be passed over to me yet?' she asked.

'Not quite, actually. We have recently done some work outside of the province, on the Balkan Peninsula, Bosnia to be exact. I have been sending some of my team out there to give them a change of scenery and to support MI6 with some of their intelligence tasks. It has been quite productive, and it has created a positive working relationship that didn't previously exist. Prior to deployment there, all my staff attend a course that Special Branch holds in Morocco. It would be a great experience for him if Carl were to attend it, and I think he needs a bit of time to settle down. Let's give him some time to find his feet before we tell him what we are expecting of him. Call it R and R if you like, but it will only strengthen his skills to prepare for you to take over.'

'How long are you suggesting? Just so that I can put things in to place at my end,' she asked. Sarah knew the Colonel was right, and this would also give her the time she needed to clear her own caseload. Mac had insisted that once Parsons was handed over to her, there must be no distractions for either of them; she was to dedicate all her time and effort to the task.

'A month, maybe two. I can fit in with your plans, but I would give it at least a month to be safe. He's currently at home on leave for the Christmas period and isn't due to return until the New Year. I can arrange for him to be on the first course that Special Branch run in January,' the Colonel offered.

'Perfect, let's aim for me to have him by mid-February and we can meet again before then to discuss his transition from you to me. It might not be as easy as we're expecting if he doesn't agree. Sending him away on this course is actually a good idea. It will prevent him from forming any strong friendships with your guys. It's perfect Colonel.' Sarah smiled as she made plans in her head. But for now, she had a flight to catch and her homeland to return to for her favourite time of year, Christmas. 'Italia, here I come,' she thought.

WHEN PARSONS LEFT the S.O.N.I. training camp, he didn't have any military residence or posting to return to. He was no longer a part of his old regiment and he was still awaiting his deployment to the unit at Gerrick barracks in Lisburn. He was informed that he had been granted annual leave for the Christmas period and that he should be ready to fly out to Northern Ireland on Monday 3rd January. He returned to his sister's home to spend the time with her and their parents who lived close by. It was the morning of Christmas Eve, and he had just returned from walking to the shop to buy a newspaper, when his sister told him he had received a telephone call while he had been out.

'Who was it?' Parsons asked her.

'A girl, she sounded nice,' his sister replied. 'Is she your girlfriend?'

'What was her name?' he asked as his sister walked away from him and into another room.

'I didn't ask her. What is your girlfriend's name?'

'I haven't got one. Are you sure they asked for me?'

'Yep, her number is next to the phone. She wants you to call her back. Little brother has got a girlfriend, woo.' His sister, who was older than him, had spent far too much time in the past trying to set him up with girls, and he wondered if this was going to be another of her attempts.

He looked at the number and saw that it had an area code that he didn't recognise. He dialled it anyway and waited as it rang.

'Hello,' the phone was answered.

'Hello, it's Carl calling back. You've left a message with my sister for me to call you,' he said.

'Ah, your sister. So, you haven't got a wife that you've been hiding from me then. How are you?'

'Rebecca, is that you?' Parsons asked as he recognised the voice.

'Yes, of course it's me. Who were you expecting it to be?' she replied.

'I don't know, to be honest; I just wasn't expecting to hear from you.'

'Oh well, I've made your day for you then, haven't I? How are you?'

'I'm good. I'm bored daft, but good thanks. How about you?'

'I'm fine. Why are you bored?' she asked him.

'Well, the Colonel asked me to try to not speak with any of my old friends, so there's not a lot to do,' he told her.

'How come you can't speak to your friends?'

'He said that it would be difficult to say what I'm going to be doing from now on and that I would have to lie to them. So, he said that I should just avoid it.'

'You really take everything so literally, don't you? He means to just avoid talking about work from now on. It's easy, you'll soon get used to it. Anyway, more importantly, you've had some good luck,' she said, changing the subject.

'What is it?'

'Well, first you are going to have to meet up with me, so I can give you some joining instructions for a course that you are going to be going on straight after Christmas.'

'A course? How is that good luck?' he sighed.

'Meeting up with me is the lucky bit! I will ignore the fact you didn't see that for yourself. And also..., I'm coming on the course too, so for you that is more luck than you could have possibly hoped for!' she told him.

He didn't reply, and she thought he was actually disappointed.

'Well, say something then, Mr Grumpy.'

'Er... wow, really?' he eventually asked. It was far more luck than he could have possibly hoped for. He couldn't believe it. 'That's brilliant. Are you being serious? I mean, what course is it and where is it?'

'I can't tell you over the phone, so when are you free to meet up?' she asked him, relieved that he now sounded a little more enthusiastic.

'I've got nothing on. Whenever you like.'

'I didn't ask you what you were wearing, but it's nice that you feel you can share these things with me' she giggled, as her words tailed off.

'You know what I mean,' he said, blushing, then breaking into a grin.

'Well, I'm free too, so whenever suits you.'

'How about lunchtime then?' he suggested, hoping that she would say yes. He hadn't expected to see her for a while, but now that he had the chance to, he had a sudden urge for it to be sooner rather than later.

'I'm over in Lincolnshire and you're in Staffordshire. How can we do that?'

'I can drive over if you like. I'll have a look at how far it is if you give me a minute,' Parsons replied as he tried to remember where his road atlas was.

'Eighty-one-miles.'

'Pardon.'

'It's eighty-one miles.' There was the briefest of hesitation in her voice when she continued, 'From you to me I mean, about eighty-one miles, or thereabout, I think'. She realised she had just given away the upper hand, and that he must surely now know how much she had wanted to see him.

After a second he replied, 'That's nothing, I could be there in an hour.'

'Does your sister have a Ferrari or a helicopter?'

Parsons laughed. 'She is probably on the other phone listening to us right now,' he said.

'What's her name?' Rebecca asked him.

'It's Carol, why?'

'Hi Carol. I'm Becky,' she said in a friendly voice.

'Hi Becky, nice to meet you. Look after my little brother for me,' Parsons' sister replied.

'Oi, get off the phone,' Parsons told her through the handset.

'Nice to meet you, too. I'll look after him, I promise. Have a lovely Christmas,' Rebecca replied.

'Seriously, you two are horrendous. Carol, can you please hang up?' he said, only slightly annoyed.

'Ok, I'm going. Make sure that you come around for dinner sometime, Becky. Don't let him hide you away! Merry Christmas, bye.'

'Bye Carol,' Rebecca said.

'Did she really just listen in to our conversation?' Parsons asked, embarrassed by his sister.

'She's nice. Argh, I've got to look after you now, I've promised.'

'Ignore my sister. She does things like this, and you haven't got to look after me. Where should I meet you?' he asked.

'It's so sweet. Are you ready for the address?' Rebecca asked him.

'It's not sweet, yes, I've got a pen, ready when you are.'

'Well, I think that it's sweet. It's Abbeyfield House,

Wolseley Lane...' Rebecca gave Parsons the address, and he said that he would see her in a couple of hours.

After he had hung up the telephone, he was met with a never-ending list of questions from his sister, who was convinced that Becky was his girlfriend.

'She's a friend from work, that's all,' he told her.

'Carl, you are a soldier. They don't have women in the army. I knew you were different this time when you came home. Come on, tell your big sister all about her,' she insisted.

'You are so old-fashioned - Of course, they have women in the army. Anyway, I'm off to Lincolnshire to meet my friend,' he said mockingly as he got his stuff together and headed out of the door.

'Be careful and wear a condom if you do anything.'

He shook his head in shock and laughed at his sister as he opened the car door. 'Thank you for that advice. I'll call you later, love you, you nosey cow.'

Carol laughed at him as she watched him go. He was her little brother and he might have a girlfriend. She was pleased with him.

IT TOOK Parsons just over two hours to get to the address that Rebecca had given. As he stopped outside, he saw her come out of the house and walk to his car.

'Hey, how was the drive?' she asked as she got into the passenger seat.

'It was good. I think that it's quieter because it's Christmas Eve. There wasn't much traffic at all. You look good.'

'Good? I've just spent two hours getting myself ready, and good is the best that you can come up with!'

He looked into her eyes and was about to speak, but then her lips were on his. She kissed him softly, then pulled away.

'Do not say the word, "tasty" or I will kick your ass,' she threatened.

Although she was smiling, he wasn't sure whether she meant it. 'Beautiful, I was going to say beautiful,' he told her.

She smiled and kissed him again. 'That will do for now. You can work on it while we are in Morocco.' Her smile grew when she saw the shocked expression on his face. Before he could speak, she went on, 'Come on, I need some lunch. Let's go driver.'

Grantham was a pleasant place, and after lunch, Rebecca showed Parsons around the town. He asked her if she would help him choose a Christmas present for his sister.

'Oh, I would like that. Carol and I are friends now,' she told him. 'How much can I spend?'

'Any amount, just so long as it's something special,' he said.

'How much money do you have in your bank?' she asked him, pretending to be serious.

'My sister has a Ferrari and a helicopter, remember. She doesn't need anything expensive,' he replied, and it made her smile.

'Wow, she is beautiful,' he thought. He looked at her and felt a connection he had never felt before.

'What?' she asked.

'What?' he replied.

'What were you just thinking? You looked at me funny.'

He thought about it for a moment and decided to tell her the truth.

'I think I would like to marry someone like you,' he said.

She laughed and hit him playfully. 'What are you saying, you nutter?'

'One day I mean,' he elaborated.

She shook her head and then took his hand in hers. 'You are the strangest person I've ever met'. He made her feel happy, and she liked it. 'Come on, let's spend all of your money on your sister,' she giggled as she led him away to a shop she had in mind.

The afternoon slipped into early evening and as it went dark, the high street was lit up with Christmas lights. They walked the length of the lit-up decorations and, as they did, Parsons saw a homeless beggar huddled in a doorway. They had been walking with linked arms and Parsons made to break his arm from Rebecca's grip slightly. She knew what he was going to do and gripped his arm tighter, but altered her direction towards the beggar. Parsons gave the beggar ten pounds and asked him if he was alright. The beggar was delighted and thanked him. They spent a few minutes talking with him and by the time they walked on; the beggar was laughing and wished them a Merry Christmas. Rebecca noted how Parsons had got down to the beggar's level and had not leaned over him. It was a simple but caring little detail; she thought. Although neither of them was hungry again, they went for dinner in a pub, as neither of them wanted their time together to end.

As they ate, they learned more about each other, and Rebecca told Parsons that she envied him for having siblings.

'What is your sister like?' she asked him.

'Nosey, she's nosey', Parsons answered. 'My brother is

the opposite to her; you wouldn't believe that they are twins.'

'Twins, really? Are they close to each other?' she asked, excited by the idea of twins.

'Yeh, I suppose they are. We have lots of twins in our family. I think that it usually skips a generation, but not in mine. There is at least one set of twins in each generation if you include my uncles and aunts.'

'Double the trouble, that seems to describe you to a tee.' Rebecca smiled at him.

'I'm not a twin though, I'm a one off.'

'Thank God,' Rebecca commented.

'How come you are single?' Parsons asked.

'How do you know I am single?' she asked, raising a brow in question.

'How come you are single, Miss single old cat lady?' Parsons replied now, with a grin.

'I do actually have a cat. That's quite impressive for you,' she replied. 'Seriously though, how do you have a relationship when you do our work? It's not exactly normal, or easy to explain to people. I have dated guys I've worked with but it never lasts.'

'Yeh, I can see work being an issue.'

'What about you? No girlfriend?' she asked Parsons.

'No. If I'm honest, I've never had a serious relationship. Nothing more than a couple of months, anyway.'

'I'm surprised by that,' Rebecca said.

'Why?'

'I wouldn't have thought that anyone would have put up with you for as long as a couple of months.' She took a drink from her glass as she finished speaking, but he could see her smile.

'Remember what you promised my sister? You are meant to be nice to me.'

'I promised her I would look after her little brother, not be nice to him. Plus, I chose her Christmas present, so she will love me no matter what,' Rebecca laughed.

As Parsons laughed along with her, he knew his sister would love her if they were to meet. Her personality was engaging and as he gazed at her, he made himself a promise that she would meet his sister.

He realised he was daydreaming and so changed the subject. 'You still haven't told me about us going away on this course, you know,' he told Rebecca.

'Oh my God, I haven't. You have been here for hours and we haven't even mentioned it'. She was surprised by how naturally they had spent the time together. He really was different. She felt as though she had known him for far longer than she had.

She told him everything that she knew about the course, including that it started on 17th January. They needed to arrive the day before and would be there for two weeks. The Colonel had suggested that they spend the days leading up to it in Gibraltar and had asked Rebecca to use the time to bring Parsons up to speed on MI5, MI6, and Special Branch. He didn't want Parsons walking into the course blind, and to be fair to him, he was still extremely new to the world of covert operations and espionage.

'Will I become the new James Bond after this?' Parsons asked Rebecca.

'You might become the monkey from the Brooke Bond advert, if you are lucky,' she offered him. 'Anyway, who are you with for dinner tomorrow?' she asked him.

'My sister's, boyfriend's, sister's family.'

'What?' She looked confused.

'My sister's boyfriend had already arranged for them to go to his sister's house for dinner. So, I'm going there with him and my sister as a plus one. What about you?' he asked.

'My parents have gone to stay with family. They didn't know that I was coming home.'

'So, who are you going to be with?' he asked her.

'No one, I'll be on my own. I could have gone with my parents, but if I'm really honest, I've not spent a Christmas at home in four years, and I kind of want to wake up on Christmas morning in my own bed, at home.'

'Me too,' he replied.

'What? You want to wake up in my bed?' she said, teasing him again.

'Yes, please,' he laughed with her. After they had paid the bill, they drove back to Rebecca's house.

Rebecca's parents hadn't expected her to be home for Christmas. They had already planned to stay with her grandparents and family in Dorset when she gave them the news. They had begged her to go with them, but she had insisted on spending the time at home. She had promised that she would spend New Year's Eve with them as a trade-off, and they were happy with that. They had left earlier in the day and wouldn't be back now until New Year's Eve morning.

'Park on the drive,' Rebecca told Parsons as he drove up to the house.

He pulled up the handbrake and wondered if she was going to invite him inside. She soon answered any doubts he had.

'Well, you can either come inside or I can tear your clothes off right here. But we will be a lot more comfortable in my double bed.'

Their eyes locked. When their lips met, Parsons felt a

crackle of electricity. Rebecca put her palm on his chest and pushed him away. 'Quick, let's get inside,' she said, catching her breath. Parsons couldn't unbuckle his seatbelt fast enough, and they raced into the house.

Clothes were hurriedly discarded as they made their way up the stairs to the bedroom. Rebecca lay down on the bed and Parsons marvelled at how sexy she looked in her lacy black knickers and bra. His cock strained at his boxers, so he shrugged them off. Naked, he rested his knees on the end of the bed and held Rebecca's feet. Circling her ankles with kisses, he took his time and kissed his way up her legs and over her knees. Rebecca moaned softly. He remembered the first time he had laid eyes on her in the classroom and how desperate he had been to get his hands on her arse. Now, he wanted so much to see it naked, to turn her over and drink in the sight. That could wait for now.

He shifted up the bed and lightly kissed along the inside of her thighs. Rebecca opened her legs wider and reached down to grip his hair between her fingers. Her skin was so soft and tasted as sweet as he had imagined it would. A faint trace of her perfume caused his cock to harden even more. He felt her shudder slightly as he rubbed his nose over her silk knickers, which were damp.

With a low groan, Rebecca slid her hands around the back of his head and pulled him in closer. He moved his hands to her hips and pulled down her knickers. His cock twitched when he revealed her perfect, wet pussy. His nostrils were filled with the smell of her and he couldn't wait any longer to taste her, so removed her knickers and threw them on the floor. He touched her clit lightly with the tip of his tongue, and her hips bucked. As his tongue continued to move in circles, her stomach flattened and her chest rose. The sound of her panting turned him on and his cock was rock hard. He gripped her thighs, and her juices soaked his chin as he took her clitoris fully in his mouth and gently sucked. Rebecca's hands gripped the sheets as she squirmed uncontrollably. He lowered his mouth, just enough to allow his tongue to slip into her wet pussy. With a gasp, she pulled his head up and whispered, 'I want you inside me. Now.'

She took her bra off quickly and carelessly threw it. Her eyes never left his while she guided his cock to her entrance. She sighed as he pushed it in, then sighed again as he filled her completely. They were a perfect fit. He held himself there for a moment before slowly sliding his cock out and in, slowly at first, then gradually faster. Her hands roamed over his shoulders and down his back, feeling every tensed muscle with her fingertips. As she clutched his backside, he lifted his upper body, and she looked into his eyes, seeing his pleasure.

She smiled as she pulled him deeper inside her; first with her hands on his backside, and then with her legs.

'Fuck me, Carl, fuck me'. He didn't need asking twice. He steadied himself, then began thrusting, harder now and somehow even deeper. The sensation of him both filling her up and rubbing against her clitoris was almost too much. She rocked with him and felt her orgasm building. He kissed firmly along the side of her neck, which made her legs tremble. He lowered his head and took one of her breasts in his mouth. She bucked and cried out as he sucked gently.

'Fuck, yes, yes, that's it.'

He felt a tiny element of pain as she scraped her nails down his back, but it only excited him more.

'Come with me,' she said and as she lifted his head from her breast, 'Come at the same time, together.'

Those words drove him wild, and he thought his cock was going to burst. He lowered himself and her hardened nipples brushed against his chest. He kissed her beautiful mouth. She turned her head and moaned loader as he nibbled behind her ear.

'Fuck, fuck, yes,' Rebecca shouted out.

He felt it. First, she gripped him with her arms and legs, then he felt her muscles clench around his cock.

'Carl. Oh God, now!'

He slid his hand beneath her, taking her buttock in his grip. With the next thrust, he exploded, and she clung to him. Her moans matched his.

'Oh, God, Becky, oh my God,' he groaned with closed eyes as he felt himself orgasm like he had never before. He opened his eyes. There was a sexy sheen of sweat on her face and her breasts.

'Merry Christmas,' she whispered to him, still looking into his eyes.

He smiled as his cock continued to pulsate inside her.

'Merry Christmas.'

They lay together, exhausted and satisfied. Rebecca turned to face him, on her side with her leg over his, and rested her head on his chest. Listening to the other one breathing and feeling the beat of their heart, they both knew they had a special connection. It was based on trust as well as lust. Parsons could not wait until the morning so he could give Rebecca the necklace, which she had been duped into choosing, believing it to be for his sister. He smiled and kissed her on the head before slipping into the most comfortable sleep he had enjoyed in years.

8

Giselle was their contact who met them when they arrived in Gibraltar. She drove them to their accommodation and helped them settle into their stay. Before she left, she suggested it would be nice for the two of them to walk the Mediterranean steps, which was a walk that climbed around and up the south-east side of the rock. The following day, they set off for the Mediterranean steps with their tourist map, a packed lunch and the promise of the best view of Morocco and the Straits.

As they climbed, they heard the song of the hoopoe bird and spotted a flock of them swooping over the cliffs. They were quite a sight with their crown of orange feathers and distinctive black-and-white striped coat. Tropical trees and lush plants flourished along both sides of the path: growing in the direction in which they were heading as though to guide them on their journey. Hot and sweaty, they eventually came to a natural resting place where the path opened out to give way to the perfect viewing point. It was a formation of rock making a heart-shaped archway, which looked over the entrance to the Mediterranean and beyond. The view was so breath-taking that they could not find the words to give it justice. Including the coastline of the Costa Del Sol, West across the Striates of Gibraltar and as far as Morocco in Africa, the vista was stunning. The sun glinted off the sea, onto the rock and up to the archway where they stood, lighting it up with a golden glow.

'It's beautiful,' Rebecca remarked. They both took a moment to absorb the view. Rebecca turned to Parsons and put her arms around his waist, then looked up at his face. Neither said a word. Their eye contact was electric. When Rebecca finally spoke, the one sentence went straight to his heart.

'This is the best memory snap of my life.'

Parsons' heart was racing. He smiled, then leaned in to kiss her, pulling her close to his chest and tenderly brushing her lips with his. She sighed and rested her head on his shoulder.

The two lovers basked in the glow of the depth of their feelings. Rebecca's senses were heightened. She was aware of the warmth of the sun on her back and the gentle breeze that cooled her skin. Pressing her mouth to his again, her heart skipped a beat at the slightly salty taste of his lips. Butterflies filled her stomach, and she thought she might burst with the love she felt for this wonderful man.

She hugged him tightly and said a prayer under her breath as they clung to each other. If her prayer was answered, their love would be sealed forever.

Another walker stopped to enjoy the view. Rebecca asked him to take a photograph of them. Willingly, he did, and Rebecca was delighted to have the perfect moment captured forever. As Gruber handed the camera back to Rebecca, he also secured the moment in his mind.

Their time in Gibraltar passed too quickly, and before

they knew it, they were to leave for Marrakesh the following morning.

Again, a faxed message was sent giving an update. 'SUBJECT TWO TO ARRIVE AS PLANNED. SUBJECT ONE NO UPDATE.'

WHEN REBECCA and Parsons arrived in Marrakesh, they were surprised to find that the course that they were attending was held in a hotel. They were given separate hotel rooms, which were both doubles, so their sleeping arrangements remained as they had back in Gibraltar, sharing a bed. Each morning, Rebecca made sure that both of their rooms appeared to have been used and the beds slept in.

The attendees of the course were mainly UK service personnel from the military, home office, and police. It was very low key, and they were told that they should know the facility was a regular hotel with public guests. The ages of the attendees ranged from Parsons, who was the youngest, to a woman who celebrated her fifty-fourth birthday during the course. Her name was Pippa, and she was a reporter for a national paper in the UK. During her introduction, she told them she had been with British troops throughout the liberation of Baghdad. She was now working for the same paper, reporting on the Bosnia conflict that in her opinion was escalating in to mass genocide that was being orchestrated by its top military commanders. She said that she was on the course for her own safety, but she was there at the request of some government department.

When during a conversation, Parsons mentioned he was only nineteen years old, Pippa stated she was old enough to be his grandmother. She later jokingly scolded him when he said that he was amazed by how old she was. Pippa, who liked to be addressed as Pip, instructed Rebecca to give Parsons some tips on how to be tactful with women when discussing their age. She said that his innocence was sweet, but that she doubted he would live to be twenty-one if he continued to be so honest, to her at least.

'He actually looks a little older than he is, don't you think?' Pip suggested to Rebecca when they took a coffee break during the first day of the course.

'I do. I think that it's his height. And when he doesn't speak, when he's not speaking at all, he behaves quite mature,' Rebecca said with a smile.

'Yes,' Pip replied. 'He is mature for his age. When he's not making me feel old, I mean. He's very handsome Rebecca, don't let that detail slip by you. If there is one thing that I can tell you, it's to never look a gift horse in the mouth.'

'I don't understand,' Rebecca replied.

'I saw you both arrive yesterday. And from what I've seen in the short time that I've watched the two of you together, I would say that this young man has eyes for you. Just watch him for a minute.'

Rebecca and Pip looked across the room to where Parsons was talking with several of the other attendees. After a short time, he looked across at Rebecca and his face lit up with a smile.

'There it is. Look at the way he looks at you,' Pip told Rebecca. 'That's the look of a man with feelings. Yes. If I'm not mistaken, I've already missed the first part of this story.' Pip looked at Rebecca now. 'It's there in your eyes as well. Oh, now I see it. Good for you girl,' Pip congratulated Rebecca with a knowing wink.

Rebecca looked at Pip and was about to speak when she felt a connection between them. It felt good to not feel guilty for the first time since she had grown to care for Parsons. She resisted her instinct to deny what Pip was suggesting and felt good at that moment.

Pip winked again and smiled before saying, 'Oh, to be young again.'

ALL OF WHAT they were taught at the beginning of the week was to be practiced over the following two days, during which they were to go about their own business, in the hotel and the surrounding areas. Their task was to blend in and to see what they could learn about anyone and anything without being compromised.

Pip spent the time around the hotel pool, reading and catching up on some much-needed relaxation. She declared the lead instructor 'the most wonderful man that she had ever met' and told him that his methods of teaching were second to none.

Parsons and Rebecca looked around the city to learn as much as they could about its infrastructure and facilities such as hospitals, government buildings and anything that could interest a foreign party. Although the city was new to them, they were able to learn much, and gather what they thought would be useful intelligence.

On the Friday afternoon, they joined Pip around the hotel pool, and were surprised to see that she had all the hotel staff at her beck and call. Every thirty minutes, waiters would enquire whether they could get anything for her. Each time that they fetched a drink or a snack for her, she would converse with them, asking questions about their personal life and showing interest in them. Many of the hotel staff were from villages out of the city and were living away from their families. Pip seemed to make them feel at ease and listened with interest when they spoke to her about their home life and family. Even the hotel manager gave her special treatment and came to check that she had everything that she could desire.

'Abbas, I must introduce you to my friends,' Pip said as the hotel manager came near. 'This is Rebecca and Carl. They are such a lovely couple.'

Abbas came and introduced himself to them and asked them how they were enjoying their stay. They told him it was lovely, and that they had been in to the city and had seen many of the sights.

'Have you been in to the desert?' Abbas asked them with great enthusiasm.

'No, we never thought of it,' Parsons replied.

'You must, it is the most beautiful location on the whole of earth. To watch the sun set from the Agafay desert is a magical experience. Would you like me to arrange it for you?'

'Of course, they would Abbas, they are free tomorrow if you can have something in place for then,' Pip replied for them. 'In fact, I think I would like to go along too, if that would be possible.'

'Yes, Miss Pip. But I would advise an early start so that you can get away from the city before it awakens. My nephew will collect you from the reception at seven o'clock if that suits you,' Abbas suggested.

'Perfect Abbas, we will be there. What is your nephew's name? Is it Youssef, your sister's eldest son?' Pip asked him.

'Yes, that is right. He is the archaeologist that I told you about,' Abbas confirmed.

'What an adventure it is going to be, I can't wait,' Pip proclaimed as she took another sip of her gin and tonic and smiled at the couple.

'Very good, have a lovely evening all of you.' Abbas left.

'Youssef is the assistant curator at the city's museum. Abbas told me that his nephew studied in England, and that he occasionally runs these little expeditions into the desert and to the Atlas Mountains. He was in the military here for a short while, too. I think he could be the perfect person to help you fill in any gaps that you have in the information that you have been building. He will know of all the government departments and have knowledge of the current politics,' Pip told them.

Parsons looked at Pip and smiled. She was a machine. He was sure that she was capable of listening in and gaining more information than the whole of the American Central Intelligence Agency. She was a natural at it, and he imagined what her work had previously entailed. She had told them she had been in the Gulf during the war with Iraq, but he was sure that she had not told them the full extent of her role there.

Pip smiled back at Parsons and gave him a single wink of her eye. He liked her, she was a part of the new world that he was discovering, and he liked her a lot.

THAT NIGHT PARSONS and Rebecca went out in to Marrakesh for dinner. Before setting off, Parsons had gone to sit in the hotel bar to wait for Rebecca, who was finishing getting dressed. Whilst in the bar, Abbas came to chat with Parsons and asked him where they were planning to go for dinner. He suggested a place that Parsons should take Rebecca and he said that he would call ahead and book a table for them. Abbas assured Parsons that it was where the best food in the whole of Morocco was served and that the owner was a friend of his.

As Abbas returned from making the arrangements, he saw Rebecca exiting the lift and walking in to the bar. 'Oh, my world, jameela, yes?' he said to Parsons, awaiting his response.

'Pardon,' Parsons replied as he looked across the bar at Rebecca.

'Jameela, she is beautiful. Miss Rebecca, you are a gazelle. Stop, wait there for a moment'. Abbas walked over to where Rebecca was now standing, waiting for him. Abbas took her arm, linked it with his, and walked her to Parsons. 'Mr Parsons, your beautiful lady is ready, Allah mahaba.'

'What does that mean?' Rebecca asked Abbas, slightly embarrassed by his fussing.

'In English, it means God is love, or maybe love is God,' Abbas told her.

Rebecca's smile lit up not only her face, but the room as well. She looked even more radiant than Parsons had ever seen her before. She wore a blue dress that shimmered in the reflection of the lights. Her hair was wavy and fell down her back, leaving her shoulders bare and her neck line exaggerated by the necklace that Parsons had given her. Her skin had a tanned glow to it from the previous day's sun, and the faintest trace of freckles adorned her shoulders and face. Parsons looked at her and searched for the right words.

'You are the most beautiful person I have ever seen,' he said.

'Jameela,' Abbas agreed. He handed a street map to Parsons and explained to him where the restaurant was situated.

They set off for their evening and walked from the hotel, through the streets and into the city centre, which was a fifteen-minute stroll away. Using the map, they navigated their way through back streets and alleyways, rather than taking the busy main route. They saw dogs lazily sleeping and children playing together. As they passed the many homes that had doors and windows open to lose some of the day's heat, they saw snippets of the lives of the occupants. Meals were being prepared and families were coming together. To see life taking place felt good and made Rebecca think what it would be like to one day have a home and a family with Parsons. She said hello and waved at a young girl who was sitting on a small plastic chair, playing with a puppy as she watched them walk by. The young girl smiled and shyly giggled as she took hold of her puppy in a tight hug. Rebecca took a packet of mints from her bag and gave them to the girl who took them instantly, recognising what they were. She immediately lost all interest in the couple and ate the mints with help from the puppy.

As they walked away, the girl ran in to her house shouting out to her family through a mouth full of mints.

After a few more minutes, they came out in to a large open area where the night market, with its famous souks, was coming alive. This was the Jemaa El-Fnaa, the largest of the markets where it was possible to buy anything. For generations, traders had passed along the many routes that brought them to Marrakesh, where they exchanged their goods. There were souks selling ceramics, dyes, clothing, and every herb and spice that existed. The street was a clamour with food sellers working from their stalls, pushing their produce in to the faces of passerby. No one spoke quietly or even at a reasonable volume. Every word spoken was raised in competition with the neighbouring voice.

'Oh my God,' Rebecca said as she froze and pulled Parsons back by his arm. 'Is that a real snake?' she asked, as she looked at a Cobra performing its hypnotic dance. There was a crowd of men in a circle around the snake that was staring at its charmer as he used a flute to entrance it.

'Shit, look how close they are to it,' Parsons commented. At that moment, the snake spat out and lunged towards the surrounding circle. Not one man moved an inch, and the snake returned its gaze back to the flute and was again transfixed by its tune.

'Come on, let's go,' Parsons suggested, as he took Rebecca's hand in to his and led her in the direction that they needed to go. 'I bloody hate snakes,' he told her.

As they walked, they were pestered continually by the traders who attempted to pull them into their souks and chased after them, calling out ever lowering prices for their wares. As they passed through the market, they saw several animals, including monkeys and camels, all of which were for sale.

They eventually got to the street where Abbas had marked the restaurant on the map. Parsons checked the map again and looked up at the street name, confirming that they were in the correct place.

'Is it here?' Rebecca asked doubtingly as she looked along the street. It was now dark and the narrow street was dimly lit.

'It's the one that Abbas has marked. Let's have a look,' he said, leading her further down the street. There were no people around, and they were starting to believe that Abbas had marked the wrong location on the map. Then they suddenly heard a voice from above them.

'Maybe it is up there,' Parsons said, as he looked up to the roof of the building where the voice had come from.

There was a doorway into the building, but no sign of a restaurant.

They went into the doorway through which they had to both duck their heads to avoid hitting them. They climbed two flights of stairs and were relieved when they found a room that had tables and chairs set out in it. But there was no one there, and it looked closed, maybe even shut up for good. Then they heard footsteps and a voice, getting louder as it came towards them.

'Hello,' Rebecca called out, just as a man came walking into sight from the far side of the room.

'Hello, Carl and Rebecca, welcome,' the man greeted them as he came to meet them, now aware that they had arrived. Ahmed was the owner, chef, waiter, and everything else at the Casa Bazaar Restaurant. He had worked there with his wife, since they had married, twenty-eight years previously, and had never taken a holiday during that time. He lived for his restaurant and was happy, nowhere else.

'My name is Ahmad. Come, let me show you to your table. Also, you must meet my wife. Come,' he said as he beckoned them to follow him. They went through another doorway at the far side of the room and up another flight of stairs that led onto a roof terrace.

As they walked out onto the roof terrace, they entered what appeared to be a mini oasis above the city. It was far from what they had imagined it would be. The floor was a rich, terracotta colour, and the walls that were low enough to see over were whitewashed and adorned with pretty painted plant pots and flowers that gave off a vibrant and fresh feel. There were seven tables laid out on the terrace, each with chairs for two people. They were shown to a table at the end of the terrace that overlooked the city lights and the many historic buildings that cast silhouettes to create a mesmerising skyline. The terrace was lit with only candles that were seated in traditional Moroccan lanterns; their glow cast on to the walls in flickering changing patterns. The evening's heat was warm but comfortable and as they took their seats, they felt as though they were in a magical kingdom, a hidden paradise.

'I have reserved for you the best table that we have. The chief of police is dining tonight and wanted this table, but I told him it is reserved for my special guests.'

Ahmed was clearly overjoyed to have Rebecca and Carl in his restaurant and intended to make them as welcome as he did all of his guests. 'The views from here are the best in the whole of Marrakesh. You can see the Koutoubia Mosque just there,' he said as he pointed to its sandstone tower. 'And also, here is the Bahia Palace. You still have to see the most spectacular sight in the whole of Morocco though.'

Already stunned by their location and the sights that Ahmad had shown them, Rebecca and Parsons were intrigued to see what he was going to show them next.

'Safaa,' Ahmad called out to his wife. 'Safaa, come and meet our guests, that Abbas has sent to us.'

At the news that the young couple had arrived, Safaa came out from the kitchen to meet them. Saffa, like her husband, was in her early fifties and had spent much of her adult life building the reputation of their little restaurant that she adored. She was small, rotund, and beautiful. Her energy and warmth were tangible, and she radiated positivity as she entered the terrace wearing a chef's apron over her clothes.

Ahmed put his hand out to her as she approached them and said, 'Here is my sunshine, this is Saffa, my wife and my eternal love.'

As Saffa got to him, she gently hit him with her palm.

She smiled at him and said, 'You are my eternal mischief, my love.' Saffa was taken into Ahmad's embrace and she looked a perfect match by his side. 'Welcome to our little home,' she told Rebecca and Parsons. 'You will have beautiful children one day. I can feel this,' she added, looking at Rebecca.

Rebecca looked back at her, surprised, and Saffa gave her a knowing look as she placed a hand on her shoulder and spoke again.

'Come now, I know these things. And I also know that you young Gazelle wish to one day have a daughter.' Neither Rebecca nor Parsons said anything to deny what Saffa had said, as they both knew that she had read the thoughts that they had been having separately for some time.

'You see Ahmed, the old hen is wise and you should listen to me whenever I speak,' Saffa teased, making him laugh at her.

'Saffa, I only ever listen to you my love, your voice is the only voice that my heart knows,' Ahmed replied to her, causing her to hit him again.

'Then listen to me now and fetch drinks for our guests or else we will lose them to thirst before they have even had the chance to taste our food.'

Ahmed told Saffa that he would do it right away and left with their drinks order. Whilst he was gone, Saffa asked how they had enjoyed their time in the city and was pleased to know that they liked it there. Saffa was then distracted by a father and his daughter who arrived to dine. She showed them to a table and then returned to the kitchen where, with the help of Ahmed, she prepared a fine dinner for their guests.

'This is the most unlikely place I could have imagined,'

Parsons told Rebecca. 'It's completely hidden away, and it's wonderful.'

'I think Abbas is the man to know in Marrakesh,' Rebecca replied.

'We still have the trip in to the Sahara yet, I'm looking forward to that.'

'Have you travelled much before?' Rebecca asked.

'No, my mum doesn't enjoy travelling, so we never went away when I was a kid. What about you?'

'We went abroad most years when I was growing up. Every summer we would go to a different place. Every few years, we would go to Australia for a month to stay with my dad's brother and his family. I was really lucky, I guess.'

Rebecca knew she had had a much more privileged upbringing than Parsons. She had seen his personnel file that gave details of his childhood. His family had lived in rented accommodation and had struggled when his father had become ill and had to take a long time away from work. Although Parsons never spoke negatively of his childhood, Rebecca had seen the reports from teachers who had commented on the condition of his clothes and that in their opinion the family must have been struggling to manage financially.

'Where would you go if you could go anywhere?' she asked him.

'Spain,' he answered without hesitation.

'Then we should go,' Rebecca suggested.

She saw his expression change and remembered that he had once hoped to live in Spain. 'When do you think we could go there?' Parsons asked enthusiastically.

'Well, we could try to book leave together in the summer and go then, maybe.'

'That would be amazing. We could take two weeks and drive to different places,' Parsons suggested.

'I've been thinking about things actually Carl,' Rebecca said in a more serious tone. 'When we get back, neither of us is allowed to be in any kind of personal relationship with anyone that we work with. It's a rule that has always been in place at the unit. So, we are going to have to either cool things down between us when we are there or tell them, and see what they say.'

Parsons thought about what she had said and asked, 'What can they say? I mean, if we just say that we won't end it, what can they do?'

'I'm not sure. No one has ever done that. They could technically post one of us to somewhere else so that we have no choice.' Parsons was sad at the thought and wondered what that would mean for them.

'I don't want to be apart from you Bec,' he said, as he let it run through his mind.

'Me neither. And I'd struggle to hide my feelings for you when people were around us.'

'I love you,' he said.

'I love you; I just want to be with you.' She reached across the table and took hold of his hands in hers.

'We will be together. No matter what we have to do, we will be together,' he assured her with a smile.

'God, that feels good, to know that you love me too,' Rebecca said. 'I haven't felt like this before, and I was scared that you might not feel the same.'

Parsons leant over the table and kissed Rebecca. 'I do feel the same, and we won't let anyone separate us.'

That night, their lovemaking differed from before. Not only was it more intimate, but there was a deeper emotional connection. When Rebecca's orgasm finally came, it felt like her body had exploded and then immediately melted into a peaceful exhaustion. As Parsons lay on top of her, she clung to him to stop him from withdrawing from her. She wanted that sensation to last and she could only describe what she felt as that they had moulded in to one body. They both now knew that their feelings for each other were not in vain, and let the security of that knowledge consume them.

GRUBER LISTENED to Terhi Johanson as she gave him an account of the conversation Parsons and Rebecca had shared during dinner. Their age gap was proving useful in allowing them to pose as father and daughter, and although Gruber had heard the conversation for himself, he wanted Terhi to recite it to him. She was exactingly accurate in her account and he could not help but feel proud of her ability.

'Is he left or right-handed?' Gruber asked.

'Right.'

'How can you be sure?'

'It is his dominant hand, and it is unmistakable,' Terhi replied, as though it were a silly question.

'Good. You didn't include your opinion on his child-hood, which could have been useful. I want you to consider it next time.'

Terhi looked slightly disappointed at her teacher's criticism, but knew not to show it. She would not make the same mistake again.

'I must go now if I am to meet Youssef before he leaves the museum,' she told Gruber as she stood up.

'Remember that he is not one of our own and that you cannot trust him completely,' Gruber cautioned her.

Terhi looked back over her shoulder and smiled. 'I do

not need to trust him; I simply need to seduce him so that he falls under my spell.' She left the room and Gruber considered the situation he had placed her in. She was barely eighteen, and he was using her as one of his own agents. She was going into dangerous situations and could be killed at any moment.

'She is barely an adult,' he thought. 'Nevertheless, her life has improved since she met me. Plus, she is so good, she will be fine,' he decided.

9

_____

Youssef arrived at the hotel five minutes late and was met by his uncle Abbas, who gave him a picnic hamper filled with food and drinks for himself and the guests to enjoy during the trip. Youssef looked a little tired and rushed, but his uncle said nothing.

Rebecca, Parsons and Pip met them in the hotel's reception and were introduced by Abbas. Their belongings and the picnic hamper were loaded into the Toyota Land cruiser that Youssef was driving, and they set off into the morning sun. Youssef was as excited as his passengers as he relished these rare opportunities to show people what his country offered in the way of natural beauty. He took them away from the city and into the open landscape of Morocco.

They were surprised that the area outside of Marrakesh was not as barren as they had expected. Youssef explained to them that a great lake had been constructed some sixty years earlier, and that it was the primary source of water for Marrakesh. As the water supply made its way from the Lalla Takerkoust reservoir to the city, it fed many villages and created mini oasis' where vegetation grew and animals could water. He told them they would visit the lake at lunch time. First, Youssef took them to a viewing point from which they used binoculars to survey the Atlas Mountains whilst he pointed detail out to them and told of its history. He said that the mountains stretched out over two thousand five hundred kilometres from Morocco to Tunisia and to a height of over four thousand metres. He described how the Berber people have survived living in the mountain range for thousands of years. When they drove on, Youssef continued to point out historic facts and detail of the area.

'Youssef, how is your work funded at the museum?' Pip asked him.

'The government fund some of the work, but the greater portion of our funding comes from the UNESCO heritage group,' he told them.

'Who are these UNESCO people and what does it stand for?' Pip asked.

'It is the United Nations Education Social and Culture Organization. Its purpose is to protect world heritage sites from destruction and through treaties, its work is legally protected.'

'You certainly have a passion for your work,' Pip complimented him.

After they had been driving for a while, Youssef took them to a Berber village where they were welcomed and given sweet tea to drink. Youssef explained that the route they would take during the day was not well known and that these people did not see tourists often. He said that in tourist areas, makeshift Berber villages had been set up to appear genuine and that they were purely for commercial purposes and for tourism. No Berber had ever lived in them and each evening they were left empty until the following day, when the next busload of tourists would arrive. As a preserver of history, this disappointed Youssef, as it did the Berber tribal leaders.

They eventually drove on and Youssef told them they should try to find the hidden mirror, but refused to give them any further clues about what they were looking for. It was as they drove over a steep ridge that they first saw Lake Lalla Takerkoust, shining like a gigantic silver mirror. As they got closer to the lake, they saw it in all of its watery glory. Its banks that went in to the distance, where they were filled with an array of luscious trees and plants of various greens. There were birds in the trees and in the sky, and there was a gentle relieving wind that softly blew at their faces. They stopped on the bank of the lake and ate dinner in the sun. Parsons and Youssef used binoculars to look across the lake at a group of Berber herders and their animals. Pip and Rebecca sat watching the pair, enjoying a cold glass of wine in the midday heat.

'My goodness, this definitely beats reporting on some awful atrocity from a tiny little room in a war-torn hellhole of a country,' Pip proclaimed.

'Sorry,' Rebecca said, having not quite heard Pip.

'I said, this is far better than working. It may soon be time for me to find myself a rich oil tycoon to travel around the world with.'

'Do you know any oil tycoons?' Rebecca joked.

'Several,' pip said before taking a drink. 'But none that I would wish to spend a moment longer than necessary with, let alone travel the world with them,' Pip laughed.

'Are you from MI6 Pip?'

'My dear, you are in Morocco on a training course that should teach you the art of spying. What on earth makes you think I would answer a question like that now?' Pip replied.

'I don't know, I just wondered,' Rebecca answered honestly.

'Do you see our Youssef there?' Pip said to Rebecca as she looked over to where he stood with Parsons.

'Yes, he's lovely.'

'Do you think he works for MI6?' Pip asked seriously.

Rebecca looked at Pip with an expression of confusion on her face. Surely Pip was being cynical.

'Because he doesn't know that UNESCO stands for the United Nations Educational, Scientific and Cultural Organization.' She paused and looked at Rebecca, who was missing the point. 'When I asked him earlier, he said that it was the United Nations Education Social and Culture Organization. It's only a minor variation, but if it was important, for instance, because they funded you, it's not an error that you would make. I am in contact with UNESCO occasionally as part of my reporting. I get to see things of interested to them during my travels,' Pip explained.

'Bloody hell'. Rebecca looked over at the two men, who were deep in conversation. 'Then who is he?' Rebecca asked, still watching him.

'That is the tough question. If you look at the detail, you will eventually find gaps in it for sure. But finding the answers to the questions that you then raise, that is a totally different problem. But you just have to gather what you can from the gaps in the details and create intelligence.'

As Rebecca looked at Pip, she noticed her briefly smile, before continuing.

'A far bigger question is, what are the two of you doing here?' Pip said.

'We are here so that we can be used in Bosnia in the future.' Rebecca stopped talking when she saw Pip's facial expression.

'Rebecca, you are a woman with far-reaching abilities, who I know has a long and productive career ahead of her. Are you telling me you don't find it particularly unusual for your newest recruit to be on this course? A course to prepare him for something that he shouldn't be doing for a long time from now, if at all. If I was a cynic, I would suggest that there are plans afoot for Carl. And you need to protect you heart and your career if that is the case.'

Rebecca thought about Pip's words. The Colonel had put them both on the course as the work in Bosnia was increasing and it was logical to have as many trained staff as possible that could be deployed there, wasn't it? She looked from Parsons to Pip several times as she thought it through.

'If you knew something that would affect me and Carl being together, would you tell me?' Rebecca asked.

'I know that the two of you are madly in love. And that should be the only thing that can affect you being together if it is true love.' Pip smiled now and reached over to Rebecca, rubbing her arm. 'Come on, let's swim'. She stood up, stripped naked, and casually strolled down past the two men and into the shallow water.

'One word about my arse Carl, and I will see that you are fed to the crocodiles,' Pip warned, as they watched her in stunned amazement.

'Are there crocodiles in there?' Parsons whispered to Youssef.

'No, but don't mention her ass, because I think she will hurt you Carl. She is tough, I am sure of it,' Youssef remarked seriously.

Rebecca joined her, and as they swam, they laughed at the shocked faces of Youssef and Parsons. Rebecca put any worries that she had to the back of her mind. They would soon be back in Northern Ireland and back to normal.

LATER IN THE DAY, they got to the dunes of the Agafay desert. They were struck by the endless pattern of transverse ridges, one after the other, peaking higher and higher. The afternoon had passed, and the sun was dropping below the horizon as the evening fought to take over. The sand dunes gradually changed colour from the golden yellow they had been a short time before, to a deepening tone of red as the sun's rays took on a new life. The side of the Land cruiser appeared pink as it absorbed the light that shone on to its pearlescent painted finish.

Youssef took photographs of them using Parson's camera. Afterwards, he took the picnic hamper from the Land cruiser and urged them to climb, quickly, to the top of a high dune before they lost the sun. He lit a lantern and left it on the roof of the vehicle as a marker for where they would return to.

At the top of the dune, Youssef flattened a small area of sand and lay a traditional rug out for them to sit on. By the time Pip got to the top of the dune to join them, Youssef had set out their own little desert oasis and had arranged the food and drinks for everyone.

'My dear Youssef, I shall owe your uncle Abbas for an eternity for bringing you to me'. As she took a glass filled with wine from him, she toasted, 'Saha wa a fiab,' and they each joined her in her words and drank with her. Seeing Youssef drink and empty his glass of wine, Rebecca looked at Pip, who simply winked at her. If Youssef was a Muslim, as he had told them he was during the day, his religion would strictly forbid him to drink alcohol. It was certainly not a sign that he was a spy, but as Pip had now taught her, it was a gap in his story.

Rebecca and Parsons held hands as they sat and watched the sun sink lower, the sky grow redder, and the shadow of darkness eventually take its place. Another memory snap had been made.

ON MONDAY MORNING, when they reconvened back on the course, they were asked to prepare a report on the previous week's intelligence gathering. Rebecca and Parsons had made their notes during the previous week in such a format as to make it easy for them to use for this task, having guessed that it would be necessary. The students were given the whole of Monday to complete the reports, which they had to present to the group over the following two days.

It was Wednesday, immediately after lunch, when Pip presented her report. She began by listing almost every member of staff in the hotel, detailing their hometowns and information about many of their families. As she gave the information that she had gained, she graded it as reliable or not, depending on its source. She then moved on to other guests in the hotel, but not just the details that they had given her. She could tell what room they were staying in, their daily patterns, and how they had arrived and left the hotel. She must have watched every single movement in and out of the hotel from the moment that she had arrived. She even detailed the routines and patterns of the instructors.

She was able to say that they had eaten out on three of the evenings of the previous week and the names of the places where they had eaten. The instructors were surprised by her knowledge, especially when she added they had paid the bill on each of these occasions using a credit card that she believed was registered to MI6. She had so much detail that it was almost embarrassing for the subjects of it.

Her final instalment was to detail much about the other students, including telephone numbers that they had called from their rooms during their stay, the table that they preferred to sit at in the hotel restaurant and even how much alcohol they did or didn't consume. The only information that she gave no detail of was that of Rebecca and Parsons. She didn't mention them at all during her presentation.

When Pip had finished, she walked to her seat and as she did so she saw Rebecca make eye contact with her and whisper the words, 'Thank you.' Both Rebecca and Parsons knew that she had been kind to them by not disclosing all that she could have done about their relationship.

They were all praised for their work and told to meet at 9am the following day when they would have guest speakers. As they were leaving, Rebecca asked Pip if she would like to join them for dinner and suggested returning to Casa Bazzar.

'Oh, I would love to. How you have described it to me has created so many images in my head. I would love to see it,' Pip said.

Parsons spoke with Abbas, who made the reservation for them and booked them a taxi too.

They relaxed together on the bed in their room, passing the time that they had before dinner, chatting and reflecting on the course so far.

'I've decided that Pip is the female equivalent of James Bond,' Rebecca concluded.

'I think she would eat James Bond alive. Or feed him to crocodiles,' Parsons remarked, making them both laugh.

'I wonder who she actually is. I mean, who she works for though?' Rebecca puzzled.

'I think she is a civilian version of the Colonel. Like a stand-alone version that just blends in to any environment until she takes out her enemy,' Parsons replied.

'Oh, don't say that,' Rebecca said sadly. 'I don't want to think of her killing people. I like her and I want to keep the image that I have of her being sophisticated and ladylike.'

'I'm sorry Bec, but I think she is with the Russians and that she has a death toll longer than your arm,' he told her in a comical tone.

'You shouldn't joke,' Rebecca replied as she softly slapped his bare chest, that her head was resting on. 'She has already got your card marked for making her feel old, so if she is Pippa Bond or whoever, you might not be around for much longer.' She lifted her head and looked at him, raising her brow as to invite his response.

'The thought of this perhaps being my last few hours before I meet my fate of being fed to non-existent crocodiles by an old lady is strangely arousing me,' he told her.

'No, it isn't. It's the fact that we are naked and my leg is rubbing against your cock that is arousing you,' she corrected and kissed him as she took him erect in to her hand. As her head slid down his body and she took him in to her mouth, he groaned and closed his eyes. It was twenty minutes later as she got in to the shower, that she scolded him for making her sweaty and late.

'I'm sorry,' he lied, looking at her bare backside, dismissing the idea of going once more with her.

'You are not,' Rebecca accused him with a smile as she admitted, 'Neither am I though, I loved every second.'

PARSONS WAS SURPRISED to see Pip already waiting, alone in the bar, when he went down ahead of Rebecca to get a drink. He suddenly remembered that she was constantly working and gathering more detail. He realised he should not have been surprised that she had come to the busiest place in the hotel to watch and listen. Pip smiled as she saw him walking towards her and was genuinely pleased that he was joining her.

'You look amazing,' he told her, noticing that she was wearing a dress and heels. She had done something different with her hair and although he wanted to comment about it, he knew that if he did, he would get it wrong and he didn't want to say anything that could offend Pip.

She looked at him and paused. 'What is it?' he asked, concerned that he had done or said something awful.

'Nothing, I was just expecting you to say something unnecessary, and you didn't. My, my, you are learning,' Pip replied with a laugh.

'I was going to say that your hair looks nice, but I can't tell what is different about it so I di-'

Pip leant forward and put a single finger on to his lips, causing his mouth to close. 'You were doing so well, not another word.' She leant back in to her seat and said, 'You know, it is quite sweet that you say exactly what you are thinking. But, remember to think about what you are saying and the situation in which you are saying it'. She nodded, and he copied her.

'Yes, I do often say the wrong thing.'

'No. You often say the right thing. But you say it when you don't need to. Even though something is correct, it doesn't mean that you should say it.' She looked at Parsons and saw that he was thinking it through. 'It's fine to just think it, rather than say it out aloud'. He nodded more positively now, as he understood what Pippa was telling him. 'Be more aware of the situation and your surroundings,' she added with a wink, happy that he was finally listening to her.

'Would you excuse me for a minute, please?' Parsons asked and then left Pip in the bar. He went to the reception and spoke with Abbas briefly. When he returned, he saw Rebecca must have passed by him, as she was now in the bar with Pip.

'Hello again,' Rebecca said to him with a smile as Parsons joined them.

'Hello beautiful,' he replied before he gave her a kiss. He reached out to Pip and handed her an envelope.

'What is it?' Rebecca asked as she watched Pip take it from him.

'If I'm not mistaken, it's Carl taking in the situation and his surroundings!' Pip said, looking at him approvingly. She opened the envelope and took out a birthday card. In it was written, 'To Pip, Happy Birthday, Love Carl and Bec xx.' 'I know how hard it must have been for you to not be cheeky, and to resist writing a comment relating to age in there. So, I am very pleased with you, and really quite touched. Come here,' she said and gave him a kiss on his cheek.

Rebecca was also touched by Carl's thoughtful deed. As Pip gave her a kiss too, Rebecca wished her a happy birthday and asked Carl, 'How do you know that today is Pip's birthday?'

Parsons delayed his response and thought about it. 'A lucky guess,' he told her.

'Good lord, you are learning quickly Carl. You are a new man,' Pip said. Rebecca looked at them both, puzzled, as they laughed. 'I'll explain it to you at dinner,' Pip assured her.

Abbas appeared at the entrance to the bar, signalling that their taxi had arrived.

AHMED AND SAFFA were waiting for the trio as they walked up the stairs and out onto the terrace of the restaurant. Saffa hugged Rebecca when she saw her and already knew who Pip was, having been told by Abbas that she would be their guest this evening.

'Miss Pippa, it is lovely to meet you. Abbas has told us you are celebrating your birthday today. 'Eid milad saeid', we are honoured that you share it with us,' Saffa told her as she embraced her. She had wished Pip a happy birthday in Arabic.

'Azul,' Pip replied, which was a way of saying 'hello' in the traditional Berber language. 'Tamussni n lxir'. This meant, 'it's nice to meet you,' and upon hearing it, Ahmed and Saffa were delighted.

'Do you speak in the Amazigh tongue of our ancestors?' Ahmed asked her, with astonished respect.

'Oh no Ahmed, I have only a few words I learnt during my stay here. Amek tellid?' she asked of him. This meant, 'how are you?' he was overjoyed to see that she was trying to learn to speak his ancestor's language. Few people spoke in traditional Berber, as it was a language made up of several other dialects and was difficult to grasp. Arabic was the widely spoken language, and both Ahmed and Saffa appreciated hearing her attempt at the language that they loved.

'Igerrez, tanemmirt,' Saffa replied, saying 'fine, thank you.'

Rebecca and Parsons looked on as Pip charmed her new friends, and they could see how she could go anywhere in the world and instantly blend in and be accepted. They dined at the table at the end of the terrace, with the views over the city. The food was even tastier than it had been during their first visit and Pip insisted it was the best meal that she had eaten since arriving in Morocco.

'You weren't exaggerating this view, were you Rebecca?' Pip said, as she looked out over the city and the vanishing sun. 'That is a sight that I will take away with me,' she remarked.

'It's a memory snap,' Parsons commented.

When Pip enquired what a memory snap was, Rebecca explained Parsons' theory to her. Pip laughed and asked him whether memory snaps really made awful situations better.

'Yes,' he assured her.

'Give me an example of when you have used one of your memory snaps in the past, Carl,' Pip said.

Parsons thought about it and then began, 'I used to go to Piccadilly Circus at night and sit there, below the statue. I would watch the people and the traffic passing by, just sit there, listening to what was going on, while eating sweets.'

'Eating sweets?' Pip asked him.

'Yes, I would take sweets with me. I like sweets.'

Rebecca joined in the conversation by saying, 'He eats a lot of sweets.' Pip shook her head, wondering where his story was going.

'I used to sit there and watch the advertisements changing on the large video display boards across the road. When the lights in the display change colour, everything changes colour. The lights reflect off of all the buildings and passing traffic. It's beautiful.'

Pip and Rebecca could see that he was deep in thought, and from the smile on his face, they could see that this was a happy memory snap that he was reflecting up on.

'Do you know what that statue is named?' Pip asked him.

He broke from his thoughts, 'The Shaftesbury Memorial Fountain. It's actually Anteros, the brother of Eros. Most people are mistaken and say that it's Eros because he's more commonly known.' Pippa could not help but smile at Parsons.

'Where did you learn that information?' she asked him. She was intrigued how he knew the statue's subject was indeed, almost always mistaken for his brother, Eros.

Carl looked at Rebecca, having told her only weeks before of his time in London. He hadn't told her he used to visit Piccadilly Circus or that the location meant so much to him.

'Can I tell Pip why you went to London?' Rebecca interjected and pleaded with him. 'And then you can tell us both about the statue and how you know so much about it.'

'Go on then, I'll see if you were listening to me when I told you and the Colonel,' he challenged her.

Rebecca took great pleasure in telling Pip of how Parsons had gone AWOL from the army and had lived homeless on the streets begging. She recounted all that Parsons had told her, and it was clear to Pip that this woman loved him even more for his experience.

'But you've never told me about Eros, so I'm desperate to hear it,' Rebecca told him.

'Well, because there are always people there, at Piccadilly Circus, it is safe, and it is light as well. There is always something to watch, a street performer or tourists. It's never lonely there. I would go there every night before the sun went down and sit there until just before midnight.'

'Why until midnight? Where did you go then?' Pip asked.

'To the soup kitchen,' he replied. Rebecca recounted what Parsons had told her of the soup kitchen at Charing Cross station and Pip listened intently to the story.

'But you haven't explained how you learnt the difference between Eros and Anteros, the statue,' Pip said.

'Oh, I just learnt that.'

'But how did you learn it?' she asked.

'I spent all day walking around and learning about the places that I saw. And if the weather was bad, I went to museums and libraries to get out of the rain. I researched the places I was interested in and learnt about them. In the past I have taken a few friends on a tour of places to see in London, mostly the places I learnt about while I was living there.'

Pip looked at him and tried to imagine just how he would change in the years to come. She smiled at him and had an overpowering urge to protect him and to say something, to warn him. He reminded her of someone from her past. Someone who she had loved with all of her heart, someone she still loved with all of her heart.

'Carl, do you know the difference between Eros and Anteros in mythology?'. Pip asked him this to satisfy herself that he really was as important as she believed he was.

'Yes. Anteros' is love unreq-'

She interrupted him mid-sentence and said, 'Ok, Ok, you've learnt your stuff, we believe you'. She smiled at the couple and proposed a toast. 'To requited love.'

'To requited love,' they repeated and, with the touching of their glasses, they heard singing.

As they turned to look back at the terrace and the other diners, they saw Ahmed walking towards them, followed by Saffa, who was carrying a birthday cake. The rendition of Happy Birthday was taken up by everybody and as it ended, Pip blew out the candles and briefly closed her eyes.

'Did you make a wish?' Rebecca asked as she placed her hand on to Pip's arm.

'I did,' she said as she nodded. She had wished for Rebecca and Carl to be happy. She didn't believe in wishes, and neither did she believe the couple would be happy. But she still made the wish for them anyway.

ON FRIDAY MORNING Pip had to leave to catch her flight back to London, but before she left, she said goodbye to Parsons and Rebecca.

'Can I ask you a question?' Parsons asked Pip.

'You can. But I haven't felt the urge to murder you for a long time now. Are you sure that it will not make me change my mind?' she asked him with a mock serious expression.

'What did Youssef and the Berber elders speak about when we visited their village?'

'Why?' she asked him.

'I think you are right about Youssef, and I think the Berber told him something of importance. Am I right?'

'Yes, you are,' she told him honestly.

'What was it?'

'I'm not telling you.'

He looked at her with an expression that resembled something between disappointment and heartbroken sadness.

'Learn to speak languages for yourself if you want to be nosey.'

'To speak Berber?' he replied.

'Well, if you want to listen in to Youssef's conversation,

then yes. But something like Russian would be much more practical and is far more widely used. Anyway Rebecca, here is a telephone number that you can call to leave a message for me if you ever need to. Keep it safe and thank you both for making my birthday one to remember. Take care of this cheeky chappie,' she said to Rebecca as she gave Parsons a kiss on his cheek. When she hugged Rebecca, she felt strangely emotional. 'And you take care of this young lady, do you hear me? I know of a lake filled with crocodiles if you don't.' Her warning to Parsons made them all laugh as they parted company.

'She's feels like a mother figure, don't you think?' Rebecca remarked to Parsons as they rode the lift to their room.

He considered it for a moment and then shook his head. 'No. She refused to tell me what they discussed with Youssef. Plus, I've seen her naked, and she is after any excuse to feed me to crocodiles. Definitely not a mother figure.'

They laughed at his response and went to spend the rest of their last day in Morocco together.

10

For Sarah Rantsu, Lower Belgrave Street was home. Although she much preferred to be in her native Italy, here was where she now spent most of her time. She had found the property quite by accident whilst in the area and had fallen in love with it as soon as she laid eyes on it. The place had stuck in her mind and she had had no choice but to return to it months later to speak with the owner and persuade them to sell it to her.

She was now in the first floor sitting room, pouring drinks for herself and the Colonel, who was there to discuss the final arrangements for her to take custody of Parsons.

'They'll arrive back in to Gibraltar tomorrow,' the Colonel told Sarah.

She walked over to him and handed him a glass of whisky as she joined him on the sofa.

'Do they have any instructions on where to go from there?' Sarah asked.

'No. It was quite a surprise to me when Rebecca told me of their relationship yesterday. I thought it best for you and I to speak before I decided.'

'Yes, I can imagine that you were surprised. It throws a spanner in to the works, doesn't it?' she replied.

'Yes, it does. I reminded Rebecca of the policy on relationships within the unit, but she said that they have discussed this and that if necessary they are both willing to give up their careers to be together.'

'Oh gosh, it is a mess. Neither of them has any idea what this is all about, and that they can't be together,' Sarah said sympathetically.

'A bloody mess,' the Colonel agreed as he took a swig of his whisky.

'I think that we will have to be cruel to be kind. In this instance, I can't see how else it can be done. They were aware of your policy and they should never have let themselves get carried away as they have.'

'Quite.' The Colonel had slept very little during the previous evening. He was angry at himself for not foreseeing the possibility that Parsons and Rebecca could start a relationship. He was also troubled by the knowledge that he would have to prevent them from being together at any cost.

'I would suggest that he is the one more likely to accept any story that we create. Taking him away with me will help to prevent Rebecca from being able to communicate with him. Once they arrive back here, in the UK, that should be the last time they see each other. We can, in time, turn them against each other, so that it becomes no longer a problem, it won't take long. In fact, I think that this might just work to our advantage. I have an idea.'

The Colonel was not happy with the situation, but it was not his doing and he had no other option but to let Sarah put her plans in to place.

~

PARSONS AND REBECCA arrived back in to Gibraltar on Saturday morning and were given the same accommodation as they had shared on their earlier visit. They were to fly on to England the following morning, so they spent the afternoon browsing the shops on the main street and had an early dinner in the marina. Over dinner, Rebecca told Parsons that she had a gift for him.

'What is it?' he asked, intrigued.

They hadn't spent a moment apart, and he wondered what she could have for him. She took a box out of her bag and put it on to the table.

'Open it,' Rebecca said.

Parsons picked it up and gently shook it. 'Should I guess what it is?' he teased.

'No, please just open it,' she said. She appeared suddenly serious, and so Parsons unwrapped it. He opened the box that was inside and took out a watch.

'It's amazing. I actually wanted one of these,' he said as he fitted it on to his wrist.

'I know you did.' She smiled at him as he fastened the strap on the watch and looked at it.

He was everything that she had ever dreamed of.

'You are the best girlfriend in the world, you know,' he told her as he leant over and kissed her.

'Carl,' she said as she took hold of his hand.

'Yes,' he replied, seeing that she was serious.

'I love you more than I ever thought possible.'

'I know you do; I love you too,' he said. He saw her eyes fill with tears and asked her, 'Bec, are you ok, is something wrong?'

'No, nothing is wrong. I just want you to know that I love you.' He went to speak, but she stopped him. 'Will you promise me something?'

'Anything, I'll do anything for you,' he replied as one of her tears fell.

'Will you wear the watch for as long as you love me, keep it on, so that I always know that you still love me?' She asked him, trying to not cry.

'Hey, are you OK?'

'Carl, promise me, so that I will always know if you love me,' she urged him, taking both of his hands in to hers.

'I promise Bec. I promise I will always wear the watch and that I will always love you.'

'No, promise that you will only wear the watch for as long as you love me, Carl.'

'Yes, I will wear it for as long as I love you,' he replied. He looked at the necklace around her neck, the one that he had given her as a gift, and she read his mind.

'And I will wear this for as long as I love you,' she told him as she took hold of the necklace.

He pulled her from her seat and onto his lap. They sat there hugging for a long while and although he knew she was softly sobbing, he just held her. She was his entire world and he would never remove the watch if he could help it.

THE COLONEL HAD ARRANGED flights back to Heathrow for Rebecca and Parsons the following day, and they arrived as planned at 1135 hours. He met them at the airport and told them Parsons had a medical that he needed to attend before they caught the evening flight to Belfast. The Colonel dropped him off at the medical centre that was a twenty-minute drive from Heathrow in a territorial army camp. He told Parsons he and Rebecca would go grab a coffee while they waited for him and that he would be collected in about an hour. As the Colonel and Rebecca drove away, Parsons felt happy that the Colonel had not been off with them. After all, Rebecca had told him of their relationship during a telephone conversation and he had not said a word about it when he had met them at the airport. Maybe he was going to turn a blind eye to them being together, probably not allow them to deploy operationally as a pair, but ignore it so long as it didn't cause any issues.

The medical centre appeared empty other than the receptionist, who asked Parsons to take a seat and said that he would shortly be called through by the doctor

'Private Parsons,' the doctor called out his name. He went through to the doctors' room with him and sat down in a chair.

'If you can wait one moment,' the doctor said, and left the room. After just a moment, he returned with a female.

'Hello Carl,' she said as she reached out to shake his hand. Parsons noticed she was carrying a paper folder and smiled at her as she took the seat opposite him. The doctor left the room and closed the door behind him.

'My name is Janice, and I have been asked to see you today.' She smiled back at him. He had thought that the man was the doctor; but, upon realising, felt guilty for having presumed that a doctor would be a male.

'Hello doctor,' Parsons replied.

'Carl, I am not a doctor, I am from a department that manages personnel records.' He looked at her, surprised, but listened as she continued to speak.

'I am here to speak with you about yourself and Rebecca, actually about your relationship,' she told him. He felt his heart stop for what seemed like an eternity. He had no response.

'Carl, you are aware, it is strictly forbidden for you to have intimate relationships with any other person serving in the same unit as you, aren't you?'

He was prepared for this question, and he knew the answer that he had been considering for a while. 'Yes, I am aware of that. We are, I mean. We are both going to leave the army if we have to.'

'Carl, you can't leave the army. You know that it doesn't work like that,' Janice told him. 'You can't just decide that you are going to walk away because you don't like the rules.'

'We can, once our service ends we can leave.'

'That is three years away Carl - you are not considering this. Are you going to throw away all that you have worked for, for a fling with a colleague?' she asked him.

'No, it's not a fling. We are in love, and we will leave if we have to.' Carl was certain of his decision and he knew Bec was, too.

'How long have you known Rebecca?'

'Since September.'

'Carl, you haven't. You met her briefly in September, but you didn't know her. Carl, you still barely know her. You are not seeing reality here'. She was speaking to him in a manner that was sympathetic rather than condescending. He looked at her and saw that she didn't know what he and Rebecca had together.

'I know her well enough, I'm happy to take the chance.'

'Have you had a girlfriend before?' Janice asked.

'No. Why would that matter, though?'

As she looked at Parsons, she felt genuine compassion for him and sorrow for his young love. He wouldn't listen to any reasoning that she attempted to explain to him and she knew that Sarah Rantsu had been right in her briefing, she would have to hurt him.

'Carl, Rebecca is already in a relationship. You have been a temporary distraction for her. This is not the first time that she has done it, and you are not the first person to fall for her. The rules have already been ignored so that she could be with him. He is part of the unit in Lisburn.'

She saw the expression on his face turn to disbelief as he began to shake his head.

'No, I don't believe you,' he said. 'You are lying.'

'I'm not Carl. Rebecca has had relationships with people in the unit before and they have been disciplined for it. A little over a year ago, she began a new relationship with Johnathon, her sergeant at the unit. The Colonel forbid them from continuing with it, and they too threatened to leave unless he turned a blind eye to what they were doing. Because it wasn't the first time that Rebecca had done this, the Colonel thought it would blow over quickly. So, he turned a blind eye, expecting it to take its course and to end as quickly as it had begun. But it hasn't, and they are still very much together. They are discrete and it has caused no problems until now. When you return to the unit with Rebecca, we will have an issue. Your new sergeant, Johnathon, her partner, is not going to just welcome you with open arms now. And if you think that maybe she loves you now, rather than him, that still won't make the situation any more workable.'

He sat in silence, perplexed and unable to work it out in his head. 'Was this why she had been crying at the marina in Gibraltar, because she knew it was ending, that he would find out about this Johnathon?' Parsons thought silently.

'I didn't want to show you these, but you need to see them.' Janice passed A4 sized photographs to him, one at a time. They showed Rebecca with a man who he presumed to be Johnathon. There were dozens of them, holding hands as they walked through streets, sat in a car kissing, eating at restaurants. He could see the smile on their faces as they looked at each other in the pictures.

In one photograph, Rebecca was reaching across a table, holding one of the man's hands in both of hers. She did this, Parsons knew she did this. She had done it to him many times when they had been together in Gibraltar and Morocco.

'Please, no more,' he said as he refused to accept any more of the photographs and handed what he had already seen back to her.

'I'm sorry, Carl. You had no way of knowing. This isn't your fault,' she told him. The tears ran down his face and she could see the energy draining from his body. They sat there in silence for a while and Janice waited for him to speak first.

'What happens now?' Parsons asked as he dried his tears and tried to gain some composure.

'What do you want to happen?' she asked him.

'Can I see Bec?' he asked.

'Let me go and see. I'll make a call and I'll bring you a drink, is that alright?' she asked him. Parsons nodded.

Janice left the room and didn't return for nearly fifteen minutes. She handed Parsons a glass of water, which he drank straight away. His throat was dry, and he had the headache from hell that wouldn't go away.

'I've made the call, Carl. Rebecca doesn't want to see you right now.' As Janice said this, he could not believe her words. He went to speak, but she continued, 'She has been told that you know about her and Johnathon. She says she can't see you right now. She wants to think things through, to decide what she should do. She has just spoken with Johnathon on the telephone and she has asked me to tell you she is confused. She didn't think that she would feel this strongly about him. She wants to see him without you there. I asked her if she would talk to you on the telephone and she said that she feels too guilty to speak with you right now.'

'Why is she going to see him? She is here. She could see me first. Where is she? Is she with the Colonel? Can he not talk to her and bring her here so that I can speak with her?' Parsons asked, pleading, almost begging. You could sense the passion and confusion in his voice.

'The Colonel cannot get involved, Carl. He is going to be investigated for allowing this to happen. The Colonel should never have allowed Rebecca to fall in love with Johnathon and for them to be a couple, let alone the rest of this mess. He isn't in a position to do that.' Janice looked at him and watched as the dilemma to sank in. 'What do you want to do, other than see Rebecca?'

'I don't know. Am I still going to the unit, to Lisburn?' he asked.

'Not at the moment, Carl. Your presence would bring their work to a standstill and that cannot happen. Would you like me to find you somewhere that you can go, out of the way for a while?' she offered.

'Yes please,' he nodded as he began to sob.

IT WAS a little more than a week later when Parson was informed of the impending fate that he had been trying to predict.

The Colonel was to stand trial in a Court Marshal for his negligence, and Rebecca would remain at the unit due to the operational necessity. Johnathon had been reduced in

rank to corporal and would also remain working in the unit.
Rebecca had not spoken with Parsons, she had refused to do
so, but had sent him a letter instead. Janice came to give the
letter to him and left him while he read it.

Dear Carl,
I want to start by telling you - I am sorry. I meant to tell you
about John, but the right time never seemed to come. The
longer things went on, the harder it became to say something. I enjoyed every moment I spent with you, and you
really are a wonderful person. It always had to end at some
point though, and I now know how foolish I was to lead you
along, as I did. I have another chance with John and he is
the person who I want to spend my future with. You meant a
lot to me and I hope you will forgive me one day and understand that I made a mistake. I know soon you will meet
someone who will adore you and that they will make you
happy.
Take care.
Bec

By the time Parsons finished the letter, he was crying, as
he had each day since she had gone. He read it once more
and then folded it back in to the envelope. He stood up and
went to the window. He looked outside at the grey clouds
and the pouring rain. He hated it here, this place was miser-
able. He was to be returned to his unit in Chester and he felt
as though his world was ending, but slowly and painfully.

As Janice came back in to the room, Parsons went to sit
back in the chair. As he did so, he picked up the envelope
that contained the letter from Rebecca. Janice sat down also
and asked him if she could read the letter. He handed it to
her; she read in silence.

'You've been handed a shit deal here. I'm sorry, I don't know how I can make it any better for you.'

'You can't, she's made her mind up,' Parsons replied emptily.

'But you have lost everything because of her Carl, it seems so unfair. Nothing has changed in her little world, but for you,' she tailed off her words and looked at him, trying to find something constructive to say.

'Carl, I have a proposal,' she said.

He lifted his gaze up from the floor and asked, 'What?'

'I told you before that I work in a department that deals with personnel, didn't I. Well, I have access to all of the military vacancies that come available. I've seen something that might help you out.'

'What is it?' he asked.

'I'm not sure exactly, but there is a requirement for an agent to be in Italy. I looked at the eligibility requirements and because of your training you could apply for it.'

'But I've just been thrown out of S.O.N.I. before I had even got there. They wouldn't allow me to apply,' he reminded her, in case she had forgotten the events of the last week.

'Can I trust you Carl? I'd like to tell you something, but I have to be able to trust you,' Janice told him.

He shrugged his shoulders and said, 'I guess so, yeah.'

'The Colonel doesn't want any more detail of your departure than is absolutely necessary to be kept on record. He has asked me to deal with the whole thing and to use my discretion as I see fit. I'm meant to be making contact with your old regiment to arrange your return, and once that is done, I'm to write up your file.'

'What are you saying?' he questioned her.

'I think you are a nice guy and that you shouldn't be

getting punished when you have done nothing wrong.' He looked at her, wondering if he had missed something important. 'Carl, I am the one who will select the person for this job in Italy. I could choose you,' she said.

'How could you do that? They have said that I have to go back to my regiment,' Parsons told her.'

'The only thing that they want, Carl, is for you to be gone. The Colonel won't be enquiring where you are. He is facing a court martial and he will be hoping to never hear your name again. You have already left your regiment, it's only if I contact them that they will know anything about this. I've thought it through and we wouldn't be doing anything wrong. You are not assigned to any department; you are qualified for the posting and I am sanctioned to make the decision and choose you or anyone else that I see fit.'

She smiled at him and saw that he was considering it, she needed to push him further. 'Yes, it's all very convenient that I choose you, but would it be more ethical to give it to someone like that bastard boyfriend of hers, Johnathon?'. She appeared upset and Parsons could see that she was trying to help him and was willing to take a risk to do so.

Since he had met Janice, she had looked out for him in every way that he could have hoped for. She could have easily rushed through his return to his regiment, but she had helped him.

'Also, if you still want to leave the military as soon as you can, this will give you some opportunities to start building a civilian career. You could learn something new, start to train, get some civilian skills. It's not a uniformed role you would be doing,' she told him.

'What do you know about it? What exactly is it doing?' he asked her.

'It's a civilian role, so it will involve living in a town, away from the military. You would have to do some intelligence building and report writing. Probably the odd bit of travelling to meet people, but not too much. You would be living in the sun and be able to go to the beach each day. It sounded like a dream when I read through the bulletin.'

'When would it start?' he asked her.

'Straight away, they need someone who is available immediately. So, you see, you are perfect for the position, Carl,' Janice told him. 'It seems like fate, as though it was meant for you.'

'Are you sure you won't get in to trouble, and that we could do it?'

'I know we could. I won't get in to trouble,' Janice assured him.

He had a feeling of loss in his heart and an emptiness in his soul; he was broken. It didn't matter what happened anymore, things would never be the same again. But if this was the case, he had nothing to lose by taking a chance.

'Can you arrange it for me please, will you try?'

'You'll be leaving tomorrow,' Janice said. 'I'll see you in the morning.'

A new fax message was created and sent. 'SEPARATION COMPLETED. SUBJECT TWO HANDED OVER. INSTRUCTIONS ON RK.'

11

The pilot used the plane's public address system to announce to the passengers that they would shortly begin their descent into Naples International Airport.

Parsons looked through the plane's small circular window, down onto green crops in the fields. These were dotted with an endless number of tiny buildings with distinctive bright red roofs. Everything was drowned in sunlight and it made him feel warm. He instinctively put his hand into the line of the sun's rays, shining in through the window. It felt good to feel the sun on his skin again. However, when it shone onto his watch and reflected into his eyes, he moved his hand away again. The pilot set the plane onto a straight course and Parsons felt his seatbelt tighten as they lost height on their descent. A young woman across the aisle from Parsons looked nervous and clutched the arms of her seat. She was pale and wide-eyed, and he felt sorry for her.

'It's OK. The pilot is just preparing to land,' Parsons told her.

'Thank you. I'm terrible at flying,' she said. 'Are you travelling alone?'

'Yes.'

'Me too. I think that's why I am so nervous,' Terhi Johanson explained.

'We are nearly down now,' Parsons reassured her with a smile.

From two rows of seats behind, Gruber smiled, content that he had taught her well.

Within minutes they had landed and were disembarking the plane into the midday heat.

When Janice had driven him to Heathrow that morning, she had told him he would be met at Naples airport by a woman who would display a card with his name on it. Not seeing his name displayed inside, he walked out of the airport and looked around to see if anyone was waiting for him out there. He heard a car's engine racing, the screech of tyres and a horn beep twice. He turned around and saw a woman in a car that had just pulled up on the road directly outside the terminal. She waved and was looking in his direction. He looked around to see who she was waving at, but there was no one else around, so he pointed at his chest, asking if she meant him. She nodded and smiled, beckoning him to go to her.

As he got closer, she opened the door, got out of the car, went to the boot and opened it. Parsons stopped next to the open boot and looked at her, wondering if she had mistaken him for someone else. The car was a 1980, baby blue Mercedes-Benz, SL 280 cabriolet, that shone in the sun. The hood of the car was down so that he could see the expensive tan coloured leather seats inside.

The woman walked to him and touched both of her cheeks to his, as though she had known him for all of his life. 'Pop your case in here Carl', she said, returning to the boot and holding it open. He thought that the likelihood of her being here at this precise moment to pick up someone else named Carl was very slim.

'I'm sorry, they didn't tell me your name,' he replied.

'Sarah, I'm Sarah and you are Carl, they told me'. She smiled as she helped him squeeze his case in to the boot. 'Jump in,' she added, pointing to the passenger seat.

Parsons watched her as she skipped past him and got in to the driver seat. She wasn't what he had been expecting. As he got in to the car beside her, he placed his seatbelt on.

'Oh, don't worry about that. No one uses them here,' Sarah said as she drove off and joined the passing traffic. He removed the seat belt, feeling that he had, in some way, offended a local custom.

'So, you are going to be with me for a while, Carl. We had better get to know each other. I want you to think of some things that you can tell me about yourself and something that you want to know about me,' Sarah said. She looked across at him as she drove and said, 'I will begin by telling you, should I? I was born in Italia, but I now also live in London. Your turn.'

He thought about it for a moment and replied, 'OK. Well, I was born in England, but I also now live in Italia'. He looked at her and she sniggered at his reply.

'Oh, I am going to enjoy having you around.' She already liked him and smiled to herself. 'Come on, let me show you the place on this earth that God created first.'

'Where is that?' Parsons asked her.

'Vico Equense, my hometown. You will love it,' Sarah answered.

For the rest of the drive along the beautiful coast road, they swapped questions and answers with each other, and it provided the light-hearted fun that Parsons so desperately needed.

Vico Equense was the first town on the Sorrentine Peninsula. It was on the edge of the sea, surrounded by hills and was some six kilometres from the larger and busier Sorrento. Although hilly, the area was fertile, green, and offered endless clifftop vistas overlooking the town and the sea beyond. On the outskirts of the town, there were many traditional farms with groves still in production. There were two large beaches and several smaller, secluded ones that were usually less populated. Its small marina was littered with prettily painted fishing boats that brought in their daily catches to be sold to the many restaurants. As they drove into the town, Sarah suggested they should stop for a drink. She parked the car and asked him if he was hungry.

'I'm always hungry, are you?' he asked in response.

'Am I always hungry?' Sarah said.

'No, I meant,' he stopped himself when he saw her grin, 'are you hungry now?'

'Yes, let's get a bite to eat. You will then know what pizza should taste like. This way,' she said as she crossed the road in front of a motor scooter that was being ridden by two young males. The horn sounded, and they had to take evasive action and swerve around her.

'Ehi pazzo!' they shouted as they passed her, again peeping the scooter's horn.

Parsons had seen the scooter and had stopped, waiting for it to pass. He crossed the road after her and asked, 'Didn't you see that coming?'

'Of course I did, otherwise I would have been hit by it. It wasn't even close to me. Come and keep up with me or else you will get lost.'

They passed through several streets and then walked out

in to a square with a water fountain at its centre. The walk-ways around its edge were wide and were filled with bars, cafes, and shops. There were a variety of vehicles passing by, many that Parsons had never seen before, older traditional vehicles that were not sold in the UK. There was a three wheeled Citroen van that had a cab at the front and an open flatbed at the rear. It was painted grey and reminded him of a vehicle that would be seen in a wartime film.

The next vehicle to pass by was a brand-new BMW, and then a dirty works van, and then another three wheeled wreck that looked dangerously unsafe. The people in the square were all going about their business and the town had a feeling of energy and life about it.

'Here we are,' Sarah announced as she stopped at a café on the square. They sat at a table in the sun, looking out to the square and the grand buildings that surrounded it. 'How hungry are you?'

'I had breakfast but nothing since, so pretty hungry.'

'Good, we can share a pizza. Vico Equense is the birth-place of the metre-long pizza. We invented it right here in this town.'

'Pizza was invented here?' Parsons asked, surprised.

'No, silly. We invented the metre-long pizza, rather than a boring circular pizza.'

'Oh, I see,' Parsons said.

Sarah ordered pizza and a bottle of wine, her favourite. She was secretly celebrating, and this justified her breaking her 'no alcohol before 6pm' rule. The café that they were sitting at and all the others in the square were filled with people and were thriving. It was riposo time, and hungry locals were meeting and eating together before they returned to work for the last part of their working day. When Parsons asked Sarah if it was always this busy, she explained to him that the Italian version of taking an after-noon siesta was called riposo and that it was taken anywhere between one thirty and four, lasting for about an hour and a half.

'I could get used to this,' he told her.

'You will get used to it. Before you know it, you will love this place as much as I do, and then you will never want to leave.' She raised her glass and was smiling. 'Come, make a toast Carl.'

Parsons picked up his glass and tried to think of a toast. 'To a new way of life.' They touched glasses and drank. He was feeling better about himself, and although he knew that the sun was partly responsible for that, he felt things would improve here. Sarah was older than him, but she was stunningly attractive and, most certainly, pleasant to be with. If he had to spend time with her in a beautiful, warm location, he would happily do so. For queen and country, he would cope with this 'awful' new lifestyle. He smiled on both the inside and the outside as he thought how lucky he was right now, considering what had recently happened. Maybe it was fate, as Janice had said. Maybe this was his future, his chance to start again.

When the Pizza arrived, Parsons eyes almost popped out, and Sarah laughed at him.

'Is all of that for us?' he asked.

'Most of it is for you. I will have this bit here, and then watch you struggle with the rest of it,' she told him, taking a small piece for herself. 'Get started, you have a lot to get through,' she cheerfully suggested.

During their meal, Sarah explained to Carl that her house was a few hundred metres out of the town, a short distance up the hillside. She explained that she also still owned the house that she had grown up in, which was in the town, close to the centre. In time Carl could move in to the town house if he wanted to, but for now he would stop with Sarah. She told him that her house on the outskirts of town was much bigger, and that it had a garden, which made it more pleasant to stay at. Although she had cherished growing up in the town as a child, she now appreciated having a home on its outskirts where it was quieter and more private.

As they left the town centre in the car, Sarah pointed out to Parsons a footpath that was a shortcut from her house to the centre of town. She recommended he use it if he were on foot, as it was a much quicker journey than to follow the road. Once on the edge of the town, Sarah turned the car off the main road on to a minor road that she followed for a few hundred metres before turning again on to a much smaller tree-lined, gravel track that was barely wide enough for the car.

'This is narrow. What do you do if another car comes the other way?' Parsons asked Sarah.

She looked at him and then answered very simply, 'Shoot at it.'

He looked at her, shocked by her answer, as she seemed serious. 'I mean, is there somewhere to pass another car or something?'

'No. This is private land. If anyone is here, they shouldn't be. If you have to pass anyone here, shoot them, Carl.' She raised her brows and smiled at him.

'What do you really do?' he asked again after a pause.

She looked at him and then reached over to his side of the car, to the glove box, which she opened. As it opened, he saw a pistol lay inside. 'Shoot them.'

She closed the glove box and there was a silence as Parsons tried to decide whether she was being serious. After a minute of travelling along the track, they came out of the trees and in to a clearing. When he saw the house stood before him, he immediately thought that it was like a scene on a postcard.

The gravel track that they had driven along ended where it met a clearing and was replaced with light brown stone slabs that formed a courtyard. This led, all the way up, to the house and around the side of it. To the left side of the court-yard were garages, which had once been a stable block, but had since been converted. There were several other smaller buildings beyond the garages that looked too small to be anything other than outhouses for storage. To the right side of the courtyard was a two-storey building, that was separate from the main house and appeared to be an annex, possibly a living quarter. Running the full length between the main house and this building was a white painted, single storey height wall that had plants growing from its base, winding up and along its length. Beyond the wall, in the near distance, there were tall trees that appeared that they might form the boundary of the far side of the property's grounds.

The main house, like all the other buildings, was made of sandstone that varied in colour and shade. It reminded Parsons of a tortoise pattern; the sun shone on to the stone, reflecting from its many angles and creating colour varia-tions. There were three upper floors he could see. Below these, the ground floor was set back behind six wide arch-ways that formed the entrance to a cool covered terrace with terracotta tiles on the floor and white painted walls that housed a door and windows. Above this, on the first floor, each of the rooms had a small Juliet balcony, accessed from double doors that opened inwards to allow a passing breeze to flow in to the building. The second floor only covered two-thirds of the floor below, the remainder of it being an upper terrace that was open to the sun. The top floor was covered with red tiles that rose to a ridge on the roof.

'This is the back of the house. Wait until you see it from the other side, you will like it then,' Sarah told Parsons. She parked the car in one of the garages and waited for Parsons as he collected his suitcase.

'Come, leave your case here and let me show you the garden,' Sarah said as they passed by the rear entrance to the house. She led him through an ornate doorway in the wall that ran from the main house to the annexe. As they passed through the doorway and along the side of the main house, the gardens came in to view. Immediately in front of the house was a large terrace area that ran its full length. This led to an immaculately manicured lawn that went all the way to the edge of the property's boundary and gave way to a view of the coast and the sea below. The lawn was interrupted by a glistening swimming pool that had another, smaller terrace to its righthand side. This terrace accommodated a large dining table and chairs that were shaded by a gigantic parasol. The tall trees that Parsons had seen from the courtyard ran from the boundary where the lawn ended, back along the sides of the perimeter, concealing the house and its grounds from view. It was a secluded cocoon, a paradise with a view that took Parsons' soul to a place of safety.

As they stood at the edge of the pool, looking out in to the distance, Sarah asked, 'Do you like it here?'

He nodded as a tear formed in his eye. He felt a lump in his throat that prevented him from speaking. He stood there silently, looking in to the distant horizon.

Eventually he spoke and said, 'It's perfect'. Sarah smiled and was pleased that he had accepted his situation.

Parsons turned to face her and said, 'Let's get my things

put away, and then maybe we can come back out here with a bottle of wine so that you tell me what my new job is all about.' Sarah nodded in agreement, she was impressed by his maturity and resilience.

OVER THE FOLLOWING DAYS, Sarah explained to Parsons the role that he was to fulfil. She told him a redacted version of the work that she did and said that he would be her new partner. She explained he would act in any role that she required him to, roles that would assist her in completing the tasks that she was given.

Sarah explained to him that one element of his work would be to infiltrate the lives of the various females linked to their targets, who were some of the top criminals around the world. Criminals who posed a threat to the UK, in one way or another, a serious threat. His targets would be their wives, girlfriends, daughters, staff, anyone who could unknowingly give away valuable information. Sarah explained to Parsons that using him in this way would reduce the danger of her having to get too close to the main targets themselves. If he could get the information or evidence that they needed from the girlfriend or secretary of a criminal, this would remove the necessity for Sarah to become involved and, in turn, reduce any risk to her.

'So, you will teach me everything that I will need to learn and I will work for you?' He asked her as they sat next to the pool late one afternoon.

'Not quite. I will teach you, but you won't work for me. You will work for my employer. I will pass on their instructions when they have a problem and want you to do something for them,' Sarah corrected him.

'What if I can't do it? What if the women don't like me?' he asked her.

'You don't need to worry about that. Carl, as I've told you; I can show you how to make people like you. This all boils down to whether you are happy to deceive those who will trust, and possibly even come to love you. Play on their weaknesses and manipulate these. Doing this comes more naturally to women than it does to men. You might feel awful at first, Carl. But if it's not in your nature and you want to go back to the UK, you can leave.'

He thought about her words, 'It did come more naturally to women, Rebecca at least.' He thought of returning to his regiment in the UK for a further three years before he could leave.

'And you are sure that they are all bad people?' he asked.

'They are the worst vile people, Carl. You wouldn't be targeting anyone that didn't deserve it. I wouldn't do it myself if I didn't believe I was doing the right thing. Plus, you would benefit financially from the risks that you would take - the pay is unbelievable. Where do you think all of this came from?' she asked him. Parsons looked around at the gardens and back at the house.

'This is all mine, Carl, paid for in full. And anytime I want to stop, give up working and call it a day, I can. You could eventually be where I am now if you take on this role.'

Parsons had never longed to be rich. But he knew the value of money, and this was an opportunity he doubted he would get again.

'I will do it then,' he told her. 'But can you ask them if they will give me a pay advance, please?'

'How much do you want?' Sarah asked.

'Fourteen thousand pounds, maybe fifteen.'

'Yes, I can get that for you. How do you want it, cash or a

bank transfer?' she asked him.

'Cash,' he answered. He then thought about it and said, 'Actually, I'm not sure'.

'Do you want to tell me what it is for?' Sarah asked him. So that she, perhaps, could advise him what would be best.

'To pay my mum and dad's mortgage off. I'm not sure whether they owe fourteen or fifteen thousand,' he explained.

'Would it be better if I just arranged for their mortgage to be paid in full? That way they won't have the trouble of dealing with it.'

'If you would please.'

'Fabulous, it's decided then. A toast, but this time it's mine to make.' They both lifted their glasses and Sarah was truly delighted as she proposed, 'To my new, and first ever partner'.

Sarah and Parsons spent several weeks introducing him to the area. They walked around the whole of the town each day, and Sarah took him to several eateries and places of interest. Soon, Parsons knew the town like the back of his hand and was confident that when he was alone, he would be able to find his way around.

ONE MORNING DURING BREAKFAST, Sarah announced to Parsons that his training was to now begin, and that it would start with him learning to settle in to a new environment. She suggested today they should go down to the marina for lunch. It was mid-February and although the summer season had not yet begun, the marina would be busy with families from the surrounding area, coming to dine together. Sarah told him he would like the atmosphere in the marina and that it had some of the area's best restaurants. She asked him to be ready to leave by ten thirty, as she had something to show him she thought he might like. She suggested he should wear something different on his feet, rather than the ragged worn sandals that he had become accustomed to wearing every day.

When Sarah came to Parsons' and saw that he was ready to go, they headed over to the garages.

Parsons asked her, 'Are you going to let me drive your car?.'

'Not a chance. If you were to crash her, I would never forgive you,' Sarah replied with honesty. She pressed the button on the garage remote control and the door at the end of the garage complex opened. 'You can drive my second car, though,' she told him.

As the garage door slowly lifted, Parsons stooped down to see what the second car was. Sarah tutted at him and told him to be patient. There was a dust sheet covering a square shape that looked too small to be a car.

'Is that it?' Parsons asked, disappointed as he looked into the garage.

'You haven't seen it yet. Come, I will help you take the cover off. You go that side and I will go this way.' Sarah walked into the garage and towards what was the front of the car. Parsons mirrored her and they both took hold of the cover, which they pulled backwards. The first thing that Parsons saw was the colour, yellow. The bright yellow paintwork was old and dull, but it was the brightest thing that he could remember ever seeing. The cover came off and revealed a tiny yellow box shaped car that Parsons immediately thought was too small for him.

'I will never fit in there,' he said, amazed at the idea.

'It is a family car, of course you will,' Sarah told him as

she laughed at his expression.

'It's the smallest thing I've ever seen, you have to be joking.'

'I thought you would like it, it's you Carl.'

'How is it me? It's yellow, tiny and old. I'm six foot two and not yellow, for God's sake,' he told her.

'No, you are green and not yellow, but I can change that,' she told him with a grin on her face. 'Come, sit inside and you'll see that there is plenty of room,' Sarah suggested as she opened the passenger door and sat in the car. Parsons opened the door on the driver's side and stooped down to get inside. He managed to get into the seat, just about, but if he sat up straight, his head touched the roof.

Sarah was laughing so much that she could not get her words out, and had to catch her breath before she spoke again. 'Carl, you need to see what you look like in this car. It was designed for you; it is a perfect match.'

'You are winding me up. This isn't really for me, is it?' he asked her.

Sarah told him it was for him, but that it was purely so that he could learn to drive on Italian roads. 'Once you get the hang of driving on these roads, we can get you another car. But this is perfect for now. Come on, start her up and pull her out in to the sunshine. Sarah was still laughing at Parsons five minutes later when the car was out of the garage and he was walking around the outside of it, looking at it in horror.

'How old is it?' he asked Sarah.

'It's probably just a little older than you. This is part of your work for the next few days,' Sarah told him.

'What is?'

'Driving. You have to learn how to drive on the right side of the road, safely.'

'It's a death trap. What if I crash?' he said.

'That is why you must learn,' Sarah told him. 'Anyway, stop talking about crashing, it's not lucky. We can go out for a little drive in your new car and then you can take me to the marina in it for lunch.'

Parson looked at the rear of the car. The badge read, 'Fiat 126.' 'Of all the Italian classics that you could have chosen, you went for this one,' he told Sarah.

'I'm glad that you like my choice,' she replied with sarcasm. 'Let's get going and go steady until you have got used to the power.'

Parsons had been driving for almost an hour when they had to stop for fuel at a service station. Sarah spoke in Italian to the attendant who came out to serve them, and then went in to the shop to buy a cold drink. As Parsons stood next to the car, looking it over, the service attendant spoke to him.

'I'm sorry, I don't speak Italian, English only,' he apologised to the attendant, who he could not understand.

The attendant, an older guy, continued talking as he pointed at the car, seeming oblivious to the fact that Parsons didn't have a clue what he was saying.

Sarah came back out to them and spoke again with the attendant, who had now filled the car's tank with fuel. She thanked him, and they continued on their journey, driving along the twisty roads that seemed to get more dangerous as they went.

'What was that guy trying to tell me?' Parsons asked Sarah.

'He told you he liked your car. He said that when he was younger he had one of these himself, and that it was very reliable and simple to repair, unlike modern cars.'

'I feel ignorant when people try to talk to me, and I can't

reply to them.'

'Would you like me to teach you to speak Italian?' Sarah asked him.

'Would you?'

'Of course, I speak many languages and I would enjoy teaching you,' she told him.

'Russian, do you speak Russian?'

'Da,' Sarah answered him.

'How many languages can you actually speak?'

'Fluently? Seven. But I can understand more, just not so well.'

'Can you teach me Russian as well?'

'Let's start with Italian for now, and we can look at Russian once you have the hang of that,' Sarah suggested. 'Si?' she asked him.

'Si, bene,' he said.

'Molto bene,' Sarah congratulated him with a smile.

Parsons parked the car in the marina before they then went to a fish restaurant that overlooked the sea. As they ate, Sarah told Parsons that his parents' mortgage had now been paid off in full, and that they would soon receive a letter from the bank confirming this. He thanked her for arranging it.

'Why did you want to pay off your parents' mortgage for them?'

'My dad hasn't been well for a while, and they have struggled to pay it because he had to take time off work,' he explained to her.

'Are you close to your parents?' she asked him.

'Not really close, but I love them and I'd do anything that I could to help them. My mum says that I am her baby, and she would smoother me with love if I let her. It's a bit annoying sometimes, so I limit my time with them.'

Sarah smiled at the thought of his mother fussing over him. 'They are lucky to have a son who would do something so kind for them,' she said.

'What about you? Are you close to your parents?' Parsons asked.

'My Parents both died when I was younger, that is why I moved to England to live with my grandmother.'

'I'm sorry, I didn't mean to-'

'It's fine Carl, you haven't offended me. It was a long time ago now, and to answer your question, I was very close to my parents'. Sarah smiled as she spoke and remembering them brought back many happy memories.

'Have you ever been married?' he asked her.

'Good grief, no,' Sarah answered.

'I just thought that you might have been by now.'

'How old do you think I am?' she asked him with mock surprise.

'Not old, but people get married at a certain age, don't they?'

Sarah told him she was deeply offended and demanded to know how old he thought she was.

'Somewhere between twenty-eight and thirty,' he replied.

'I am thirty-one years old; you have ever so slightly redeemed yourself young man.'

'Have you ever been in love?' Parsons now asked.

'What is love?'

'When you love someone,' he told her.

'Yes, but what does that mean?'

'That you care for them, that you want to be with them, to marry them.'

'You can care for lots of people and want to be with

them, but that doesn't mean that you love them, does it?' Sarah asked him.

'That's different, I mean a more intense love.'

'Love is just a feeling; it doesn't actually exist. It can change at any moment and then it is gone,' Sarah told him.

Parsons thought about this and wanted to argue his point.

'Have you ever been in love, Carl?' she asked him.

'Yes, I think so.'

'But now something has changed, and it is gone, yes?' she suggested.

'Yes, I suppose so,' Parsons reluctantly agreed.

'Love is an emotion that we cling to when we are vulnerable or weak. It allows people to take advantage of us and to manipulate us. I don't believe in love. I have had people in my life that I have enjoyed being with and I have even cared for them. But I don't believe in love. It is a silly notion, and people abuse it and hurt you if you let them,' Sarah told him.

Her response had cut his conversation short; he had not expected the answer that she had given. Sarah was perhaps the most physically beautiful human he had ever seen, and he had presumed that she would have had many admirers who would have loved her. Since he had been in her company, he had seen her at various times of the day and night, and she had only ever looked immaculate. With or without make-up, wearing pyjamas or a fine dress, it didn't matter. Her natural beauty and something about her persona made her stand out and allured men to her.

He considered what she had said and decided that maybe she had been hurt by some lover in her past. Even beautiful people can have their hearts broken, he considered.

Sarah had been correct; the restaurant was busy and the families who had come together were loud and animated as they excitedly shared stories amongst themselves.

'Carl, listen to the conversations surrounding you,' Sarah told him. 'Identify the most frequently used words and watch the people as they say them.'

Parsons listened and watched as multiple conversations surrounded him. He recognised a few of the simplest words.

'Look at their body language as they speak. If you were to suddenly become deaf, but could still see, you could guess some of their words, just from their body language and reactions,' Sarah suggested.

Parsons watched and began to appreciate what she meant. He did not know exactly what the conversations were about, but he could tell when listeners were surprised, in agreement or vice versa.

Sarah went on, 'Body language is important. You can read it. It will help you learn a new language, but also it can tell you what a person is thinking, feeling, or even what they are about to do. It is often more reliable than the words that are said.'

'Si, no, io, ma, they are the most popular words I can hear,' he told her.

'Yes, no, I and but. Watch what their bodies do as they say those words. Shakes and nods of heads, arm movements, changes in voice tone. It helps you to understand what they are saying.'

Parsons saw it now. He watched a couple at a table further away and saw that the man was speaking fast and said, 'Ma', a lot.

'Are they arguing over at that table?' he asked Sarah.

She turned to look at the couple and listened to them for a few seconds. 'He is complaining about their son.

What can you read by her body language, Carl?' she asked him.

'I think she is just listening for the sake of it. She isn't attempting to reply to him.'

'Describe to me about her body language. You are right, but what is it about her you can see rather than hear?'

'Her shoulders are forward but she is sitting back in her seat, her arms are folded on the table and her face is blank,' Parsons replied.

'What do you think she is feeling?'

'Bored, tired of listening, uninterested'. The woman looked around the room as though to confirm this. She made eye contact with Parsons and looked away, embarrassed. 'She looks a little annoyed now,' he added.

'Yes, she is becoming annoyed at him because he is repeating himself. She has turned her body at a slight angle from him look. She doesn't want to listen to him any longer.'

Parsons agreed and found it interesting. He had always been a people watcher, but trying to work out what was going on in other conversations fascinated him. He looked around the restaurant, and it was easy. He could read how people were feeling, happy, sad, frustrated.

'You are good at this, because you have a lot of empathy, so you will see people's emotions,' Sarah complimented him.

He found it hard to stop watching people, and for the rest of their time in the restaurant, he kept listening and watching the other diners. After dinner Parsons drove again, and by the time they arrive back at the house he had grown to like the car a little.

'Do you have a hosepipe and some bits to wash it?' he asked Sarah, as he stopped the car in the courtyard.

'I knew it. You like her, don't you?' she accused him.

'No. She looks and drives like a lump of cheese. But if I have got to drive around in Miss Edam, then she needs a clean and polish,' Parsons replied.

'Miss Edam, you adore her already. I shall cancel the Ferrari that I have ordered for you'. Sarah waited for his reaction and watched as Parsons stopped himself from rising to the bait at the last second.

'I will look through the garages, there will be something in there,' he replied as he walked away, ignoring her.

Sarah left him to it and went into the house to make a call. While they had been out at the marina, she had noticed a girl. The same girl who she had spotted at other locations when she was out with Parsons. She wanted to check that it was pure coincidence and nothing more. She reported this and was assured that it would be looked in to without delay.

IT DIDN'T TAKE LONG for Parsons to learn to speak Italian and to confidently engage with the people that he met. He still walked into the town most mornings, and he could now speak with the waiters in the cafes and the shopkeepers. He returned to the fuel station where the attendant had asked him about Miss Edam on his first drive. Now that they could understand each other, Pepe, the attendant, advised Parsons how he could improve the car and even gave him some spares that he had lying around.

Sarah tested him on his Italian constantly and taught him more each day. Eventually she spoke to Parsons in just Italian, unless it was absolutely necessary not to. They also continued to people watch, to read situations and body language. Sarah taught him much more, including how to cook a wide range of food dishes and the right wines to accompany them. He had a flare for cooking and she looked forward to the meals that he prepared for them. She taught him how to dance and when he eventually matched her skill level, Sarah enrolled him in to dance classes with an instructor in Sorrento.

Soon Sarah sensed a change in Parsons. He was maturing and becoming more refined. She coached him how to treat a female, how to be a gentleman. He was instinctively attentive, and it took little time to show him how to look for the subtle cues that were there if he was aware of them. Sarah pointed out to Parsons when a female they encountered took a liking to him. At first, he found it embarrassing, but with her help and advice, he became far more confident and she even accused him of becoming a flirt. She set him tasks of speaking with women and would listen in to his conversation to later give him feedback.

'Make her feel important. Make her believe you are interested in her as a person, Carl. Listen to what she says to you, and use her body language to help you.'

He practised this on his dance partners during the classes in Sorrento, where he was one of only eight men in a class of over thirty students. The dance instructor, Maria, was in her late thirties and Carl sensed she was fond of him. When he told Sarah this, she suggested he should ask Maria if she would give him additional private dance lessons. He did this, and once a week, on a Wednesday evening, Maria taught him Latin America dance. He was tasked by Sarah to find out everything that he could about Maria's life. Her entire past, but also what she liked and disliked, her favourite colour, favourite film, and meal. Intimate detail that he could only learn by asking probing questions. When Sarah asked Parsons if Maria had any tattoos, he told her he had no idea.

'Ask her at your next lesson,' Sarah said.

'It's personal. I don't want to ask her that,' Parsons replied.

'She will tell you.'

'I still don't want to ask her,' he replied.

'What if she does have a tattoo, and it is somewhere sexy, don't you want to know then?' Sarah asked, looking at him across the table as they ate breakfast on the terrace.

Maria may have been over fifteen years older than Parsons, but she was fit and attractive. When he danced with her and his hands passed over her body, he often had to distract himself from imagining her naked.

'No.'

'You liar. You fancy her as much as she fancies you,' Sarah told him.

Parsons looked at her across the table. He had lived with Sarah for nearly four months now, and he knew that to deny the truth to her would be futile. She knew him well enough.

'Finding someone attractive does not mean that you feel the need to ask them personal questions, Sarah.'

'What is her favourite sexual position?' Parson ignored the questions. 'Does she like it rough or is she a dominatrix?' Sarah continued.

'You are crazy,' Parsons told her.

'You like this woman, and it would not be unreasonable for the two of you to have sex. Come on Carl, if you feel uncomfortable just to ask her if she has a tattoo, how are you going to do your job in the future?' She looked at him seriously as she asked the question.

'Soon, you are going to have to get information from our targets by deceiving them, by any means necessary. And you may be embarrassed by the questions that you have to ask them too, but this is what our world is about, Carl.'

12

Parsons adored Sorrento and looked forward to going there each Wednesday. It was his birthday tomorrow, so he was especially excited to be in his favourite destination today. He arrived in the early afternoon and went down to the beach for a few hours to sunbath and to snorkel in the sea. He ate at a beachside restaurant called the four sisters, and had pasta with a cold beer. The food was always good, and he liked to ask the sisters about their recipes, which he then replicated for Sarah.

Sarah had said she had a birthday surprise planned for him for tomorrow, so he must not make any plans of his own. After their conversation around Maria and tattoos, things had initially been a little frosty between himself and Sarah. But that had been several days ago, and it was forgotten about now. He did not know what Sarah was planning, but she had been very secretive and had grown more excited by the day as his birthday approached.

As he ate, a jet ski came on to the beach and Parsons had an idea. Since arriving in Italy, he had been paid five thousand euros each month into an Italian bank account that Sarah had set up for him. He waited until the rider of the jet ski came closer and asked him about it. The rider told him they had purchased it in Sorrento and where the shop was. An hour later, Parsons was the owner of a new jet ski, and had he not had a dance lesson to go to in a few hours, he would have insisted on taking it with him there and then. But, instead, he arranged to collect it the following day.

IT WAS 7PM WHEN PARSONS' private lesson with Maria began and in all honesty he was too distracted to give it his full attention. Maria quickly sensed his mood and told him to concentrate and to put more effort in to his dancing. It was only when he said that it was because he was excited for his birthday tomorrow that she relented and cut the lesson short.

'What are you doing for your birthday?' she asked him as she collected her music from the CD player.

'I'm not sure. Sarah has something arranged, but it's a surprise.'

'She is you girlfriend, Sarah?' Maria asked him.

'No, she is my work colleague,' Parsons told her as they left the dance studio.

'She is older than you. I should have known that she is not your girlfriend,' Maria replied.

'That wouldn't matter, I like women older than myself'. As Parsons said this, he felt a small rush of adrenaline passing through him.

Maria smiled at him and said, 'Really, how much older?'

'This much,' he said as he pointed at her.

'You like me?' Maria now asked him.

'Yes, a lot,' he told her. 'Would you like to grab a drink?'

Maria nodded. They went to a bar in the town where they chatted and laughed together. Parsons asked Maria all about herself and after a while, he wasn't sure whether he was asking her so many questions because he wanted to, or whether it was what Sarah had taught him to do. He wanted to know all about Maria, but his questioning felt like a script to him now. The one thing that he learned was that she was fun and good company. After they finished their drinks, Maria asked him if he wanted another.

'I have to drive back home but I will have a cola please'.

'It is a birthday drink I am buying you. It cannot be cola,' she told him.

'But I am driving Maria.'

'Why can you not spend the night at my place?' She asked, as she shrugged.

'Are you sure that is OK?'

'Yes, sure,' she told him.

Parsons called Sarah to let her know he was staying out for the night and that he would be back early in the morning. She told him to have fun and to call her if he needed anything. Maria then gave him a tour of the bars that the locals drank in and when they heard him speaking Italian, he was accepted as one of them. Maria could not believe that he had learnt to speak the language so well, so soon.

Only one person seemed to not warm to Parsons. It was the man he had spoken to in the restrooms while paying it a visit. Parsons said 'hello,' in Italian and when the man didn't respond, Parsons spoke in English, but still the man did not reply. He looked familiar and Parsons was about to ask if they had met before. Suddenly, he was gone, leaving the restrooms and the bar. Parsons asked Maria about the man, but she was clueless as to who he was talking about.

For Gruber, it had been a wonderful insight into Parsons' character seeing him in the bar. He had learnt that Parsons was sociable and talkative. But he was also weak, Gruber thought as he compared Parsons to his own prodigy, who he knew would be the successful one.

It was nearly midnight when they got back to Maria's small apartment, that was close to the central train station. Parsons recognised the area around the station, as he had often travelled in to Sorrento from Vico Equense, using the Circumvesuviana regional trainline.

Maria poured them both a brandy that they sat down in her lounge, drinking.

'Do you have any tattoos?' Parsons asked Maria.

'Yes, I have two,' she told him.

'What are they?'

Maria stood up and removed her top to reveal her bra. Parsons' eyes lingered on the tantalising swell of her cleavage. She turned around, and he saw a tattoo of a bird below her left shoulder blade. It was a stunning Cuban Tody, in full colour, complete with the distinctive green body, pink flank, red throat and blue ear patch of the species.

'Wow, a bird, lovely. What about the other one?' he asked, admiring her slender back and deeply tanned skin.

Maria turned to face him and lowered her trousers. She pushed them down her thighs and he could see that she was wearing a red G-string. She pulled the front of the G-string to one side. A small tattoo of a love heart sat just above her pubic bone.

Parsons leaned in to get a closer look. Maria hooked her thumbs into the G-string and pushed it down along with her trousers until both were on the floor. Stepping out of them, she reached behind her and unclasped her bra. She slipped it off her shoulders and dropped it onto the floor, freeing her ample breasts. Parsons reached out and took hold of her buttocks. With a firm grip, he pulled her towards him and buried his face between her legs. Her pussy was hot and wet. His erection hardened. He flattened his tongue against Maria's entrance and she began to grind her pussy on his face. Once her legs stiffened and her breathing grew heavier, he leaned back slightly, just enough to flick his tongue over her clitoris. Maria used one hand to keep his head in place and moaned loudly. Her other hand squeezed her left breast and rubbed her nipple.

Parsons' cock jumped: he was desperate to be inside her. He pulled his shirt over his head, took off his trousers, then boxers, his hard cock ready to enter her when she spoke.

'Wait a second,' Maria told him as she twisted around and got on to her knees, facing away from him. She leaned against the arm of the sofa; her backside raised invitingly. Parsons wanted to feel her around him, and he pushed forward with his erection until he felt his tip touch the wet entrance to her pussy. His body stiffened as she pushed backwards, taking him inside her. Maria arched her back and groaned with pleasure. Parsons slid one hand along her back, beginning at the groove between her buttocks, using his thumb and then his fingers, following the line of her spine. Her skin was so soft and smooth. Reaching forwards, he cupped one of her breasts in his other hand. Maria lifted herself up until her back leaned against his chest. Clutching the back of his neck, she moved her right hand down between her legs, rubbing at her clitoris.

'Squeeze my nipple,' Maria demanded, and he responded immediately, rolling the erect bud between his thumb and finger.

He felt her pussy tighten around his shaft in response.

'Harder, squeeze it harder,' she groaned.

Parsons squeezed her nipple harder still and pressed his mouth into the side of her neck, kissing a line from behind her ear down to her shoulder.

Maria moaned, and she dug her nails into the back of Parsons' neck. He instinctively reacted to the pleasurable pain by squeezing her nipple harder before bouncing her harder onto his cock.

With a cry of 'Oh God,' Maria orgasmed hard before her body relaxed.

'Lie down,' she said as she turned around and pushed him back on to the sofa.

Maria straddled him and put his cock inside her again. She rode up and down, never taking her eyes off his. Parsons clenched her thighs tightly and raised his hips to meet her, enjoying the sensation of her buttocks slamming into him.

Kissing him deeply, Maria moaned into his mouth. She ran her tongue over his bottom lip and across the top of his teeth.

'Get on top of me,' Maria whispered. 'I want to feel you on me, please'.

Watching Maria rub her pussy while she lay on her back, waiting for him, drove Parsons wild. She saw the hungry look in his eyes and smiled.

With his cock in her pussy, he watched her breasts move as he thrust. He raised Maria's arms above her head and held both of her wrists in one hand. Watching Maria come again underneath him tipped him over the edge and he exploded inside her.

～

WHEN PARSONS ARRIVED BACK at the house at 7am, Sarah was already up and dressed. There were two small suitcases in the hallway and he sensed that she going somewhere.

'Good morning,' he greeted her.

'I think that good night is probably more apt,' she said with a knowing smile.

Parsons felt a flush of colour in his face, but resisted the urge to reply to her.

'Happy birthday, you old dog,' she said to him with a grin.

'I'm not old,' he replied, surprised by her words.

Sarah walked to him and gave him a kiss on each cheek as she handed him an envelope.

'The emphasis was on the dog part lover boy.' She looked at him and added, 'I have a feeling that you are more of a man this morning, and not just because of your age.' She smiled as she saw his reaction and the grin that he could not hide.

'You are nosier than my sister. I am telling you nothing,' Parsons replied.

'Open your card quickly. I cannot stand the suspense any longer,' she demanded.

Parsons opened the envelope and took the card out. It was a birthday card from Sarah, which he thanked her for and gave her a kiss. There was a second envelope inside that he also opened.

'Oh my God, is this for real?' he asked her.

'Yes, I am going to teach you Russian, just like you asked me to,' Sarah told him.

'These are tickets to fly to Moscow today,' Parsons said as he looked at the flight tickets that he had taken from the envelope.

'Yes, remember how you learnt to speak Italian? You

watched and listened to it being spoken. We are going to do that in Moscow, if we don't miss our flight. Come on, you dirty stop out, get a shower and hurry up, you have thirty minutes until our taxi arrives'.

'Sarah, this is amazing, thank you'. He kissed her again and hugged her tightly, genuinely delighted with her gift.

'Urgh, you stink of sex. Get off me and go get ready. You can tell me all about your night of passion during the flight. I can't wait to learn whether she has a tattoo,' Sarah told him. 'I will bring a coffee up to you. Hurry, go get ready.'

THE FLIGHT to Moscow passed quickly and Parsons eventually relented to questioning, describing Maria's tattoos to Sarah.

'She is a temptress, and she will teach you to dance in the bedroom; as well as on the dance floor. I feel that your dance lessons may be more strenuous in the future.'

'I told you about the tattoos. That's enough for now. It is my birthday. Stop teasing me,' he joked with her.

'It is your birthday, I'm sorry,' Sarah apologised. 'I cannot wait until you see your present.'

'I thought that this was my present, coming to Russia,' he said.

'Don't be silly, this is training. You are learning a new language for your work,' Sarah explained.

Parsons looked at her in amazement and then remembered his jet ski. He was due to collect it today. He explained this to Sarah, and she told him that once they landed, she would call the shop in Sorrento and rearrange it for him.

'My goodness, is this a new you?' she asked him.

'Is what a new me?' he replied.

'Impulse buying, a red-hot lover, you really are becoming Italian, aren't you!'

Parsons laughed at her and shook his head. 'I'm not an impulse buyer,' he eventually replied with a grin.

'You were very careful to deny just that one. I shall therefore presume that you are now ready to be unleashed on the female villains of the world,' Sarah told him with a raised brow and a cunning smile.

As she looked at him, she was confident that he was ready. He had developed and matured beyond belief since he had arrived in Italy several months ago. He had listened to all that she had told him and had quickly learnt what she had taught. He absorbed everything and put it in to practise willingly; he was ready and he would soon have to prove it.

13

———

Moscow was everything that Parsons had expected and more. The buildings and the architecture fascinated him. From the moment that they left Domodedovo airport and caught the train for the thirty-mile journey in to Moscow, he was in awe. Little details such as the height and width of the trains, compared to those that he had seen before, impressed him. Even though Parsons had previously studied soviet tactics, back at his old army regiment, nothing was quite as he had imagined it would be. When they arrived in Moscow centre, they took a short walk through the busy streets to get to their hotel.

'Everything is huge, the road is six lanes wide, and it's all just... huge,' Parsons commented as they stood at a pavement waiting to cross the road.

Sarah had travelled to Russia many times before and now remembered back to her first visit to the country. On that occasion she had gone to St Petersburg; however, she remembered being just as impressed as Parsons appeared to be.

'Wait till you see the rest of the city. The Kremlin and St Basil's will blow your mind,' she assured him. 'In fact, the Metro, that is possibly the most surprising sight for many visitors, wait and see.'

Sarah enjoyed seeing Parsons so happy and excited. As their time together had grown longer, she had seen his personality in a different, deeper way. She felt a tinge of guilt for her part in his selection for the role he would fulfil.

'Can we visit the Bolshoi theatre; will we have time?' he enquired.

'Yes, we are here for a few days, so we should be able to do that,' Sarah assured him.

They were staying in the hotel Baltschug Kempinski, that was set on the south side of the river Moskva. The building dated back to 1898, and was amongst the best hotels in Moscow, if not the best. Its original, neoclassical facade was well maintained and decorated with ornamental figures that watched over the river and the city beyond. The hotel was by far beyond any luxury that Parsons had ever experienced. The reception and public areas reminded him of a palace with marble columns and fine artwork on the walls. From their room, they had spectacular views of both the Kremlin and St Basil's Cathedral.

'Are we sharing a room and a bed?' Parsons asked Sarah as he looked around the luxurious private space, that was filled with grand furniture and an enormous bed.

'Yes, I thought it would be nice to spend the time together. It would be silly to have separate rooms when we have a bed the size of a small country,' Sarah answered him. 'It has been a long time since I have had somebody to spoon with.'

Parsons looked at her, uncertain which of the questions he had in his mind he should ask first.

'Don't worry, I promise I can resist you. You will be safe in a bed with me,' Sarah said, seeing his expression. 'Even now that you are a male floosy.' She was smiling, but she now changed her tone slightly as she added, 'Also, as I have a task that I need you to complete whilst we are here in Moscow. At some point you will need to move in to a hotel on your own, so this will only be for one or two nights.'

'A task? What is it?' Parsons asked.

'We have to retrieve some information for our employer, but not now. Today is your birthday, and we are on holiday.' She finished checking herself in the mirror, and in a heavily Russian accented voice said, 'Come comrade, let's go and explore mother Russia.'

It was late in the afternoon when they set off from the hotel to look around the city, and as promised, Sarah took Parsons directly to Red Square to see its sights. Once there, they saw the brightly coloured, onion-shaped domes of St Basil's and the high perimeter walls of the Kremlin. She told him that the name Kremlin meant fortress inside a city. He was fascinated by the history that Sarah knew, and as they walked through the street, she gave him an in-depth insight in to the culture and history of a country that captured his imagination.

'At the end of 1991, the Union of Soviet Socialist Republics collapsed, Perestroika and Glasnost had caused the revolutions of 1989, and the end of the Soviet Union was inevitable. A new Russia and the end of the cold war. Things are changing and the financial investment is visible. Look around you, there is the emergence of a free market here now,' Sarah explained.

'How do you know all of this stuff about Russia?' Parsons asked her.

'It is my job to know about it. To know about all the countries that pose a threat to the UK and her allies'.

'But you said that the cold war was over. The threat from the USSR has surely gone now,' Parsons suggested to her.

'Maybe, but that has opened the gates to capitalism, and with that comes an even bigger threat. The elites, the rich and powerful oligarchy, are seizing control. They are a network of entrepreneurs, businessmen, criminals who are stealing the country's wealth from the people and from the state.'

'Why doesn't the government and the military leadership take control of things and stop these people? They have the KGB, surely they can stop them?' Parsons said.

'The people here have changed, as a result of that, the government and the FSB, which has replaced the KGB, are weakened. Many of the former senior officers of the KGB are aligning themselves with the wealth and criminality. Some of them are themselves becoming very rich, very quickly. And many government officials have realised that they prefer money to power, so they are also becoming corrupt and working with the oligarchs. At least when it was the Soviet Union, things were controlled by the state. Now the state is controlled by the wealthy elite and the criminals who support them,' Sarah told him.

Parsons listened to her and considered how these oligarchs would grow in to the most powerful people in Russia and maybe the most powerful in the world.

'How can a country so large and so rich in natural resources have a single poor citizen?' Sarah said out aloud.

Parsons nodded and understood the predicament that threatened Russia, a threat that could be far more damaging to the people than anything before it. They had been walking for a while when Parsons suggested they should stop for a drink and a snack.

'Can you tell me about the task?' he asked Sarah as they drank coffee at a popular café.

'If you really want me to, but it is your birthday and we shouldn't interrupt it with talk of work,' Sarah replied.

'I do want you to, please tell me.'

Sarah ensured they were not overheard before she began. 'There is a Russian businessman by the name of Nikolay Turgenev. At the moment he is in London, attending meetings and arranging the purchase of a home for himself and his secretary, come mistress. He is a former criminal boss, who has registered numerous new companies, both here, in Germany and back in the UK. For a man who appeared to be of no great wealth two years ago, he suddenly has many millions of pounds to invest. The new companies are registered as being concerned in the production and export of oil. However, he has no historical links to the oil industry here in Russia.'

Although Parsons nodded as she spoke, Sarah saw he had a question to ask her, and so paused for a second.

'Where does the money that he has invested originate from? Who does it trace back to?' he asked.

'To him. Several bank accounts, with falsified lengthy accounting histories, have been created in his name. For someone with the right access, historic bank records are easy to fabricate and easy to make look genuine. But we were watching for Russian investment in the UK markets and his activities were flagged up by one of the intelligence agencies. He has invested over three hundred million pounds through his companies and he is looking to invest more.'

'If he is a criminal, why is the British government allowing him to register businesses in the UK?' Parsons asked.

'He is no longer a criminal. All records of his previous convictions have been deliberately deleted from records. Even from FSB archives, which really is a difficult thing to achieve,' Sarah commented.

'How do you know that?' Parsons asked.

Sarah raised her brow, surprised that he had asked such an obvious and naïve question. The British had their own spies inside the FSB as they had in the KGB previously. Before she could answer, Parsons understood and moved on.

'Is he linked to any other people that might indicate where the money has come from?'

'Not that we know of, but that is our task,' Sarah told him.

She saw Parsons sudden increased interest and told him the plan that she had.

'Nikolay is staying in a hotel in London and is under surveillance. We will know if he leaves the UK and heads back here. He isn't expected to return for another week, next Thursday, to be exact. He has a wife, Tatiana, who lives in St. Petersburg, along with their two children. The family is protected at home by his private security team, so we have not been able to get in there to plant any listening devices or cameras. Nikolay is very security conscious and knows that his activity is drawing the attention of the authorities in the UK. To get close to him is almost impossible and even if we could, it is very unlikely that it would be very fruitful. He is forty-six years old and has spent all of his adult life surviving in the toughest criminal underworld possible. He is far from a fool. His weak point, however, is Tatiana. She is our way of finding out what we need to. She is your task.' As Sarah finished speaking, she watched for a reaction from Parsons and was pleased when he spoke.

'What can I do then? How do I get what we need?' he replied.

'Tatiana is aware of Nikolay's soon to be purchased, new home in London, and that it is his young secretary who has chosen it. She accepts this and all of his other indiscretions so long as she can continue with the lifestyle that she enjoys, and that she is not caused any embarrassment in public. She is a few years his junior, she is forty. But this is quite old for the wife of someone like Nikolay. She knows that the day will come when he will divorce her. It is inevitable.'

'The poor woman,' Parsons said as he listened.

'Far from it. Tatiana is named on the board of several of the new company's and is, to some degree, involved in their running. By all accounts, she is known to be quite a ruthless businesswoman herself. Nikolay appears to be cautious of his mystery investor or investors, and has made sure that some of his new wealth is secured in a name other than his own. Perhaps in case things turn ugly between himself and his new businesses pals. Tatiana is a wealthy lady on paper at least, and knows how to enjoy herself, both with money and with male company.'

He nodded as he began to realise how he was to become involved. He had a question, more of a problem. 'If she is Russian, how the hell am I of any use?'

'You mean you can't speak Russian?' Sarah asked him.

'Yes, how will I speak with her?'

Sarah flashed her dazzling smile that he had come to recognise. 'Non lo farai. Lei parla italiano'.

'She speaks Italian?' he asked.

'Yes, she adores Italy and would live there in a flash, if it were possible. For the last two years, she and the children have been to Florence for their summer holidays. She also speaks a little English but her Italian is better.'

'Shit, is my Italian good enough?' Parsons was suddenly panicking, but Sarah had anticipated this.

'You know that it is. You have even developed a regional accent when you speak. And remember, she is Russian. Italian is a second language to her, a holiday language. You speak it every day, plus she will know that you are British, so between the two languages you will be able to communicate easily. Maybe you will be able to help her improve her Italian,' Sarah suggested.

He felt confident when Sarah told him things. She was right. He watched Italian television programs at home, and only really spoke English when helping out a tourist or calling his family back in England.

'How do I get to her?' he asked.

'Tatiana arrives in Moscow tomorrow, and won't be leaving until Monday. She is here for a short break, to spend time with her girlfriends and to shop. They will get together at several points during the weekend, but a large portion of her time will be spent in her hotel room with a lover. You will take his place.'

Parsons looked surprised. There were so many questions. 'Take his place?'

'Yes. I will see to that he never arrives, and you will fill the time for her.'

'Sleep with her?' he asked.

'If you like, she is very attractive. Whatever you feel comfortable doing in the process of gaining her trust,' Sarah said.

'I can't sleep with her.'

Sarah shrugged and drank from the mug that she had in front of her on the table.

'She is beautiful. Maybe you will want to,' she said as she placed the mug back on to the table. Parsons looked at her but said nothing. 'She will be going to Florence on holiday again in a few weeks. It would be an ideal time and opportunity for you to get close to her while she is there.'

Parsons looked at Sarah as he evaluated their situation and the likelihood of there being another chance to get close to Tatiana.

'You could just see how it goes. I can coordinate it so that you meet her in the hotel bar by chance and from there you can see what you think,' Sarah said, breaking the silence.

Parsons simply replied, 'OK', and picked up his drink.

In his mind, he wasn't sure how far he would go to complete the task, but it was his job and he would trust Sarah.

'Right, it's my birthday. No more work until tomorrow. Let's go have some fun,' he said with a smiled.

She couldn't help herself. Sarah leant across the table to Parsons and kissed him full on the lips. It was only a quick kiss, but she was so happy with him that she couldn't help herself.

'You are right, come, let's go and party,' she said.

WHEN THEY ARRIVED BACK at the hotel, it was after midnight and they had both had a long day. As he undressed, Parsons thought about how they were going to sleep in the same bed together. Sarah was in the bathroom and he was waiting to get into the bed, unsure what he should wear as he didn't have any pyjamas. She came out of the bathroom and saw him standing there, looking confused.

'Are you OK?' she asked.

'I've got no pyjamas. What should I wear in bed?' he asked her.

'What do you normally wear to bed?'

'Nothing, I don't sleep well if I'm not naked,' he answered.

'That's your answer then - wear nothing.' Sarah removed her clothes and underwear and got into the bed naked.

Parsons took his clothes off and also got in to the bed naked. The bed was at least the equivalent size of four regular beds and there was a gap of some five to six feet between the two of them. Sarah used the switch to the side of the headboard to turn off the lights, plunging the room in to darkness. When he thought he had heard her lie down, he suddenly felt her touch, which made him jump.

'I told you, it has been a long time since I have had somebody to spoon with. Come here or else you will fall off the edge of the bed.'

Once Parsons had slid across the bed towards Sarah, he felt her head on his chest and her body up against his side. He then felt a kiss on his cheek and heard her say, 'Good night.'

He lay there for a moment, feeling slightly uneasy to be lay naked in bed with her. But he then realised that she was sound asleep, and that she was completely content. He hadn't sensed this with Sarah before, and it gave him an overwhelming urge to protect her. He himself fell asleep, and rested for several hours, only to be woken in the morning when he felt Sarah stir beside him. She was still half asleep and looked as perfect as she always did. Her head was still on his chest and her leg was across his body.

He started to move away and saw her wake with a shocked look on her face as she lifted her head a little. She was about to jump up when she realised where she was and that she was with him. She relaxed again, and he felt her head rest back on to his chest.

'Did we spoon?' she asked him.

'I don't think so,' he answered.

'Next time I want to spoon, OK?'

Parsons hesitated and then felt her head moving on his chest as she looked up at him.

'Yes, next time we can spoon,' he replied. She squeezed him with satisfaction and relented, allowing him to get out of bed. Parsons took a shower and found that she was still lazing in the bed when he came back into the room. He threw a pillow onto the bed next to her and she lifted her head to look at him.

'Come on sleepy, you have a briefing to give to me over breakfast. I want to know everything that you can tell me about Mrs Tatiana Turgenev.' She looked at him, surprised by his enthusiasm. 'And by the way,' he added.

'What?' she said sleepily.

'You snore like an infantry soldier.'

She giggled, and buried her face in to her pillow as she did so.

BY THE TIME they had returned from a river cruise that afternoon, Parsons was fully up to speed with the plan, and knew everything that Sarah did in relation to Tatiana. He was to move into a new hotel immediately and stay there over the weekend. This was the hotel where Tatiana would stay, and where she had arranged to meet her male companion in the bar at 7.30 pm. She always came away alone when meeting male companions and would not have any security with her. Sarah would see to it that the male that Tatiana was expecting would be diverted, leaving her waiting alone and wondering where he had got to. Parsons would be in the bar at this time, and would make his excuse to talk to Tatiana. The rest would be down to him to work out, to entice her to engage with him.

As Parsons packed his suitcase, Sarah gave him details of an emergency rendezvous point and a contact telephone number that he should call in an emergency situation. She told him that as a security measure, she would shortly leave the hotel Baltschug herself and would find an alternative place to stay. Parsons had until 4pm on Sunday, at which point he must be at the café where they had drunk coffee the previous day.

He was given false documents in the name of Carl Massey, and his date of birth was altered to make him twenty-four years old. He liked the idea of being older than he was; he found it strangely satisfying. Parsons walked a short distance towards the city centre and then caught a taxi to the new hotel. He handed the piece of paper that Sarah had given to him to the taxi driver, who grunted an acknowledgement and drove straight there. Parsons was promptly booked in to the hotel and shown to his room by a member of staff. He took time to unpack his suitcase and then rehearsed his plan again.

He was using the guise of being an English teacher living in Italy. Parsons had rehearsed a cover story of how he had qualified from university as a teacher. But rather than settle down with a job at a school in England, had travelled the world a little, teaching privately to fund his adventures. He had been in Italy for a couple of years now, living in

Naples. He and Sarah had travelled there enough in the past, and he felt he could talk about it easily. He was confident that Tatiana would not doubt his story. Sarah had given him a camera to hide in his room, so that it could be used to record if Tatiana came back there with him. Once he had set the camera up in a discrete location and he had dressed, he went down to the bar.

It was 7pm when he entered the hotel bar, which was empty other than one man sat reading a paper. Parsons ordered a drink and sat at a table close to the bar as he waited. He had only been there for five minutes when Tatiana came in to the hotel reception from the direction of the street. He could see that she was carrying several bags that appeared to be filled with shopping. She glanced into the bar briefly before heading over to wait for a lift that was slowly travelling down from another floor. As the lift arrived and the doors opened, she turned back to look at Parsons and smiled. He didn't have time to return her smile before she walked into the lift and was gone again.

Sarah had been right, Tatiana was attractive. She had long, straight, blonde hair that was just a little short of her waist. She was close to six-foot-tall and had long slim legs. He had only seen her from behind, other than when she turned to look into the bar briefly, but he immediately recognised her from the photograph that Sarah had shown to him.

As the time passed, he ran through his story again in his head and tried to find any weaknesses. He looked at the clock and saw that it was now after 7.30pm. Tatiana was nowhere to be seen, and he began to wonder whether Sarah's intelligence had been accurate. He did not know where it had come from, but as the minutes rolled by, it was proving to be wrong. 8pm came and went and there was still no sign of Tatiana in the bar.

Parsons wondered whether Sarah might have failed to intercept the male who Tatiana was due to meet and that maybe he had slipped up to her room unnoticed. It was another ten minutes later when he saw the doors of the lift open and Tatiana walk out into the reception. She had made the most of her time since returning to the hotel, making herself look like a fashion model. She was wearing a figure-hugging black dress that emphasised her slender shape and long legs. Her jewellery shone in the light, and the many diamonds that she wore glistened to match her eyes. As she walked through the reception area, she glanced briefly into the bar, and then made her way to the exit, leaving the hotel. Parsons waited for a minute to see if she would come back in.

'Shit, this isn't going to plan,' he thought to himself. He drank his drink and stood up; he would have to see where she was going. As he stood up, he heard a female voice thank somebody and realised that she was coming back inside. He altered his direction and went to the bar. Tatiana came and stood at the bar herself, waiting to speak with the bartender. The tender came to Parsons first and asked him what he could get for him.

Speaking Italian, Parsons replied, 'Please serve this lady before me'. He gestured towards Tatiana and, deceptively, smiled at her in a welcoming way. She hesitated a second, and then spoke in Russian to the bartender, in a very low voice. She asked him whether anyone had been waiting in the bar, who may have asked for her. The bar tender told her that only the older male who was sitting alone at a table reading and Carl had been in the bar. She thanked the bartender and was about to leave when Parsons called out.

'Not you as well.'

Tatiana spoke in Russian, saying, 'Izvinite', meaning sorry.

'Oh, I don't speak Russian sorry, just English and Italian,' Parsons replied. 'Do you speak either of them?'

Tatiana recognised he was English and said, 'I speak a little English but not much. I can speak better Italian.' She was now facing him and he saw that she was not wearing her wedding ring. Sarah had taught him that deliberately getting caught looking to see if someone was wearing a wedding ring would show someone that you were interested in them.

Tatiana instinctively covered her wedding hand when she saw Parsons look at it, a reaction to the feeling of guilt.

'Really, you speak three languages?' he asked.

'A little,' she replied with a smile.

'Can I get you a drink?' he asked, noticing the bar tender waiting. Tatiana hesitated and Parsons said the first thing that he could think of. 'It's my birthday'.

'It is your birthday, today?' Tatiana asked him.

'Yes. No. I mean it was my birthday yesterday'. He felt that he was making a mess of the situation. 'But I didn't get to celebrate it yesterday, so I'm trying to celebrate it today, on my own'. He pulled a sad face at her and she formed a smile.

'I am meeting a friend, but I can have one drink with you before they arrive,' she conceded.

They sat down at Parsons table, and the bartender brought their drinks over to them.

Switching between English and Italian, they were able to have a conversation during which Parsons told Tatiana how he had come to be in Russia. He said that he had been scheduled to attend an interview for work as an English teacher for an Italian family, but that it had been cancelled and so he had time to waste before his flight home on Sunday. When she asked him about his Italian, he explained to her how he had lived in Italy for a few years and taught English privately. She asked him if he had been to Florence and told him how she holidayed there each summer. She never mentioned that she was married, or that she had children. Tatiana told Parsons that she was an accountant in St. Petersburg and that she was in Moscow for a weekend of shopping.

They had been talking for about forty-five minutes when the concierge came through to the bar to find Tatiana. He handed her a note and Parsons saw a flush of anger and disappointment pass over her face as she read it. Sarah had arranged for the message to be delivered, and it read that Sergei would not be joining her for the weekend.

It was true, Sergei would no longer be meeting with Tatiana or anyone else. He had been more difficult to deal with than Sarah had anticipated. She had followed him as he had exited a Metro station and had stopped to speak with him at the entrance of an alleyway. Once she persuaded him to come into the alleyway with her, there had been a conversation between them, followed by a brief struggle. Even at the mention of Nikolay's name, Sarah had not been able to persuade Sergei to stay away from Tatiana. She had broken his neck and left him slumped between two rubbish bins. Killing him irritated her. She had overreacted and could have simply put him in hospital for a while. She felt it was due to protecting Parsons that she had not been her normal controlled self and made a mental note to not let it happen again.

'Is everything OK?' Parsons asked Tatiana as she put the note away.

'Yes, but my friend is not well, it is not a problem.' It was a problem and she would have ensured that he did not get the chance to let her down again. Tatiana had become accustomed to people other than Nikolay doing what she wanted.

'Would you like another drink?' Parsons asked. They sat in the bar drinking together, while Tatiana asked him all about his life in Italy. Parsons described the Amalfi Coast to her, and said that although he had never been to Florence, he was sure that it could not be more beautiful than places such as Positano.

'You should let me know the next time that you come to Italy. I could meet you and give you a guided tour,' he suggested.

'I don't even know you. I couldn't ask you to do that,' she replied, enjoying herself and feeling young again.

'Well, get to know me, and then you can ask me,' he told her as he smiled at her. 'I would enjoy it,' he added, flirting with her.

She smiled, and as she looked at him; she wondered how old he was. He looked no older than twenty-five and that would be her youngest lover to date; she thought. The thought of a much younger lover made her feel good, and it made her think that she was beating Nikolay.

'Carl, I am unrested and hungry. I think that it's time for me to return to my room and get some room service.' She touched his leg under the table and he had to stop himself from flinching. He looked down below the table and saw her bare legs, smooth and sexy. As he looked back up, Tatiana looked him dead in the eye and waited for him to speak.

'I would like to come with you. Maybe I could help you rest, or something,' he suggested. He was sure that his voice had been wobbly as he said it and he was about to say something further when Tatiana spoke.

'I am in room 509, on the top floor. What room are you in?' she asked.

'203,' he replied.

'Five minutes after I leave, use the lift to go to your own floor. Then use the stairs to come up to my room, the door will be open'. She stood up and said goodbye to Parsons and the bar tender before making her way up to her room. Parsons waited the instructed five minutes and then left also, saying good night to the bar tender.

As promised, the door to her room was open. Parsons entered and saw Tatiana sat in a chair, silhouetted against a bay window. He closed the door behind him and locked it. He used the light panel on the wall to dim the lights and then walked towards Tatiana, who was still sat in the chair.

'Do you know who I am?' she asked, causing Parsons to stop.

He felt a surge of panic. His senses were screaming at him and he felt adrenalin rushing through his body.

'Do you know who my husband is?' she asked.

'No,' he replied.

His energy peaked, and he knew it would soon turn to nerves and overwhelm him. With a nervous excitement, he began to unbutton his shirt and walked slowly towards her.

'I don't know who you are, and I don't know who your husband is. All that I do know is that you are intelligent and sexy and I want to fuck your brains out right now.' He removed his shirt and tossed it to the floor.

Her eyes lit up at the sight of his strong, young body, and she felt aroused by his confidence. With his hands, he released the belt from around his waist and undid his trousers.

'Come here,' he told her as he looked into her eyes. Tatiana stood up from the chair and he spoke again. 'No, on your knees'. She froze and looked at him. This wasn't a role that she usually played; she was the dominant one. She watched as he lowered his trousers a little and the long ridge that ran up the front of his boxer shorts was revealed.

'Now, come here,' he commanded her. She felt a wave of excitement energise her body and without even thinking about it she dropped to her knees and went to him.

He guided her hands on to his covered cock and took hold of the back of her head with his hands. She was under his control and she waited for him to instruct her.

'Take my cock out,' he said.

She immediately obeyed him and felt herself strangely shaking with excitement. She went to put it in to her mouth but he stopped her. 'Wait'. There was a pause during which she felt that time itself stood still. He guided her head closer to his erection and said, 'Now, suck it now'.

She engulfed him between her lips and felt the heat of it against the roof of her mouth. As she felt the pressure of his hands increase, pulling her towards him, she let it slide deeper into her mouth. She relished being dominated as she had never before. This had not been something that she had considered being pleasurable before. Nikolay had always been a brute; she dreaded any form of sexual vulnerability with him. But Parsons was somehow respectful, demanding and strong at the same time as gentle. She sucked harder and deeper, driven by her urge to please him.

She felt him pull back and heard, 'Stand up, stand against the wall, facing it,' he said.

She did it without delay, and he lifted her arms above her shoulders, and then spread them out against the wall. He used his foot to open her legs, parting them wider. She was now in the stereotypical police frisk position and he was behind her. He reached down and took a hand full of her right buttock. She went to turn her head and he gently but quickly took hold of her chin in his hand, whispering to her to face the wall and to not move again. She nodded and realised that she was panting heavily.

It was a sudden shock when she felt the slap land against her butt. It wasn't even hard, but it felt electric and she made the softest of whimpers. Her dress had ridden up to the tops of her legs, leaving her buttocks exposed and bare. He slowly repeated the slap again and again, a little harder each time. She felt the pauses between them too long as her enjoyment grew with each one. His right hand slid down to the base of her buttocks and beneath them until she felt it touching the inside of her left leg. She felt him lower himself onto one knee and slide his left hand down her left leg, slowly stopping just above her knee. He then gripped at the leg and circled it with his hand. She felt his breath against her left buttock and saw that she had goose bumps on her arms. She had no choice but to close her eyes for a second, the anticipation was too much for her.

His right hand moved down the inside of her right leg. He was using the outside of his hand, and she could feel the contour of his knuckles, one by one, travelling over her skin. He stopped and changed direction, back up now, slowly getting higher. She sighed and almost lowered herself to his hand.

'Don't move,' he said to her sharply, but with no annoyance. She froze and waited for him to go on, but he remained still.

'I won't move. Please keep going,' she said, hoping and encouraging him to go on.

She felt him twist his hand as it reached the top, and the

palm of it encased her. She had removed her underwear before he had arrived at the room, leaving her bare and ready. She could now feel his wrist against her anus, his palm against her perineum and his fingers covering her clitoris and the opening of her pussy. She moaned out as his fingers jerked forwards and backwards against her swollen, wet mound. He stopped, and she instinctively nodded, knowing that it was his order to remain silent. She felt the friction of his hand reduce against her skin as she became wetter, lubricating the two surfaces.

It was too much for her when she felt his fingers enter her pussy; she groaned and felt the air pushing from her chest as she did. As his fingers slid in and out of her pussy, she sensed his thumb moving back over her perineum and then onto her anus. Gently, he pushed at the opening and she felt it. His thumb broke through and entered her anus, up to the first knuckle. As he rocked his hand between her legs, he entered and exited her pussy and anus in a rhythmic motion. She felt her legs becoming more ridged as her body tightened from its core. She knew she was close to her orgasm and the stiffness in her legs turned to shaking. He gripped tighter on her leg with his left hand and put his face to her left buttock to steady her. But it was no use. As she felt her orgasm come, she could not hold herself and she dropped onto him. She was shaking and her legs felt heavy; she moaned out and let the overwhelming sensation of the orgasm take her.

Parsons sensed the moment and used his right shoulder to support her weight. He removed his thumb and fingers as he steadied her and slowly stood up behind her, sliding his hands up her torso, using them to support her trembling body. He picked her up and carried her to the edge of the high bed, where he lowered her so that she was standing once again. He bent her forwards at her waist and positioned her lower so that her torso was on the bed. The bed was the right height for her stomach to rest on, her hips just slightly higher than the top of the mattress when both of her feet were on the floor. Parsons raised her dress up past the area of her hips and her stomach, to the area at the top of her back, and left it there.

As he looked down at her body, he appreciated her feminine shape and the beauty of her skin; she was as womanly as was possible. He had to be inside her, but he had to make her wait. This was how it would be with Tatiana - this was how he would maintain some control. He moved behind her, to within millimetres of her, until he could feel his cock at her entrance. She sensed how close he was and enthused to meet him in a slow backwards motion. It was harder than before, but the slap on her buttocks made her moan in ecstasy, and she longed for him to do it again. She instinctively pushed back, knowing what her exhilarating punishment would be. She felt it again and gasped at the tingling that his hand left. Before she could push back again, he was inside her. She felt her legs give way and her weight rest on the mattress. With his hands on her hips, he lifted her to her feet and steadied her there, bent over the bed. She felt his rhythmic movements increasing in speed and power, and she cried out again in sync with them. His hands slid up to her waist, and he held her tightly, pulling her back to him each time his hard cock filled her.

She felt herself losing control and wanted to orgasm again. This was intensified when she felt him take hold of her hair. He wrapped her long silky mane through his fingers and around his hand, gently but with confidence. The feeling of her hair tightening on her scalp was bliss. It felt as though it was connected to her clitoris and the feeling travelled all the way down and through her body. With one powerful movement, he pushed her forwards and her feet came free of the floor. As her stomach came to rest on the bed again, she again went to stand on her legs. But now he had followed her and was there, restricting her from moving backwards. He pushed into her, faster and harder. She felt the supportive pressure of the mattress on her stomach, and it heightened the feeling of him deep inside her. She felt herself tighten inside, and he sensed it too, as she tensed her grip on his erection. He let go of her hair and slapped her buttocks twice before taking her by the waist. He pushed harder now, and she could hear him groaning, almost painfully groaning, with each push. She felt his cock pulse as he came inside her. He finally dropped flat on top of her and she lay there beneath him, feeling the muscles of his chest against her naked, sweaty back.

He kissed her once on her back and withdrew himself from within her, as he stood and moved fully onto the bed, exhausted.

Tatiana took a second or two before she moved and then, as she tried to control her breathing, she went to the bathroom to clean herself. When she returned to the room, she joined Parsons where he lay resting on the bed, half lay down and half sat up against the headboard. As she moved close to him, she smiled and kissed his forehead.

'I know you well enough now. You can give me that guided tour when I come to see you in Italy,' she said.

He rolled her on to her back, and leaning above her as he kissed her intensely on her lips. As he lifted his head and looked at her, he said, 'You will know me a lot better by the time you come to me in Italy.' He rubbed his hand up the inside of her leg and held it against her pussy. 'A whole lot better,' he added. She smiled, growled and pulled his head to hers and kissed him back.

OVER THE NEXT THIRTY-SIX HOURS, Parsons and Tatiana spent several hours in both his and her hotel rooms, occasionally talking but mainly engaging in sexual experimentation. He acted on instinct and his newly discovered dominant side pleasantly shocked him. Tatiana allowed herself to be directed and immersed herself in the liberation that she felt. They agreed they would meet again when she came to Italy for her holidays in a month, but that she would stay in the area around Positano rather than Florence.

Tatiana gave him a telephone number and said that it would not be a problem for him to call at any time. She told him of Nikolay and her children and revealed that she wasn't an accountant, but was a wealthy business owner. He acted surprised at first and she reacted by apologising for misleading him. She described how her marriage was in all senses over, and that Nikolay was an awful man who she longed to be rid of. Parsons portrayed empathy towards her and said that he understood.

As Parsons prepared to leave the hotel, Tatiana came to his room to say goodbye to him.

'My husband is a bad and powerful man; he must not know of us.'

'What about you? Will you be OK?' he asked her. She was touched by his concern for her and smiled at him.

'I am far too valuable to him for me to have to worry, in terms of money at least'.

They parted and Parsons caught a taxi to the airport.

Once he was a distance from the hotel, he made his excuse and got out of the taxi, thanking the driver and paying him for his troubles. He then headed to meet Sarah, to update her on all that had taken place. Well, nearly all!

That evening, the latest fax was sent. 'SUBJECT DEPLOYED. CONTACT INITIATED. SUBJECT ONE LOCAL.'

14

Once they received confirmation that Tatiana had boarded her flight back to St. Petersburg, Sarah and Parsons completed their sightseeing in Moscow. They spent seven nights there, and Parsons practiced using many of the Russian sentences that Sarah taught him. During this time, he fully debriefed Sarah on the events that had occurred whilst he had been with Tatiana and she was overjoyed when he gave her the telephone number at Tatiana's home. He described how he had taken the dominant role in their sexual encounters, and how she had willingly played the submissive role. Sarah told him it was perfect, but that now they must prepare for when Tatiana came to Italy.

Returning to Vico Equense felt good; like home, and Parsons was glad to be back. He took delivery of his new jet ski and Sarah gave him the birthday present. She had told him before they set off to Russia that she had a surprise birthday present for him. It was a red Ducati Monster motorcycle. He had previously told her he had got his motorcycle licence immediately after passing his car driving test, but had not had the opportunity to buy one since then. He was ecstatic and desperate to get out and ride the Ducati straight away.

Sarah told him he had to wait until the following day when a friend of hers, a local police officer, would take him out on escorted rides. When he asked her why, she told him that Gino had been a police motorcyclist for many years and that he was going to show Parsons how to ride safely. Also, Gino was going to show Parsons around the Amalfi coast, as it was where he had grown up, and he knew that area better than anyone.

For the next two weeks, Parsons rode the Ducati for several hours each day, constantly learning from Gino. He was taught advanced riding skills, how to use the motorcycle safely but at high speeds, and, importantly, how to conduct counter surveillance. Gino was a character and Parsons liked his sense of humour. He was a charmer and could not help but talk to every attractive woman that they encountered during their frequent refreshment stops in the towns that they passed through. Each time that they were stopped by the police for speeding, Gino would simply show his police identification and explain that they were on official training. It was a lie, but Gino was so charismatic that he was never challenged and he usually had the officer laughing and joking with him.

During this time, Sarah received the update she had been waiting for that confirmed Parsons was being watched. It took Sarah four days to lure the threat into her trap. As Parsons and Gino left one of their stops on their motorbikes, Sarah lay in wait. She had asked Gino to deliberately repeat visiting this location each day.

The girl appeared almost as soon as they left, making her way from a nearby building, she started walking over to a carpark. As she passed down the side of a large truck, Sarah, who was now following, took the opportunity. Striking the girl across the back of her head, Sarah knocked her unconscious, but was careful not to do her any serious harm for now. A car pulled up alongside and with the assistance of the front passenger, Sarah bundled the girl into the rear seats and got in with her. The car was driven away and Terhi Johanson was once again captive and at the mercy of another.

When Johanson woke, she found herself restrained in a dimly lit room that was deliberately cold and damp. She looked across the table at Sarah and spoke in English.

'What do you want with me?'

'Tell me everything or else I will hand you over to the UK authorities so that you can be put on trial for the brutal death of your mother,' Sarah replied.

Johanson was startled by Sarah's knowledge. She realised she was a step behind and needed to find a delay so that Gruber could deal with this.

'My mother sold me to men from the age of fifteen.'

'I don't give a fuck if she was the devil. That is your past and I have no interest in it. Tell me everything you know or you will be taken to the British embassy and handed over,' Sarah threatened.

Johanson could tell that Sarah was as ruthless as Gruber had warned and that she was going to be difficult to manipulate. She would have to buy herself some time, she thought. Johanson cried and was about to feed Sarah a long trail of lies.

Sarah could see on her face just what was going through Johanson's mind. 'I've changed my mind. I won't take you to the embassy. I will take you back to the place your mother sent you. I will allow them to fuck and use you as they did before. But this time they will be pissed off and you will suffer so much more.'

Johanson felt a mixture of anger and fear fill her veins at the thought of returning to the brothel. There was no way she could possibly go back. She knew what she must do; she knew she had to talk.

'So much as one lie or the smallest detail omitted and you will be back with them, do you understand?' Sarah asked.

Johanson nodded and then went on to give Sarah an account of the events in her life since being rescued by Gruber. She detailed how he had trained her and tasked her to spy on Parsons. She genuinely knew nothing of Gruber's background or why he was interested in Parsons, but she knew that Gruber constantly compared Parsons to another person and she found this strange.

'What do you mean, he compares?' Sarah asked.

'He criticises what your Parsons does and then says that Gladius would have done it better. He says that Parsons is weak and kind, like an old lady,' Johanson replied.

'Who or what is Gladius?' Sarah asked.

'I don't know. He won't talk about it when I ask, but it must be a person. I think it is someone that he trained.'

Sarah listened carefully as Johanson spoke, looking and waiting for any sign of deception.

'He often says things like, "I brought Gladius here, or Gladius got the hang of this quicker than you". I think it is someone he is proud of,' Johanson said honestly.

Sarah had first discovered Terhi Johanson by using the manifest of Parsons' flight to Italy. Johanson had used a fake passport, but sources back in London had traced who she was and that she was wanted for murder.

Johanson's mother had been a migrant, arriving in

Britain nine years ago with her daughter. She had left the Ukraine but continued her profession, working as a madam in the illegal sex trade. She had fallen out of favour at the time when Johanson had been around fifteen years old, so had started offering her daughter up to her bosses. Sarah had read the police intelligence file on her mother. It detailed how she had imprisoned many girls in various brothels, including her own daughter- at sixteen. Johanson had tried to escape but had been discovered by her mother, who stopped her and raised the alarm. Johanson had been severely beaten for her actions and subjected to events even more horrific than she had endured before. A short time after this, when Johanson had become ill, she had been escorted to hospital by her mother where they had waited for treatment. Johanson seized her opportunity and had fatally stabbed her mother with scissors, which had been left by the nurse.

Johanson had fled from the hospital but had not considered the escort from the brothel who had been waiting in a car outside. She was promptly caught and taken back to the tiny, dank room where she had been kept isolated for several weeks until she broke and agreed to return to servicing the customers that arrived day and night. Meanwhile, the police searched for her, releasing CCTV images of her to the national press and listing her as "wanted on a European arrest warrant."

Sarah felt for her and knew that had she ever have met Johanson's mother herself, she would have killed her too.

'I am sending you away to a place where you will be safe; you can stay with a friend of mine. They will primarily ensure that you stay with them and out of mine and Parsons' affairs. If you leave before I tell you; they will kill you. Do you understand?' Sarah asked.

Johanson nodded and Sarah went on. 'Once I have dealt with this Gruber, you will be free to leave as you please, but not before.'

'Where will it be? Italy?' Johanson asked.

'That does not matter. But you will be well cared for and after the awful life you have had, you might just wonder if you have landed in heaven.' Sarah was about to leave when she added one more detail. 'Please be sure that if you have crossed me or if you do anything that interferes with Parsons, I will make you wish you had never escaped your old life.'

PARSONS MADE several calls to Tatiana, all of which were now recorded and listened in to by Sarah. Tatiana told Parsons that her mother would join her and the children on the holiday so that she could take time out alone with him, while her mother babysat. Tatiana said that she would arrive on July 9th, and that she would stay for two weeks. When Parsons asked where, she told him she had rented a villa in Positano, as he had tempted her with his descriptions of the romantic coastline. Parsons said that he was also looking for somewhere to stay in Positano and she offered to send him money to assist him in doing so. He declined the offer, but afterwards Sarah told him it had been a mistake. The opportunity to gain details of a bank account belonging to Tatiana that they may not already be aware of was invaluable. Sarah encouraged him to raise the subject of finances in future calls and to accept the offer if it was made again. She provided him with details of a bank account to use that was registered in his false name, Carl Massey.

During their next telephone conversation, he told

Tatiana that he had seen several places to rent in Positano but that they were all too expensive. She insisted he allow her to send him some money and argued that it was for the both of them, so it was reasonable for her to contribute towards it. He accepted her offer and gave her the bank details, only to discover twenty thousand pounds had been transferred to the account the following morning. Sarah felt that this was Tatiana's way of having some power over Parsons and he agreed with her. Their conversations took place frequently and Sarah monitored them all, happy that things were going to plan.

Each evening, Sarah taught Parsons more Russian. They practiced by watching old Russian movies and reading newspapers together. She was pleased with his progress and reminded him that for now; he was learning Russian so that he could listen in to Tatiana and that he would not be required to speak with her in Russian. He was, in fact, to pretend that he did not understand enough Russian to have a conversation. They practiced this too, and Sarah would have time slots, where he was to not respond to her if she spoke in Russian. Parsons found this difficult at first, but soon got the hang of it. Sarah told him he had to learn to not show emotion or any reaction to what he heard.

'For instance,' she said. 'If when you are with her, you hear Tatiana speaking to someone on the telephone in Russian, and perhaps say something awful about you. You must ignore it and behave as though you have no idea what she is saying.'

'I can't believe that it is possible that she would say anything awful about me,' he replied with a grin. Sarah ignored his humour, pretending that she had not heard him, although she had to hide her smile.

Sarah found a small rental for him on the edge of Positano that he went to each day. It was a tiny two-bedroom house, a few hundred metres from the edge of the town, close to the sea and an isolated beach. Parsons made a point of being seen at the house on the rare occasion that there was someone staying in any of the neighbouring properties.

This part of the town was filled with holiday lets and second homes of Italians who only came to visit during the summer and on occasional weekends. Parsons and Sarah rigged the house up with cameras in each room, and removed anything that interfered with their recording. They disabled the fan in the bathroom, as they found that when it was switched on, it was so loud that it drowned out the sound of conversation on the video recordings. Several of the light bulbs were also changed, to improve the lighting in the house, and the picture quality of the video recordings. They now had two weeks left until Tatiana was due to arrive, and they were both satisfied that Parsons' new home was ready.

'I think you should move in here now,' Sarah told him as she made the finishing touches to the new house. 'It will help you behave naturally here, and it will give us time to iron out any issues that we haven't considered.'

Parsons felt sad at the thought of moving out of the house away from Sarah, and she saw it in his reaction.

'I will come here to you each day, and we will practice your Russian. You can take me out on that little red rocket of yours if you like. Rehearse the route of the guided tour you are going to give to Tatiana,' she said, lifting his mood slightly.

It was Friday and Parsons said, 'What if I move in here on Sunday? That will be OK won't it?'

Sarah smiled and came to him, giving him a big hug. He

embraced her and hugged her back as he asked, 'Have you even got a helmet?'

'I've had my helmet ready since the day I gave you the bike. I am all prepared. And you moving in here on Sunday is a good idea. I think that we should have a weekend of relaxing, that would be nice.'

Parsons and Sarah headed back to the Vico Equense, and spent the evening sat watching 'Office Romance', a Russian love story, set in Moscow. They spent that and the following night sharing a bed again, Sarah insisted she fall asleep in his bed with Parsons spooning her. It felt right this time, and he was happy to have her there, next to him, warm and comfortable. On Saturday, they spent time around the pool during the day and went into the town to eat in the evening. On Sunday, they relaxed and lay in bed until mid-morning.

'I can't believe how much my life has changed since I came here?' Parsons said as he reflected.

'For the better?' Sarah asked as she sat next to him, drinking her tea.

'Yes, definitely for the better.'

There was a silence as Parsons thought of Rebecca and the Colonel. He had pushed her from his thoughts each time she had entered them over the previous months. He had struggled at first and had longed to be with her again. But then, his thoughts would shift to her with Johnathon and he would feel a bitterness.

'What are you thinking?' Sarah asked him, interrupting his thoughts.

He proceeded to tell Sarah of the relationship that he had shared with Rebecca and of its eventual outcome. Sarah reached and put her hand on his when he finished speaking, remaining silent herself. She eventually squeezed his hand and smiled at him.

'You know, I did love somebody once, but they hurt me.' She paused as though in thought herself and then went on. 'They made me feel I was the most important person in their world. And then I learnt I wasn't. They had been playing games all along, and I meant nothing to them. They were very good at it, I'll give them that.'

Parsons listened intently as she spoke, recognising the hurt that she felt.

'That is why I wouldn't let it happen to me again. I'm stronger now and I don't need to be loved. I see how love is used as a weapon and how people like Nikolay and Tatiana abuse it. That is why I feel no guilt using it against people like them, play them at their own game. But for a moral purpose, to stop them being able to do it to people, people who need our protection.'

Parsons had not considered it in this way before. Although he had enjoyed every moment of the time he had spent at the hotel in Moscow with Tatiana, he had still felt uncomfortable that he was deceiving her and having sex with her whilst doing so. But now he understood what Sarah was saying. He was fighting against people who broke hearts, people who hurt the good in the world. It was just sex, a way to turn the tables and stop the Tatiana's and Rebecca's of this world.

'Promise that you won't ever lie to me,' Sarah asked him. 'If you have something to tell me or you have something to say, just say it.' She looked into his eyes as she said it and waited for him to answer.

'Yes, I promise,' he replied.

'I promise too.' she said.

DURING THE AFTERNOON, Parsons took the Fiat 126 to the house in Positano. Before he left, he arranged to collect Sarah the following morning when they would go out on the Ducati, exploring.

That evening, he called Tatiana on the telephone. He could tell that she was happy to hear his voice, but sensed that there was something wrong. They spoke for a while and then she revealed what was concerning her.

'Nikolay has suggested that he should come to Italy with me'. Parsons was astonished by the idea and felt a sense of panic.

'But you said that he never holidays with you.'

'No, he doesn't normally, he hasn't for years. But he called me last night and said that he feels guilty for being away so much and that he will try to alter his schedule so that he can join myself and the children. He is going to London tomorrow and hopes to return home on the 8th of July, in time to fly to Italy with us the following day.'

'How do you feel about that?' Parsons asked.

'Uzhasnyy', she replied. Parson recognised the word to mean terrible.

'What does that mean?' he still asked.

Tatiana laughed at herself and said, 'I am sorry, it means awful.'

Parsons thought quickly and came up with an idea.

'Why don't you let him change his schedule. Tell him it is a great idea and that you want him to come. Once he has made plans, move your holiday forward by a week and fly out on the 2nd instead. That way you will have a week without him, some time before he arrives.'

Tatiana thought about it for a second and said that she

would see if it was possible, whether the villa was available a week early. She said that she had some meetings to attend during the week of the 2nd of July but that she could try to bring them forward.

'Where is it exactly that you are staying when you get here? I can see if there is anyone stopping there at the moment.'

Tatiana gave him the address, which he made a note of. He suggested she should tell Nikolay that she wanted to go ahead of him, to make sure that everything was perfect and to put in to place some activities that they could do as a family. She agreed and thought that Nikolay would understand her wanting to do this as he was always restless and bored easily. He would not want to spend his time there sat around. After the telephone conversation ended, Parsons called Sarah and gave her the address of the villa where Tatiana would be staying. When he told her that Nikolay now planned to join Tatiana, Sarah could not believe the news. She said that this changed things considerably and that she would need to update their employer on the developments. A technical team went into the property a few days later, and installed surveillance equipment similar to that installed in Parsons house, only far more technically advanced.

Parsons picked Sarah up from home after breakfast, and they set off together on the Ducati, stopping at various towns and villages along the Amalfi coast. Sarah pointed out that there was an increasing risk of danger for himself considering the changes in circumstances. As they looked around the towns, she asked him security questions.

'What would be your response now, if you were ambushed or faced with a need to escape?' She pointed out escape routes and natural features that would help him evade capture and avoid gun fire if he was compromised and had to fight his way out.

In the town of Amalfi, they sat outside an eatery, at a table that overlooked a busy road. They had just visited the Cloister del Paradiso, a marvel of Moorish-style architecture dating back to the 13th century. The cold cola that Parsons was drinking was a welcome refresher in the day's heat.

'Do you see the man walking towards us along the path?' Sarah asked.

Parsons looked in the direction that she was indicating and said, 'Yes.' She was referring to a male who had just crossed the road and was walking in their direction.

'He is pulling a gun out now and speeding up as he runs at you. What are you going to do?'

Parsons looked at her and then back at the male, watching him cautiously as he walked past them and off along the road.

'You need to be ready and watching constantly. I'm concerned for you, Carl. Tatiana is a risk in herself, and now that you have Nikolay to factor in, you need to be alert. You need to be prepared to protect yourself, constantly.'

Parsons looked at her and nodded as he appreciated the point that she was making. He stood up and went into the eatery to use the bathroom. After a few minutes, he returned to the table and sat down, leaning closer to Sarah.

'There is an exit out of the back there. It leads into a courtyard, which leads into an alleyway. Also, next to the toilets, there is a flight of stairs up to the first floor. The terrace on the first floor joins the neighbouring buildings terrace and can be used as an escape route.'

'Good.' she said. 'What weapons were to hand along both of those routes?'

He nodded again, acknowledging her thinking.

'Go back and take a look,' she instructed him.

Parsons left the table again and came back minutes later.

'There are several items that could be used in a hand fight and there are knives in the kitchen, but that only has one way in and out, so I would avoid going in there if I could,' he told her.

Sarah smiled and was pleased that he had realised the danger of entering an enclosed space. 'From now on, I want you to familiarise yourself with all of your surroundings every time you change your location. Plan escape routes and look for weapons. You will be surprised what you start to notice. The pens in the pot, next to that stack of menus, they are as good as a knife if used appropriately.'

Parsons looked at the pens that he had not seen before. He looked back at Sarah, and she smiled again.

'Under the arms, in the groin, eyes, neck,' she suggested, looking at him.

He had no doubt that she was right, and that a pen could be used to cause serious harm to another human.

'Ok, I've got it,' he told her.

'Right, let's go and find a beach,' she suggested. 'I need to swim, and you need to find somewhere romantic where you can have a picnic with your girlfriend.' He looked at her, puzzled, and she sighed. 'Next week silly, you need to find a beach, where you can have a romantic picnic with Tatiana'.

'Oh, good idea,' he said, realising what she meant.

They rode further around the coast, and after a couple of hours of stopping and searching, they stumbled on the perfect location. They found a tiny enclosed cove with a small, but sandy, beach. It was a good distance from the nearest town, and although visible from further along the coast road, it was not visible from the road from which it was accessed. To get down to the beach, they rode down a bumpy track for a few hundred metres. They left the Ducati parked up and walked along the cliff edge for another hundred metres before they saw the cove and the tiny path that led down to it.

Once on the beach, Sarah took out a towel and lay it out on the sand. She sat down and removed her clothes, beginning with her jeans. Seeing her prompted Parsons to want to swim himself.

'I wish I had brought my shorts now,' he said.

'Why?' she asked.

'So that I could swim too.'

Sarah removed her bra, stood up and lowered her knickers on to the towel.

'You can swim without shorts, you know. You won't sink'. He looked at her body as she walked to the sea. She was amazing. Her backside wobbled just a fraction with each step and as she turned to speak with him, her breasts rocked only slightly. 'If you sink, I'll save you. Come on,' she said before running into the water.

Fearing that he had become aroused, Parsons candidly undressed, facing away from where she swam. There wasn't another soul on the beach, it was completely deserted. He ran swiftly into the sea, covering up his nakedness before Sarah had the opportunity to turn and see him. Like many of the beaches along this coast, the bottom dropped away sharply to deeper waters. He dived in, submerging himself beneath the crystal clear, warm water. When he came back up, he deliberately flicked the water from his hair, causing Sarah to scream out as it hit her, and went into her eyes. She blinked and wiped her face, before shouting a threat at Parsons and swimming after him. Parsons was at the peak of his fitness, having trained more since arriving in Italy. Each day, he swam for at least thirty minutes and trained in the gym at the house before running. He rippled with lean muscle and Sarah had no chance of catching him. He only came to her when she told him she thought she had trodden on a sea urchin, and that one of its spines was stuck in her foot.

'Will you take a look for me?' she asked as she trod water.

'Lift your foot up then,' he told her.

As he looked at her foot whilst holding it, she pulled on her leg and grabbed hold of him, surprising him with her speed.

She dunked his head below the water and, when he came back up, she wrapped her legs around him.

They laughed and caught their breath. It was after a few seconds that they both realised that he was erect, and that his cock was stretched beneath her, resting and pushing up against her. There was a silence as they looked into each other's eyes, just the faint sound of their breathing and the gentle lapping of the sea on the shore. She moved her mouth to his until their lips met and they kissed.

Slowly at first and then passionately, closing their eyes and gripping at each other with their arms. Parsons kicked his legs, pushing the both of them towards the beach until he felt his feet scrape on the sand below. With just their heads above the water, he felt her move and position herself so that the tip of his erection was between her legs. Pulling her head backwards, she looked at him and with a push slid forwards, feeling him enter her. She held him there, waiting, watching to see his reaction. She was not sure what was happening. She had told herself that this must not happen. Each time she had woken during the night, whilst sharing a bed with him, she had wanted to climb on top of him. She had wanted to climb on to his often-erect cock and ride him in his sleep whilst he dreamt. But she hadn't. She had resisted and remained professional, concealing her sexual frustration.

But now it had begun, and he had not pushed her away. He was holding her and he had kissed her. At that moment, she realised he had no choice, that it was she who had kissed him and she was consumed by doubt. She used her legs to slide herself backwards, to take him out of her, to stop this mistake. As she inched back, she felt the emptiness where his cock had been in her pussy. She was suddenly filled with dread, regret, and embarrassment.

As she unwrapped her legs from his waist, she felt his arms move down her back as to let her go, but then they stopped at her buttocks. He gulped as he did this, and she felt the resistance of his arms against the sides of her legs. Parsons was pulling her to him. He moved his head towards hers, closed his eyes again, and pushed his cock into her as he held her. She kept her eyes open while they kissed. He was trembling, and she could sense his nervousness. As they kissed, he made a choking noise and broke his lips from hers as he recovered. He wanted this as much as she did, and he was now as desperate as her. She closed her eyes and kissed him as she wrapped her legs around his waist and pulled him deep into her. She had not felt the touch of a man who she cared for in many years. She knew that this was wrong, but her feelings for him had grown stronger over the previous months. A fondness, at first, which had turned in to vivid fantasies of them together in various sexual situations. She had masturbated alone in her room and had satisfied herself, but when he had gone to spend time with Tatiana, she had become engulf by a feeling of loss.

As they stood in the water, locked together in a moment

of passion, she let all the emotions that she had for him override her fears. Parsons walked them towards the beach and out of the sea. As he walked, he felt the burden of her weight and lifted her higher. She moaned as she felt him move inside her and then again as he lowered them both onto the towel. He lay there, motionless, between her legs, kissing her and exploring her mouth with his tongue. She rubbed her hands over his wet skin and down to his buttocks. She pulled him into her and then released him several times as she grinded beneath, encouraging him to join her movements. He joined her, slowly at first, progressively lengthening his strokes in time with her pelvic movements. She felt him kissing, sucking and softly biting at her neck and behind her ear with such enthusiasm that it sent shivers through her body.

He raised his body at the torso, held himself up above her with his arms, and looked down at her panting beneath him. She watched him as he looked at her breasts with fascination, deliberately making them sway by penetrating her harder. She placed a hand on his chest to support him and guided one of his hands onto her breast. He looked into her eyes as he softly cupped the breast in his hand, covering the swollen nipple that sat at its peak. The centre of her nipple was a dark shade of pink, surrounded by an island of brown that was darker than the rest of the skin on her body. She saw him looking at the beauty spots that decorated her chest and stomach. He sighed loudly as he took it all in.

Looking into her eyes, he said, 'God, you are beautiful'.

She reached up to his face with her free hand. As she ran her fingers along the side of his face, she replied to him. 'You are beautiful, you are wonderful.'

As he increased the speed of his movements, he watched her eyes close and her mouth open in response. He feared he would not last long enough for her and tried to block out the heavenly sound of her moans and the brush of her pelvis and inner thighs rubbing against him. He closed his eyes, as he knew that to watch her would only bring his orgasm closer. He felt her hand pull on the back of his neck and had to let go of her breast to support himself with both arms. Sarah went silent, and when he opened his eyes, he thought she was holding her breath and was in pain. Her eyes were closed and her face was contorted, pursing at the lips. He was about to stop when he heard her moan suddenly, and her body convulsed as she climaxed and pulled him down to her. As his chest touched hers and he felt the movements of her body below him, he exploded, feeling the individual shoots of his semen being released into her. Sarah felt it pumping into her and became confused whether it was her own body or Parsons that she could feel now shaking. It didn't matter; she kissed at his neck and held him for a long time, feeling no desire to speak or move.

THE REST of the week was busy with more preparations and passed quickly. Each day, they spent hours revisiting places and practicing speaking in Russian. Sarah suggested a list of topics that he should try to include in conversations with Tatiana if the opportunity came. These included associates of hers and Nikolay, anything relating to finance and the companies, in particular any plans that they had for the future. She told him that a surveillance team would observe him as much as was possible and that there would be an emergency extraction plan in place if Nikolay was to arrive in Italy early. Sarah said that he would be contacted during the week with details of where to meet her to debrief.

It was Friday evening, and Tatiana was due to arrive in Italy the following day. Parsons was at the house in Vico Equense, sat having dinner with Sarah. They were on the terrace next to the pool and the sun was lowering in the sky. He had prepared a chicken dish that he had discovered when he had first started learning to cook. It was one of Sarah's favourites.

'I hate you for discovering this dish. It is irresistible and makes me eat far too much,' Sarah told him as she touched her stomach, feeling bloated.

'I'll never cook it again then,' Parsons replied.

'Then I really will hate you,' she said with a smile.

She poured another glass of wine for herself and topped up his water.

'Are you sure that you won't have a drink of wine?' she asked him.

'No, You Italians have built the windiest roads in the world, and I have to ride the Ducati back to Positano later. I need all of my senses for that.'

'You could leave in the morning. You have spent every night there this week,' she said.

He looked at her and saw that she wanted him to stay tonight.

'Can I ask you something?' he asked.

Sarah nodded as he thought about how to ask his question.

'Does it bother you that I am going to be with her?'

'It is your work,' she replied.

She hadn't answered his question. He wanted to ask her again - he wanted to know.

'If it was not connected to work, I wouldn't want you to be with her. But it is, and I understand that,' she added.

Parsons knew that he would have to be content with that. It was almost certainly more emotion than she was comfortable displaying.

'Will you sleep with me in my bed tonight?' he asked her.

'No, tonight I want you to join me in my bed.'

Sarah's bedroom was her sanctuary, the one place where she allowed no one else to go. As Parsons got into her bed, he realised that this was the first time that he had been into the room. He looked around at the décor that was minimalistic and spacious, but warm and welcoming. Sarah came out of the bathroom and tidied a few items of her clothing away before she got into bed. As she did this, he watched her, and realised that everything was in its place; it was picture-perfect. She set an alarm for 7am and then turned out the lights, before sliding over to him in the bed.

'Will you hold me, spoon me?' she said.

'Of course,' Parsons said, and she turned onto her side so that her back was towards him and her backside was pushed against him.

Parsons turned towards her and she pushed back against him, so that she was encased in his shape, with him spooning her. His arms held her securely against his chest and she held on to them, pushing back a little further so that every inch of her back was in contact with him.

'Good night,' she said to him, turning her face as far as she could towards him.

Parsons lifted his head from the pillow. 'Good night,' he said as he kissed her.

IT WAS several hours later that he woke from his dream. He felt the kisses on his chest first and then realised that Sarah was straddling him. Riding him so slowly, that he had not woken initially, but had believed that he had been dreaming. She sensed him waking and sat up, almost upright, creating a silhouette of her body. He moved his hands to hold her, but she stopped him and pushed them back to his side. She wanted to do it herself; she wanted him to lie there and let her do it.

As he lay there, he watched her, and imagined his hands on her body, feeling the outline of her silhouette. When he felt her movements speed up and her breathing become heavier, he knew she was close. He could not see her face clearly, but from the contractions that he felt and the sounds that she made, he knew her orgasm was flowing through her. She reached for his hands and lifted them to her waist.

'Now', she said.

He needed no further encouragement and took up the rhythm of her hips as they gyrated back and forth. It took only minutes before he orgasmed inside of her, bucking up at her as he pulled her down onto his cock by her hips. She lay above him, still straddling him, and fell asleep. It was a long time later that he carefully rolled her onto her side and held her.

15

As Tatiana's mother, Karina, unpacked the family's clothing into the various bedrooms of the villa, she wondered why her daughter had suddenly invited her to join them on the holiday. Tatiana had changed since Nikolay had become rich. She no longer recognised her daughter and now saw a cruel edge to her. She had been a kind child and even as a young adult; she had been loving and caring. Karina and her husband had been very poor back then, but they had doted on Tatiana, supporting her in her modelling career and making personal sacrifices to fund her to live in St. Petersburg, where she had eventually become a fashion model.

When she had first entered the relationship with Nikolay, Tatiana's father had warned her he was bad news and to break it off with him. But Nikolay got his way, and they married when she was twenty-three, too young to marry, in her father's opinion. Over the years, Nikolay had gone to prison several times, leaving Tatiana to fend for herself for long periods. As a result of his jealousy, he had demanded that she end her modelling career, claiming that she was sleeping with her agent and was up to no good behind his back. In the last few years, Nikolay had made huge sums of money and behaved like a business-man. He was no businessman in Karina's opinion. He was still a street thief with dirty hands. But the change in Tatiana had been so drastic. She relished in the new wealth and the power that it gave her, making her flippant and rude.

A while ago, she had given her mother a set of docu-ments and had insisted that they should be given to a solic-itor if she were to suddenly become ill or die. Her mother knew that she was caught up in some kind of mess and was involved in something sinister, but Tatiana refused to talk to her about it or let her help. She kept the documents, sensing that one day her only child would be taken from her, and that it would be Nikolay who would be responsible.

'Mother, let's go into the town,' Tatiana said in Russian as she entered the bedroom where her mother was still finishing unpacking the clothes. Karina spoke only Russian.

'Wait child, I am working,' Karina replied, annoyed at her daughter's impatience.

'We are on holiday, let's get out of here.'

'You are on holiday, Tatian, not me. I am here to look after the children. We both know that is the reason you brought me here,' Karina replied as she looked at Tatiana.

'Oh mother, can you not be happy for once?' Tatiana said, becoming cross.

'I am tired, and I need to sleep for a while. You go out with the children and I will rest for a while.'

'I think the children are tired. Can they stay and rest with you?' she asked her mother.

Karina looked away, not wanting her daughter to see the disappointment in her eyes. Not only did she show no love to her mother, but she also neglected her son and daughter, dropping them whenever it suited her to do so.

'Yes, I will feed the children, entertain them and then rest them. You have fun, be happy, don't worry about the three of us,' Karina replied sarcastically.

Tatiana made a quick telephone call, during which she sounded happier and more positive than Karina had heard her in a long time. 'At least she is happy for once, if only she could share that happiness with the children and I,' Karina thought to herself.

Once Parsons received the call, he notified Sarah, who told him that from this point onwards he was to move in to operational procedure, meaning to assume his cover role at all times. He met Tatiana in the town, picking her up in the little yellow Fiat. She immediately kissed him when she got into the car and he was shocked by how pleased she was to see him. For an instant, he felt a pang of guilt run through him, for deceiving her.

'You came,' he said to her.

'Yes, did you think I would not come to you?' she asked him.

'Well, it's just, you know. You are special, and I feared that maybe you might have lost interest in me,' he told her gingerly.

'I have not lost interest in you; I want you more than ever now.' As she said this, she put her hand into his crotch and rubbed him.

'Come on, let's go back to my place,' Parsons suggested, smiling.

'No, take me somewhere in the car, somewhere with a view,' she insisted.

Parsons drove out of Positano and up a road that climbed higher and higher as it went. When Tatiana saw a pull in at the side of the road, she pointed it out to him and insisted that they stop there. No sooner than he had stopped, that she jumped across the car and devoured him. Neither of them worried about anyone seeing them as they fucked each other in the tiny car. They were driven by a need and the excitement of the moment.

Afterwards, she sat in the car with Parsons resting on his lap as they looked down at the sea in the distance. Occasionally, another vehicle would pass them by, but they were too immersed in each other's company to care.

'Have you ever been on a motorcycle?' Parsons asked her.

'Yes, Nikolay rode one when I first met him. We went everywhere on it,' she replied.

'Does he still have one?'

'No, that was many years ago. Why?' she asked him.

'I ride a Ducati and would like to take you on it if that is OK with you.' He watched her smile grow as she listened.

'Yes, yes please. Carl, I would enjoy that very much. I remember the feeling of the wind and the speed and acceleration.'

Tatiana had always adored the freedom of being on the motorcycle with Nikolay when they had been young. The fear and danger that she had felt when he had ridden so recklessly had been addictive. Back then, Nikolay had been dealing drugs and had often had to evade the police, using his motorcycle to get away. These chases had terrified her, but she had found them stimulating and arousing.

'I can show you all along the coast. We can go anywhere,' Parsons told her. 'How much time will you have with me before your husband arrives?' he asked.

'My mother will have the children, so I can be with you lots,' she answered.

'Won't your mother ask where you have been or say anything to Nikolay?'

'No, my mother hates him. She did not like him from the first day, she will say nothing.' Tatiana had trusted her mother with many secrets in the past and knew that she could trust her with her life.

'Do you want to see my house?' Parsons asked her.

'Yes, take me there now. I want to see it,' she said as she rubbed her fingers through his hair. 'Show me everything, your house, your life, everything. I want to see everything about you, so that I can picture it when I am not here.'

Parsons thought for a second as memory snaps came into his mind. He considered telling Tatiana that she should make memory snaps, but then he thought of Rebecca and their memory snaps. He realised he didn't want Tatiana to know about his private way of remembering special moments; he didn't want her to be allowed that close to something so special.

'OK, let's go,' he said as he kissed her.

The house was picturesque, and Tatiana was correct when she said that it was a slice of heaven. It was only now that Parsons appreciated how it was in a much sought-after location, just metres from the sea and in a quiet little alcove of several houses. The cobbled road leading down to it was original and decorative, bordered by a low green wall guarded by coloured plants that filled flowerbeds.

'It is a dream Carl, this is so pretty,' Tatiana said as she stood at an upstairs window, looking on to the sea.

'You helped me make it possible. I couldn't afford it alone,' he said as he came to stand behind her and embraced her.

Tatiana had been thinking to herself whilst back in Moscow, and she wanted to talk to Carl.

'You know Carl, I have a lot of money. More money than you think, and I could help you out again'. If Tatiana could control Parsons financially, she could guarantee that he would be hers. It would also help her hide some of her money away from Nikolay, so that when the time came to leave him, she would have less to deal with.

'I don't need you to give me any more. Other than paying for this place, I am doing fine for money,' he told her.

'But it would help you and me too,' she said.

'Giving me money wouldn't help you. You would lose out.'

'I will explain it to you another day, but it would help me greatly and you would not have to worry about money again,' Tatiana assured him.

IT WAS early evening when Tatiana was dropped off a short distance from her villa. Their time together had been filled with more sex and a meal that Parsons prepared.

'Where have you been, Tatiana?' Karina asked her accusingly.

'Seeing the town.'

'For five hours?' she asked.

'Yes, I went for a walk and the time passed quickly,' Tatiana lied.

'Nikolay called after you. I said that you had just left to fetch food. He will call back soon.'

'Thank you, mother,' she said, feeling guilty for neglecting this old woman who always supported her.

Karina was leaving the room when Tatiana called to her.

'Mother, I love you. And I know you were right about Nikolay. You and father were both right. I wish I had never laid eyes on him, but soon things will be different. Maybe then I can be a better daughter to you, and you will forgive me.' Tatiana wanted things to be different. She hoped that her mother could see that. But she knew that this would never happen.

'Maybe, maybe one day, Tatiana. For your children I pray so.' Karina left the room and went to get the children ready for bed.

Nikolay called and spoke with Tatiana. He was his usual hurried self, and she wondered whether he would actually join them. She prayed he would not, but her prayers were dashed when he told her he would try to join her sooner if he could. She went to sleep with mixed emotions. Sadness at the prospect of soon seeing Nikolay, and the anticipation of being on a motorcycle with Parsons in the morning.

Before Tatiana left for the day, she gave her mother a stash of money and walked into the town with her and the children. The children, Vlad, aged six, and Alexandra, aged four, were excited at the prospect of going to the beach with their grandmother. There was a swimming pool at the villa, but they wanted to build sandcastles and were looking forward to buying buckets and spades.

'Be careful,' Karina said, as Tatiana kissed her on the cheek. 'And be back before he calls you tonight,' she warned her daughter.

Parsons waited for Tatiana at the agreed meeting point, feeling apprehensive. He had brought a helmet with him for her to wear. As he waited, he played with it, showing signs of his nervousness. When she arrived, he hugged her tightly and kissed her for a long time, knowing that a long-range camera was being used to photograph them.

'Are you ready?' he asked her.

'I am ready. Please go-fast Carl, I like it,' she told him.

Parsons looked at her, and she explained herself.

'I enjoy going fast. Go as fast as you can, I like the feeling.'

'I'll see what I can do then,' he told her with a smile.

They took the Ducati along the coast road all the way to the beautiful town of Vietri Sul Mare. This was a long journey, but Sarah had suggested that the distance would give Parsons opportunity to see whether he was being followed. The long straights would identify any pursuing vehicles. If Parsons kept his speed down on these, any pursuer would be forced to overtake and give up their cover. Even though Tatiana encouraged him to go faster, he waited until the twisty bends before he unleashed the motorcycle's power. Once they arrived in Vietri Sul Mare, he was satisfied that they were not being followed and relaxed into the day. He spoke in Italian and taught Tatiana several new sentences that she practiced. Each time he taught her a sentence in Italian, he insisted she taught him one in Russian. He deliberately got the sentences wrong and falsely confessed to Tatiana that he had given up trying to learn Russian as he found the pronunciations too difficult.

'Shch, that is not an easy sound to make,' he told her, after he failed to say a word correctly.

'If I come to be with you in Italy, you will never need to speak Russian ever again,' she told him as they sat having lunch.

Parsons raised his glass and toasted with Tatiana.

'To being in Italy,' he said as they touched glasses.

'To being in Italy,' Tatiana repeated his words.

'Do you have to work whilst you are away, or did you move all of your meetings?' Parsons asked her.

'No work. I will speak on the telephone when I need to,

but other than that, I have no work. I left Mikhail to cover things.'

'Is he as good as you? Will he do it properly?' Parsons asked. 'I would worry that if I employed someone they wouldn't work as hard as myself.'

'He only has small things to do, but yes, he can be trusted. He is not stupid. If you employed someone, Carl, you would ensure that they worked harder than yourself. I employ lots of people and I insist that they all work hard or I fire them. Because of this I can relax and not worry.'

Mikhail was Tatiana's assistant, fixer. He was a former KGB officer who had returned from East Berlin after the collapse of the Soviet Union. He was not as bright as Tatiana gave him credit for, but what he lacked in intelligence, he made up for in cunning.

'So, you are completely mine?' Parsons said as he touched Tatiana's arm, stroking her.

'I am completely yours,' she agreed as she looked at him, pleasantly admiring how handsome he was.

Together they looked around the town, visiting the church and walking through the narrow streets, browsing the shops. They headed back along the coast to Maiori, where they toured the castle ruins above the town. An elderly Italian gentleman led them around and explained the castle's history to them. Parsons translated for Tatiana where he needed to, and she listened to his every word intently. At the church in the town, they stopped, and Tatiana remarked how the coloured domes on its roof reminded her of St Basil's Cathedral in Red Square.

The day was passing quickly, and so they made their way back towards Positano. They spent the last part of the afternoon in the house's bedroom, Parsons once again dominating a submissive Tatiana. As they lay in bed afterwards, she fell asleep and he had to wake her.

'Why do you make me feel the way you do?' Tatiana asked him.

Startled, Parsons asked her, 'What do you mean?'

She laughed and apologised for her English. 'I mean, how do you make me feel the way that you do?'

'How do I make you feel?' he asked her.

'Safe and happy.'

The guilt came to him now, and he had to dismiss it from his thoughts.

'I don't know. But you make me feel happy and important,' he replied.

'You are important,' Tatiana told him.

'And horny, you make me the horniest man alive'. As he said this, Parsons sank down onto the bed and licked between her legs. Once they were finished, they hurriedly showered together and dressed, trying to make up the lost time.

'I have to speak with Mikhail soon. I must get back to the villa,' Tatiana told him as she was putting on her shoes.

I will take you back to the villa in the car as soon as you are ready,' he offered.

This time, he took Tatiana closer to the villa so that she would not be late. When she left, he drove back to the house as quickly as he could and called Sarah immediately.

'She is about to receive a call from someone called Mikhail,' Parsons told Sarah.

'Who is he?' she asked.

'He is the person who Tatiana has left to attend to her work while she is away. He might be an assistant or something.'

'Good, I will have it traced and find out who he is. Are you OK?' Sarah asked.

'Yes, you?'

'I'm fine. You left your watch in my room, do you not need it?' she asked.

'No, not anymore.'

'How do you tell the time?' she said, confused.

'I have another watch.'

'Oh, OK. Do you need to meet at all?' she asked him.

'No, I am OK.'

'I'll get that call traced,' Sarah said.

'Great, speak later.'

'Buonanotte,' she ended.

Parsons went down to the sea to swim for a while. As he swam, he attempted to clear his head of his thoughts and to just exercise. But he couldn't empty his mind and his thoughts jumped from Sarah to Tatiana to Rebecca. He had different emotions for each, but they were all strong enough to trouble him. His emotions for Rebecca were souring, and he felt angry at her careless disregard for his love that he still knew existed for her, buried somewhere in his heart. For Tatiana, he felt guilt and perhaps sympathy. Was she a victim, or was she as bad as Nikolay? He sensed she had a bad streak in her personality, but what he was doing to her was no better than what Rebecca had done to him. Or was it? He couldn't decide. And then there was Sarah. He felt something with her, but something different from how he had felt about Rebecca. It was not as consuming, but it was strong and he felt it was sincerely mutual, equally dependant.

Parsons stopped swimming and floated face down in the water. He felt his legs slowly sinking and let himself fall. He felt weightless, and the sensation was comforting. He held his breath and made a memory snap, appreciating the feeling rather than the view. As he ran out of breath, he pushed towards the surface and lifted his head free of the water.

As he broke the surface and shook the water from his face, he saw a figure on the path leading down to the house. A man. He was stooping, waiting and watching the house. He moved closer to the house as Parsons watched, and then he went to the Fiat that was parked outside. Suddenly, he ducked out of sight. Parsons remained where he was, silently treading water. After a minute, the figure of the man reappeared and hurriedly walked back up the path and out of sight. Parsons waited several minutes before he swam back to the shore and walked up to the house, avoiding the car.

He dressed and walked into the town, which was bustling with holiday makers. He walked around the streets, circling back on himself and stopping where he could to conduct counter surveillance. He spent several minutes looking at the display in a shop window, using the reflection of the glass to watch behind. He saw no trace of being followed and so went into a small guest house. He asked the lady at reception if he could make a call and gave her ample money to do so. She agreed, and as he monitored the entrance; he called Sarah. He explained what he had seen, and she told him to not use the car until it had been checked for incendiary devices. She told him where a pistol was hidden in the house and insisted that he keep it with him tonight.

Parsons returned to the house and retrieved the pistol. It

had been many months since he had held a weapon and it felt strange in his hand. He checked it was loaded and went to bed in the spare room, keeping the pistol next to him in the bed. When he woke in the morning, he felt relieved that he was still alive, but then convinced himself that he was being overdramatic. He ate some breakfast and was interrupted by a noise outside that he went to check on. He was met by a telephone engineer who said that he was there to check the line as there had been problems in the area. He said that the neighbour, a Miss Rantsu had reported the problem, and that they shared a line, so he needed to check the one at this address too. Parsons understood the message and left him to his work. When the telephone rang, Sarah spoke first.

'You made it through the night then?' she asked.

'Yes, are we secure?' Parsons asked.

'Yes, it was just checked.'

'I know I saw him. Has the car been checked yet?' he asked.

'Yes, during the night, it's fine. I checked on Mikhail too. He is a former KGB, now he works for Tatiana. He is not a pleasant person.'

'Did you listen to their call?' Parsons asked.

'Yes, she spoke with him. She arranged for him to put a tracking device on the car. We have left it in place. It would have been Mikhail that you saw last night. He is here, staying in Positano.'

Parsons was shocked and felt anger at Tatiana's deception. This was ironic, he thought. He was deceiving her, but felt cheated to learn that she had done the same.

'What does this mean now?' he asked.

'Nothing. I don't think that you are in any increased danger. She is doing basic checks on you for her own protection. If she didn't do this, it would be more worrying. Once she is happy that you are not up to no good, she will call Mikhail off. You still have the tracker on the car, so just be cautious that you don't take it anywhere compromising. And remember that Mikhail will know where you are if you both go out in it.'

'Fine, thank you for sorting it out,' he said.

'You are welcome. I was actually checking that my little car was safe.'

'It's my car now,' he pointed out.

'It is not. It's still mine. You can choose any car you like once this is finished.'

'From me and my car, goodbye,' he laughed.

'If you hurt my car, I will push your silly Ducati off the edge of a cliff. Be careful, bye.' Sarah hung up the call and Parsons went to get ready.

Parsons sat waiting for Tatiana to arrive at their meeting point, watching as people passed by, wondering if Mikhail was amongst them. When he saw her approaching with an enormous smile, he got off the bike and walked to meet her. He gave her a kiss and tried to sense if there was anything different in her reaction. When she looked at him, he was sure that he saw nothing but affection in her eyes. Sarah was right, Tatiana was playing safe by getting Mikhail to do some checks on him.

'Good morning. Are you ready for some more fun?' he asked her.

She nodded, and they headed off along the coast road on the Ducati again, but in the opposite direction today, towards Naples. Parsons rode the Ducati hard, filtering through any stationary traffic as they passed through towns and thrashed the engine when the roads were clear enough to. They arrived at Pompeii by mid-morning to find that the crowds were already beginning to build at the world-famous archaeological site. Once inside, Parsons showed Tatiana around the once thriving Roman city, that had been buried beneath ash and pumice after the eruption of Mount Vesuvius in 79 AD. They held hands as they walked around the excavated site, looking into the remains of the houses and shops. They went in to the Lupanare, the brothel and saw the preserved menu of services painted on to the walls. These were detailed sexual illustrations that the ancient visitors to Pompeii, travellers as well as residents, used to select the services that they desired. Tatiana pointed at one illustration on the menu and told Parsons that this was her choice for later.

When they left the ruins, they went to the beach that Parsons had been to with Sarah. They also swam naked and frolicked in the sea. As they lay on the sand afterwards, drying in the warm afternoon sun and eating the picnic that Parsons had prepared, Tatiana asked him questions about his past.

'Why did you leave England for Italy, Carl?' she asked him.

One thing that he had learnt from his training was that sticking as close to the truth as possible was always a better option than inventing a lie that you might forget at some point.

'I had my heart broken,' he said.

Tatiana paused and he could tell that she wanted to ask him.

'Someone told me they loved me, and I believed them. But they were in love with someone else,' he explained.

'And you loved them?' Tatiana asked.

'Yes, I did. But not any longer.' As Parsons said the

words, he sensed the watch missing from his wrist, and it felt strange.

'I used to love Nikolay. I loved him for a long time, but after so many years we grew apart and I saw he did not love me any longer. After a while, and a lot of other women, I knew he was only staying with me for the children and to keep up the image that he wants people to see,' she told Parsons.

'That is hard. I'm not sure how you cope with that.' He felt for her, he felt for anyone who knew of love unrequited.

'It is not for much longer. I have plans to leave him, Carl. I have been planning it for a while now,' Tatiana said.

'If he is as you say, will he let you leave? Will he not stop you or leave you penniless if you go?' Parsons was trying to lead her to answer some of the hidden questions he had.

'He would let me leave, unofficially anyway. But you are right, he would attempt to leave me as a pauper. He would do everything that he could to control me. But I have allowed for this in my plans.'

'How can you do that if he is so powerful? Surely he will come after us?' Parsons deliberately spoke of him and Tatiana together in the future. She picked up on it instantly and he saw the satisfaction in her smile.

'Nikolay trusts very few people. But because he believes he controls me, he trusts me. He entrusted me with detailed records of all his business dealings. And for my security I made a copy of these, which I gave to my mother. If anything happens to me, she knows what to do with these documents, they are safe with her. He registers almost all of his investments in my name, hundreds of millions of pounds and euros all over the world. The only things that are in his name are in the UK, where he believes he will be safe if they find out what he is doing,' Tatiana said.

'The British government? They won't help him if they find out that he is stealing from them.'

'Not the British government, the Vozrozhdeniye.' Tatiana said the word as though Parsons should know what it meant.

'The what?' he asked.

'The revival or resurgence. It is a group that exists in Russia. They are the country's wealthiest men and they control everything that happens.'

Parsons deliberately looked puzzled and frowned at Tatiana. He felt reassured that she did not suspect him of being anything other than what he pretended to be, otherwise she would not be telling him this.

'Nikolay is one of them. He gets rid of money that they must hide. Money from drugs, extortion and corruption. They can only declare so much money through their business interests, so they use Nikolay to wash the rest of it for them. Billions Carl, enough money to build a whole new country.'

Parsons looked at her and waited to see if she would say more. After a while, he broke the silence.

'Surely these people will come after you? If the money is registered to you and Nikolay gets caught doing whatever he is doing, they will want the money back and will come after you and me,' he said.

'That is not important. I have been dealing with this problem. It will be fine.' She smiled to reassure him.

Parsons stroked the side of her face and smiled at her. 'I bet you don't want to go back to Russia, do you?'

'I will have to for now. But one day things will be different, and then maybe I will come to Italy and be free from him. Free to live my life as I wish to.'

Parsons leant over and kissed Tatiana. She was in some

ways a victim of all of this, and he hoped she would get her life back again someday. They returned to the house and had only a little over an hour before Tatiana had to leave to be with her family. As she dressed, Parsons asked her when Nikolay would be arriving.

'Hopefully never. Hopefully, he will vanish into thin air.' He watched as she dressed and wondered how Nikolay could want another woman. Tatiana was truly beautiful, an amazing lover and great company. When she saw him watching her, she asked him why he was looking at her.

'You are lovely,' he replied.

She laughed and asked him what he meant.

'I think Nikolay is crazy. If I was with you, I would make sure that you were as happy as I could make you,' he replied.

'You are with me, and you do make me happy,' she told him.

'I mean, if I was with you all the time.'

Tatiana came and joined him on the bed. 'Maybe you will be with me all the time. One day, once Nikolay is gone.'

'Do you think we could be together?' he asked her, injecting enthusiasm in to the question.

'Why not? The future is not yet written.'

16

Nikolay received the call from Mikhail early on Monday evening. Mikhail contacted him shortly after he had driven back from Pompeii. First, he emailed the latest photographs of Tatiana holding hands with Parsons, as they had walked around the tourist attraction. He had spared Nikolay, having to see photographs of the pair together on the beach. They would have confirmed nothing that the other photographs didn't already. Mikhail had first met Nikolay many years ago when he was a colonel in the KGB and had interrogated him. Nikolay had been under suspicion of selling weapons to Afghan rebels. These suspicions had been well founded, and it had only been by setting up one of his accomplices that Nikolay had able to draw the blame away from himself. Mikhail had always known that Nikolay had been guilty and had often thought that he should have eliminated him at the time, back then.

As he now reflected on the years, he felt bitter at how the times had changed, how the fall of the Soviet Union had made it possible for the low life criminals to take over. Mikhail accepted he had flouted the law countless times, but only for the preservation of his sacred mother land. He had been approached by Nikolay after he had left the service and recruited as a fixer. Mikhail did whatever Nikolay requested of him, intimidate, spy, kill, whatever was required. For the last year, Nikolay had given him the task of protecting his wife, Tatiana, and their children. Nikolay was rarely at home and had wanted someone that he could trust to monitor things in his absence.

Tatiana was easy to be around, and because she knew he was answerable to only Nikolay, she had not made life difficult for him. In fact, she had been very good to him, treating him as one of the family. Mikhail had divorced a long time ago and had no family of his own, so he welcomed Tatiana's kindness. In return, he had agreed to turn a blind eye to the life that she lived in her husband's absence, even himself looking after the children at times. She trusted him implicitly, and he had become her confidant and friend, giving her advice and protection beyond what Nikolay had requested. She now employed Mikhail also and paid him handsomely to deceive Nikolay. He was fully complicit in her plans.

'Mikhail, how are you?' Nikolay asked him in their native Russian.

'I am good; however, I am angry for you Nikolay. Did you receive the email that I send to you?'

'Yes, I did. Is she with him now?' Nikolay said.

'No, she is with her mother, at the Villa.'

'Good. You have done well. Are you happy with the rest of the details for when I arrive?' Nikolay asked.

'Yes, everything has been arranged and is ready. There will be no mistakes,' Mikhail replied.

'You never let me down Mikhail, you will soon be back by my side. Once this is done with, you will not need to follow that bitch any longer.' Nikolay had missed having

Mikhail around since he had sent him to watch his wife. Tatiana had believed that she had turned Mikhail, and that he had not reported back to his boss on her behaviour, her young boys that she spoiled and fucked.

'It is my work; it is what I do Nikolay. But it will be good to be away from her and the children,' Mikhail replied.

'Very well, I will arrive tomorrow evening as planned. Goodbye.' Nikolay ended the call before Mikhail could respond and he heard the line go dead.

Tatiana sat opposite Mikhail in a room at the house that he had rented for himself in the town.

'It is fine, he will arrive tomorrow evening as planned,' Mikhail said as he turned to Tatiana.

'Did he sound suspicious at all, Mikhail?' Tatiana asked nervously.

'No, he is so confident of his superiority that he wouldn't see it even if it was burning the end of his nose. He is a fool.'

Tatiana nodded, and although she knew how arrogant Nikolay was, she still had the sense of dread in the pit of her stomach.

'Good, we should continue with the plan,' she said.

'Yes, let him walk straight to his own death. It should have happened years ago, when he was helping the Afghan's.' Mikhail had a look of disgust on his face, and Tatiana remembered his hatred of Nikolay for the treason that he had committed against the state.

She nodded in agreement with Mikhail.

'Just be sure that your boy is here on time. That is essential to our plan,' Mikhail stated.

WHEN TATIANA RETURNED to the Villa, her mother was in uproar, refusing to talk calmly with her. 'You have brought me here just so that you can go out and be like a teenager. You abandon your children. You are no fit mother,' she shouted.

'Mother, I am sorry,' Tatiana tried to apologise.

'You are not sorry. You have never been sorry, not even when you broke you fathers' heart and married that monster of a man. You are not sorry, Tatiana.'

Tatiana knew that her mother was right, she had broken her father's heart. She knew also that she was not a good mother. She had no feeling of remorse at all for leaving her and the children all day. They were a weight around her neck, and she longed to be free again.

'Mother, I am sorry and tomorrow I shall spend the whole day with you, Vlad and Alexander, to show you I am sorry. Please mother, forgive me and let me make this up to you,' she pleaded as she followed Karina through the villa.

'We will see, Tatiana. In the morning we will see if you are sorry and can find a minute of your time for your mother and your children.' Karina ended their conversation, slamming the door of her bedroom shut as she passed through it.

Tatiana called Nikolay first and listened as he told her he would arrive in Italy early than planned, on Thursday.

'I will catch a taxi from the airport. I will be with you around 4pm. Then we can go out, just the two of us. Tell your mother that she will need to look after the children. She will understand that we need time together, yes?' Nikolay told her.

'Nikolay, that would be good, to have time with just you like in the olden days,' Tatiana replied. She struggled to not tell him how he was the vilest man she had ever laid eyes on, and that she would soon dance around his dead body. He thought he was coming unannounced to kill her, but he would have a shock when he learnt she was waiting for him.

'Then I will call you tomorrow evening. Good night,' Nikolay said with a bitter taste in his mouth.

'Good night my love,' she replied, matching his deceit.

The next call that Tatiana made was to Parsons at his home in the town. He was there alone, having just returned from taking a swim, when the telephone rang.

'Hello,' he answered the phone and immediately heard Tatiana.

'Hello, baby, are you missing me?' She asked him.

'Yes, I am. I have a surprise for you tomorrow, and I can't wait to show you,' Parsons told her.

'Tomorrow I cannot come with you in the day. My mother is refusing to care for the children. But in the evening you could join me at the villa. My mother will be away for the night, she is going to take the children on a trip to Rome for a few days. We could make love in a new bed and in the swimming pool. I think it would be fun.'

Parsons considered that having recordings of the two of them together in Tatiana's villa would be of good evidential value, and that he should take her up on the offer. Plus, it would give him a chance to see if there was anything there that he could recover that would be of interest to Sarah.

'But I won't see you all day. We will have to make up for it during the night,' he said.

'I promise you I will give you a night to remember. Carl, I am going to send some money to your account. I can explain what it is for tomorrow when I see you. Is that alright with you?' she asked him.

'Yes, of course. What time should I come to the villa tomorrow?'

'Can you come at 7.30pm please, baby? And then I will be ready for you,' Tatiana replied.

'Yes, I will see you then, beautiful.'

When the call ended Parsons went to call Sarah but stopped himself. Instead, he went out to the Ducati and started it up. Once he had ridden a few miles out of Positano, he pulled off the road and waited five minutes to see if he was being followed. While he waited, he inspected his bike, looking for any tracking devices. He was soon happy that he was neither being followed nor that the Ducati had a tracker planted on it. He rode as fast as he could to Vico Equense and parked in the centre of town. From there, he took a route on foot through several side streets to ensure that he was not being followed. He used the track from the town that led up to Sarah at the house. Once there, he was cautious not to startle her and called out to her from the courtyard. Upon hearing him, she leant over the upper terrace wall and told him to come inside.

She met him as he walked through the main living room and looked at him, wondering if something had happened.

'What is wrong? Why are you here?' she asked him.

'She has changed the plan for tomorrow. I have to meet her in the evening instead of in the morning. She wants me to go to the villa for the night. Her mother and the children will be away.'

'You could have told me this over the telephone. Where is your motorcycle?' Sarah asked him, a little concerned.

'I parked it in the town, and I checked I was not being followed.'

Sarah was now standing in front of him and looked concerned.

'I'm sorry you are right. It is stupid of me to risk coming

here. I can go,' he said, realising that he had taken a dangerous risk coming to see her.

He went to turn and leave, feeling embarrassed at his naivety and impulsiveness.

'Wait,' Sarah said.

Parsons stopped and turned back to Sarah, expecting her to be angry at him. She leant forward and stood on her tiptoes to kiss his lips. As she did this, she reached up and wrapped her arms around his neck. She kissed him for what seemed an eternity, and then halted.

'You have exactly two seconds to take me in to your arms. And if you don't, I am going to hit you, Carl Parsons.'

As she said it, he was sure that he could see a tear in her eye and the slightest tremble in her voice. He didn't wait for the two seconds to pass; he took hold of her, lifting her from the floor and kissed her. Sarah was glad to see him and although she knew that him being there carried risks, she just wanted to hold him for the time being.

They went to bed and experienced the most sensual love making that Sarah had ever known. She surprised herself by how intimate she felt with this young man who she had known for only months. Her fear of the lapse in her emotions intensified her passions and, although it felt counterintuitive, she leapt into this new world that Parsons had introduced to her.

As they lay in bed the following morning, Sarah updated Parsons that Nikolay would arrive in Positano on Thursday, and that it appeared that he was attempting to rekindle his relationship with Tatiana. Sarah relayed to him the evening's conversation that she had listened in on when Nikolay and Tatiana had spoken.

'How did Tatiana respond to that?' Parsons asked Sarah.

'Well, but she may have been acting for his benefit. If he

arrives on Thursday, tomorrow is going to be your only chance to find what you can inside the Villa. Documentation, electronic devices that she uses, you know what you are looking for,' Sarah replied.

'What about Mikhail? Do you think he is a threat at all?'

'I don't think so. He has been following you each day, but that is for her protection and on her orders. I think he will keep out of the way and you will be alone with her. She doesn't have any suspicions about you, or you would be dead by now,' Sarah said.

She smiled at him and he replied sarcastically, 'I most certainly aren't dead. I'm very much alive.' As he said this, he ran his hand across Sarah's body and looked at her suggestively.

'Oh yes, you are look. Let's not put that to waste, hey.' She climbed on top of him, and he was only too happy to oblige.

PARSONS PARKED the Ducati outside the house in Positano, changed and went down to the beach. It was midday, and he relaxed on the sand. He saw the lady who had been staying in one of the other houses near to his. She waved as she came down onto the beach. She walked towards him and came to join him where he was sitting on his towel, reading a book.

'Hello, what a beautiful day,' she said in Italian.

'Hello. Yes, it is lovely again, isn't it?' Parsons replied, being friendly. 'This weather spoils us, and the location too, it is out of this world.'

'Yes, my family has been here for three generations, before the town was so busy. My grandfather found this spot and when he married my grandmother, they bought the house. Sorry, my name is Greta.' She held out her hand to Parsons as she introduced herself.

'I'm Carl. I'm renting the house just there. Nice to meet you, Greta.'

'Yes, I've seen you and your friends about it's nice to meet you too,' she replied.

'Ah, that would be my friend Tatiana that you saw.'

'And the man, the foreign one, we see him too. My grandmother thought he was your father,' Greta commented.

Sarah had shown Parsons a photograph of Mikhail and he guessed Greta was referring to him.

'When did you see him?' Parsons asked.

'He has been here for a while, a week maybe. We see him in the town most days too.'

Parsons felt a touch of concern that Mikhail must have arrived ahead of Tatiana and could have been watching him prior to her arrival. If this was true, Mikhail would surely have seen Parsons together with Sarah and would have reported this to Tatiana. But as Sarah had said, if Tatiana had any suspicions about him, he would be dead by now. So why had Mikhail come to Positano so far ahead of Tatiana?

'When did you last see him?' Parsons asked, trying to not alarm her.

'This morning, early this morning. He was inside the house; did you not see him?'

'I was sleeping, I am in holiday mode and I have become lazy,' Parsons laughed with Greta.

'Well, that is OK, we all need to rest sometimes,' Greta told Parsons, before she said that she was going to swim. He said goodbye to her and collected his belongings before returning to the house. Once there, he put the radio on, loud. Then he looked around for any listening devices that Mikhail had planted, but found nothing other than the ones that he and Sarah had fitted.

Parsons was curious about what Mikhail had been doing at the house and why he was paying him so much attention. If he was simply Tatiana's protection, why was he risking coming into the house when Tatiana was not there. He felt uneasy and could not shake off some doubt that he had surrounding Mikhail's role.

Tatiana spent the day with her mother and the children in the town, making a show of spoiling them. Although Karina knew she was being bought, she welcomed some attention for the children and herself. Tatiana spoke a little Italian and conversed with the local traders when they commented on the children. This made Karina proud that her daughter was so clever and could learn a new language.

'Would you take a photograph of us?' Tatiana asked a waiter as they sat at a restaurant at lunch time'. They posed for the picture in which Tatiana hugged her mother with affection, again making Karina feel proud. They returned to the villa in the late afternoon and Tatiana sat with her mother around the pool whilst Vlad and Alexander played.

'Why will you not join me for a drink, Tatiana?' Karina asked.

'Because you have done so much for me, mother. Today you shall drink and I will care for the children.'

Karina looked at Tatiana and wondered where this new show of kindness that her daughter was displaying had come from.

'What has changed in you, Tatiana?' her mother asked.

'You mother. What you said to me last night. I am sorry for what I have put you and father through in the past.

Father is gone, but I want to make it up to you now. I want to be a better daughter and a better mother.'

'What about a better wife?' Karina found herself saying aloud.

Tatiana had loved her father dearly and had been devastated by his death two years ago. She had never had the same bond with her mother, who she felt had always held her father back in life. She loved Karina for being her mother, but she did not like her as a person. She was part of the old system that believed that the people should work for a better country and that luxuries only encouraged weakness. She criticised everything that Tatiana had ever done, her modelling, her marriage, even the way she mothered her own children. She hated the woman and wished that she could sit with her father instead, the parent that she had loved.

'Yes mother, that too.'

Karina had little faith in Tatiana's words. She had watched her ways all of her life and she would not change. But for now, this act of hers was pleasant and she would drink while she could.

At a little before 7pm, Tatiana was satisfied that her mother had drank too much vodka and helped her to her bedroom for a sleep. When Karina insisted, she needed to put the children to bed, Tatiana assured her that tonight she would see to them and that she should get some rest as they would all be going out on a trip early tomorrow. As Karina fell asleep, she prayed that this change in her daughter would be genuine and lasting.

Tatiana put the children to bed and once they were sleeping, she hurried to get herself ready for when Parsons would arrive. She had little time, but as she looked at herself in the mirror, she was satisfied that she still had the figure and the looks that men had always chased her for. She could soon use them as she wished and to have the life that she deserved.

It was 7.15pm, and she had only fifteen minutes until Parsons would arrive at the villa. Mikhail had gone to the airport to collect Nikolay and would return at 8pm as planned.

After placing a pair of gloves onto her hands, Tatiana went to the draw in her bedroom and retrieved the gun that Mikhail had given to her, along with the small container of liquid that he had prepared for her to put into Parsons' drinks.

Mikhail had agreed to help Tatiana kill Nikolay. It had been his suggestion, in fact, and he had planned most of it for her, using his KGB training and experience. He had been reporting back to Nikolay, misleadingly informing him of her affairs and encouraging Nikolay that he should catch her in the act. The original plan had been to use Sergei as the bait for Nikolay to catch her with, but that waste of space had suddenly vanished, ruining their plans. But then Carl had come along, and everything had fallen into place, giving them the perfect opportunity. Tatiana had become lovers with him and had joined him in Italia, deliberately getting away from Russia and Nikolay's influence over any investigations that would need to take place there.

Mikhail had arranged for Nikolay to come to Italia early to catch Tatiana and Parsons together in the villa. Nikolay believed Mikhail would then kill Tatiana, the children, and her mother, framing Parsons for doing so. Nikolay would claim to find Parsons in the villa with their bodies and would immediately call the police.

But of course, this would not happen, Tatiana thought to herself. Nikolay was being double crossed by Mikhail.

Instead, when Parsons arrived at the villa, his drink would be drugged by Tatiana and he would soon be dazed and incapacitated. Mikhail would then bring Nikolay to the villa, where he would find Tatiana and Parsons together. But as soon as he entered the villa, before he could do anything, Mikhail would shoot and kill him. Carl, who would be present, would be framed for killing the husband of his new lover, who had caught them in the act of their lovemaking. It was a stroke of genius by Mikhail, and she had only one other job to do before Parsons arrived.

Tatiana put music on loudly and prepared drinks for herself and Parsons. They would drink these once he arrived. She added the liquid to his drink and was satisfied that there was no trace of it visible.

Tatiana went through the villa to her mother's bedroom and went inside. Karina was sleeping on the bed and snoring. As she looked at her mother, she remembered her childhood and the happy days that there had been back then. For a moment, she wished that things could be different, but nothing could be allowed to impede her new life. The gun had a silencer fitted to it, but she still wrapped a pillow around it, as Mikhail had instructed her to. He had said that this would reduce the spread of ballistic residue released from the gun when it was fired, limiting any forensic evidence being on her own body.

'Goodbye mother,' Tatiana quietly mouthed as she put the pillow containing the gun to her sleeping mother's head and pulled the trigger. The sound of the gun surprised Tatiana, causing her to jump a little. There was an eerie silence, and then she lifted the pillow away from Karina's head to see a small hole in her temple. An awful smell suddenly hit her as she saw a red patch growing on the pillow beneath her mother's head. Tatiana left the room and walked along the corridor to the children's room. First she shot Vlad and then Alexander.

She wrapped the gun in a towel and placed it where Mikhail had instructed her to, in the electrical services box outside the villa's entrance. He could collect it from there on his way in to the villa and then use it to shoot Nikolay.

As Tatiana stood in the villa's kitchen, she looked at the clock and saw that it was 7:28 PM. Parsons would arrive any minute. As she drank from her drink, she realised she was shaking. She thought of the children, dead in their room, and wondered why she felt no sadness. There was no emotion at all and she realised Karina had been correct, she was not a fit mother and had never been. Her thoughts were interrupted by a knock on the door and she snapped back to reality, realising that Parsons had arrived. She went to the door to let him in.

Upon seeing him, she felt strangely erotic. 'Quickly, come in,' she welcomed him as she gave him a kiss.

'Hello, you look amazing,' he told her as he admired her beauty.

She was wearing a simple short dress and appeared different to him. He wasn't sure whether it was the new setting or that she wasn't her usual glamourous self. However, she looked and seemed different tonight. She led him into the lounge and gave him a drink. She sat next to him on the sofa and they chatted about how their respective days had gone while they drank.

Tatiana did not understand why at first, but she wanted Parsons so desperately. Then she realised this would be the last time they would be together. He would soon be arrested and would spend a long time in prison. He was a condemned man. The thought of him being unaware of his impending doomed fate arouse Tatiana, and she had to have him. Tatiana leapt across at him and kissed him as she lifted her dress up over her head, removing it.

'I want you. Take me here on the sofa,' she demanded of him.

They were finished quickly, and Parsons still panted as he watched Tatiana dress. She poured herself another drink and gulped it down. As he put his clothes back on, he realised that it wasn't that she looked different tonight. It was the change in her mood that he had sensed when he had arrived at the villa. Tatiana was more controlling, both during their sex and in her demeanour. He watched as she went to fetch him another drink and then returned, joining him on the sofa. She was definitely different tonight.

'Should we go out for dinner?' Parsons asked.

'Yes, give me a few minutes to get ready and we can go,' Tatiana said before going to freshen up. She was behaving strangely.

Parsons went to stand up to use the bathroom, but as he did, he stumbled and fell to the floor. He saw Tatiana come to him to help, but she stopped short and looked down at him.'

'I am sorry baby, I wish you could be with me in my new life, but I need you as part of my plan.' She walked away and went to her room to wait for Mikhail to arrive with Nikolay.

Parsons felt as though his head was spinning round and round. He knew Sarah would be listening to the recording equipment and so he shouted for her to help. He felt drunk. Each time he shouted; his speech became more slurred. He kept trying to shout, but doubted whether he would be heard through the recording equipment that he prayed Sarah was monitoring.

There was the sound of a key in the door that slowly opened. Parsons could not lift his head enough to see who it was. Nikolay entered the villa first, followed by Mikhail, who was a second or two behind him. As they entered Parsons' view, he recognised them both from photographs and he wondered if he was imagining this.

'Sarah,' he shouted out just before he felt a kick to his ribs. He was lifted and punched once, impossibly hard in his face, causing him to crash across the room, breaking a coffee table that he landed on. He heard the room around him being trashed, and he thought they must have Tatiana.

'Hello Nikolay,' he heard Tatiana say calmly. He was confused. What was happening and why was she so calm.

'Tatiana, how pleasant to see you. Has Karina been dealt with, and the children too?' he asked.

Tatiana smiled and confirmed that they had.

'Yes. And now it is time for you to be dealt with, you peasant,' she told him.

Parsons listened to the conversation and tried to move, but he was too weak and his muscles would not respond. What was happening? What was Tatiana doing?

'Really. Are you not pleased to see me?' Nikolay asked her.

Mikhail had the gun in his gloved hands and stood across the room from Nikolay, pointing it at him. Nikolay looked at him.

'What is this, Tatiana?' he asked as he looked back at her again.

'This is what you deserve. Mikhail works for me; he has done for all of this time. He knew you as a common thief and a traitor, which is what you will always be. He brought you here with the intentions of killing you, getting rid of you as he should have done a long time ago. I want you to know that once you are dead, I will live happily with your money and I shall dance on your grave.'

'Mikhail, what is she saying?' Nikolay asked as he turned to face his trusted friend.

'Do not turn away from me, you fucking pig. Look at me so that I can see your eyes as you die,' Tatiana shouted at him.

Nikolay looked at her and shook his head. He took a deep breath as though to calm himself and thought before he spoke.

'You were always a trollop, from the day that I met you. And had you not given birth to them brats, I would have had you taken care of a long time ago. I will soon become a father again, and this time it will be with a young beautiful woman who loves me as much as I love her,' Nikolay said.

Parsons was still confused by what was playing out in front of him and, although he could not stand, his senses were returning to him.

'Mikhail, shoot him quickly so that I cannot hear his voice any longer,' Tatiana ordered with a vengeance.

Mikhail lifted his arms slightly, aligning the gun with Nikolay's head. Nikolay began to laugh and shook his head at the situation.

'I promise you, you little bitch, that you won't hear my voice again.'

'Shoot him Mikhail, quickly,' Tatiana said.

Mikhail pulled the trigger and the muffled sound of the bullet startled Parsons as it left the barrel of the gun and travelled through the silencer. He moved his head millimetres and watched for Nikolay to slump to the ground. But he didn't. He stood there, unaffected by the shot. Instead, there was a crash where Tatiana fell backwards, colliding with a sideboard filled with ornaments, before falling to the floor. Her eyes were wide open, and she looked to be about to speak from her gaping mouth. But she was silent - she was dead.

Mikhail moved first, coming across the room to Parsons. He applied the safety catch on the gun and then held it in Parsons' hands, wrapping his palm around the pistol grip and putting his finger on the trigger. He did this numerous times, leaving several of Parsons' fingerprint impressions. He admired the damage to Parsons' face and complimented Nikolay on his handy work. Nikolay had gone to look in the bedrooms at his children and mother-in-law.

Parsons lay there as they moved around the rooms, preparing the scene before they called the police. He heard a knock at the door and felt the tension between Nikolay and Mikhail as they paused, waiting, hoping that whoever it was would leave. The knock came again and a muffled voice called out. Mikhail carefully looked through a window and told Nikolay that it was OK.

'It is a woman. Answer the door and tell her to call the police for you. I will leave through the back,' he said. He began to leave the room and then remember something. 'Wait.' He walked up to Nikolay and ripped at his shirt and punched him in the face. Nikolay barely flinched, but it would bruise and he understood its necessity.

Mikhail left and after a second, Nikolay went to the door and opened it as quickly as he could.

Parsons saw the opening of the door as he strained to move his head and heard Nikolay's panicked voice as he pleaded for the person at the door to call for the police and an ambulance. He was hysterical and started to cry. It was with surprise that Parsons heard him silenced and watched as he walked backwards into the room, raising his hands as he did. Sarah followed him, holding a gun to his stomach.

'Keep going, over there,' she said, indicating for Nikolay to go to the sofa. 'Move, sit down.'

Nikolay sat down on the sofa and looked at Sarah.

'I can make you rich,' he said. 'Very rich.'

Sarah cut him off as he spoke. 'Shut up,' she told him calmly as she moved towards the doorway that Mikhail had left through.

There was a sound and movement at the front door, which Sarah turned towards in response. As she did so, she saw Mikhail coming through it and realised that Nikolay was now moving towards where Parsons was lying on the floor. She saw the gun half resting in Parsons' hands and watched as Nikolay reached out for it.

Sarah fired one shot into his chest and another into his face. Before she could react further, Mikhail ran into her, sending them both crashing into the wall after stumbling over Tatiana's dead body. Sarah struggled to retain her hold on the gun as Mikhail's huge hands slowly wrenched it from her grip. Sarah drew back her head and threw it forward into his face, directly onto the bridge of his nose. As he loosened his grip and screamed out, she threw the gun across the room, knowing that if she kept it, he would soon take it from her. Sarah lifted her knee into his groin, striking him so hard that she felt the shock of it through her own body. As she did this, she pushed her thumbs into the sockets of his eyes, forcing his head backwards. Mikhail responded to the pain and raised his hands above his shoulders before driving them down onto the top of Sarah's head. She felt her neck crunch and her brain shake inside her skull. She felt dizzy and weak, but fought against the sensation of sleeping that came over her. She was helped by the blow that she received to her chin, bringing her back to her senses.

Mikhail had now got on top of Sarah and placed his

hands around her neck, tightening his grip and strangling her. She tried to twist and throw him off balance by raising a hip to one side. But he was too heavy and she could not budge him an inch. Sarah spat into his face, and he loosened one of his hands to slap her. As he did this, she took hold of the hand that was still around her neck, restraining it and with her other hand, she punched his arm at the elbow, forcing it against its natural bend. Mikhail screamed out at the pain of the damaged joint and Sarah took her opportunity, twisting the arm until she heard it snap from its joint in his shoulder. Mikhail refused to give in and swiped at her with his good arm, hitting her about the head with blows that struck with terrible, damaging force. Sarah felt one last strike and realised that she was losing consciousness. She felt Mikhail's hand around her throat and heard a bang, after which he slumped onto her, crushing her upper body. Helpless, she lay there, desperately trying to recover herself.

Suddenly, Mikhail rolled from her and she gasped for air as the pressure was lifted from her chest. Parsons looked down at her and shook her gently.

'Are you Ok?' he asked.

'What a stupid question,' she thought, but still nodded to him. As he stood, she saw he was unsteady on his feet and dazed.'

'I need to find the documents that Tatiana gave to her mother,' Sarah heard Parsons say, and he was gone. She moved a little and felt pain in her neck, but she had to get up. The police could not find them here. The recording would help them if they were arrested, but they would still face prison sentences and an international scandal beyond reproach. It took time for Sarah to get to her feet, find her gun, and then collect the one that Parsons had shot Mikhail with. She went through to the bedrooms and saw Vlad and Alexander lay dead in their beds. The sight sickened her, and she wondered what must have happened to have driven a mother to do this. Sarah had been monitoring the events from a safe house and had heard the muffled shots via the video cameras as Tatiana had executed her mother and the children.

Parsons came to her, holding a large brown paper file in his hands. He held it up for Sarah to see.

'I've got it,' he told her.

'We have to go now,' she told him and they both left the villa through the back door.

Using the car that Sarah had parked a short distance away, they returned to the house in Vico Equense. They stopped only briefly at a cliff edge to discard both guns into the sea. As soon as they got to the safety of the house, Sarah went through a routine of destroying their clothing and removing any forensic evidence against themselves.

As they showered together, Sarah instructed Parsons to scrub himself again and to start from the top of his body working downwards.

'The cameras in the villa, they were watching us,' Parsons said, panicked, realising that they were still in place.

'It's all Russian equipment. We do not need to worry about it,' Sarah said confidently. 'The authorities will think that this is to do with Nikolay's associates back in Russia and the cameras will only help with that notion.'

The following morning, the papers had an article on the massacre of a family in Positano and suggested that it was linked to organised crime. The town was awash with police investigators and Sarah said that she and Parsons should lie low for a few days until the press attention had calmed down.

The following week, word that the Russian mafia were involved spread and took away any suspicion of local involvement. Sarah sat with Parsons on the terrace, still bruised from the beating that she had received from Mikhail.

'You are looking better today. Your bruises are fading well,' Parsons told her.

'You should be ashamed of yourself to even mention them,' she replied.

Parsons smiled and said, 'I've told you, I could not move a muscle. I felt terrible watching on as you fought that big lump.'

'And as you say, you then suddenly became free of the spell and 'hey presto,' you could move again. Just as I had kicked his ass all by myself,' she said in mock disgust.

'Yes, straight after you shot him. That's right, I remember now,' Parsons said sarcastically.

'Well, at least you did that. Eventually. It was your saving grace.'

'How about I make it up to you?' Parsons offered.

Sarah looked at him and wondered what he could have in mind.

'How?' she said, smiling.

'I've been thinking. Now I am a millionaire; I could take you on a trip somewhere.'

As part of Tatiana's plan to start a new life, she had transferred ten million euros to the bank account in Parsons' pseudonym name. She had meant for it to appear to the authorities that Parsons had been blackmailing her and that when she had refused to give him any more money; he had killed her whole family. But of course, her plan had been cut short by Mikhail's allegiance to his friend and boss, Nikolay.

'Have you forgotten something?' Sarah asked him

'What?' he asked her, puzzled.

'The file that you took from Karina contains details of the Vozrozhdeniye. We have a lot of work to do,' she said seriously.

'Have you ever been to Macau or Hong Kong?' he asked her.

'No.'

'I read through the file and it appears that one of the Vozrozhdeniye has based themself in Hong Kong and spends a lot of time in Macau,' he told her. 'Maybe I could take you to Hong Kong for a while.' Parsons was smiling now, and he saw the look on Sarah's face.

'So, it would be work?' she asked him.

'Absolutely,' he said.

'Can we have a week at home first? I need a little more rest and then I will be ready to face the world.' She stood up and came to sit on his lap. 'Plus, I still haven't received a response from our employer. We are awaiting new instructions.'

'Well, I suppose it will give us time to play with my jet ski,' Parsons said, realising that his new toy had completely slipped his mind.

It was later that day the Sarah finally received a telephone call from Mac Thomason. He had read her report and was satisfied with the outcome.

'I think he was the right choice,' Mac told Sarah.

'Yes. The Colonel did well to find him,' she said, looking outside through the kitchen window. She could see Parsons lay on a sun lounger at the pool, rocking his foot as he listened to music through headphones.

'On his next task, he will work alone. How soon can he be ready to leave?' Mac asked her.

Sarah was not ready for this question and hesitated. A myriad of thoughts ran through her mind and she realised Mac was waiting for her to answer. Her breathing sped up, and she felt flushed.

'Sarah, are you there?'

'Yes, yes, I'm here,' she replied. 'Immediately I suppose.' She felt a familiar hard coldness returning, and she instinctively turned her back to the window.

'Good, I'm going to send him to meet Mark Cranborough. He will be his handler from now on. He needs to be in London in twenty-four hours for the introduction. Can you get him there for me?'

'Yes, that won't be a problem,' Sarah assured Mac. Once she had all the details she required, she said goodbye to Mac and hung up the telephone.

She wondered what it would be like to be normal. To marry, have children and a family to spend time with at Christmas and on other special occasions. To have a husband to love and to be loved back. To have a soul mate. She closed her eyes and took a deep breath before she did what she knew she must.

'Carl,' she called out as she walked out to join him at the pool.

It took Sarah less than five minutes to explain the new situation to Parsons. Even she felt that what she was doing was brutal, but she could do it no other way. When he asked if he would return to Sarah and the house afterwards, she replied she doubted he would. She told him it was too dangerous for them to remain in the same place together now.

'We may work together again in the future, but there is no way of knowing until it happens,' she told him. 'You are fully trained now Carl; you don't need me around anymore.'

PERPLEXED, confused and alone, Parsons boarded a flight to London the following morning. Sarah had hugged him when she dropped him off at the airport, but had not kissed him. He felt it was as though she had no feeling for him and that their time together in Italy had meant nothing to her. As the flight sped along the runway and climbed into the sky, Parsons realised Sarah was no different to Rebecca. She had drawn him in, letting him believe she cared for him. At that moment, Parsons vowed to never let another person do this to him again. Never would he feel this pain over anyone else. He would meet up with the contact in London and he would do what he had been trained to do.

He had not known at the time why he had taken a memory stick from the paper file he had retrieved from Tatiana's villa on the night of her death. He had given the file to Sarah, but he had kept the memory stick that had accompanied it.

As he held it in his hand he felt that it had been a wise choice. He had no idea what the information on it was but it had been security for Tatiana. He placed it into his pocket and looked out of the window. He smiled inwardly to himself when he saw the bright red roofs of the buildings that he had seen when he had arrived in what now seemed like a lifetime ago.

As Pippa left her office and entered the intel room, she

saw one of her staff remove a sheet of paper from the fax machine. He was keen to deliver it to her, knowing the importance of these messages and the secrecy that they were protected with.

'It's for you, Maam,' he said, handing the paper over. 'It says that he is coming back here.'

'ANTEROS   RETURNING.   EROS   DEPLOYED. STANDING BY.'

Pip read the message herself, understanding its seriousness and the urgency that it created.

Although her pulse raced, she smiled and calmly replied, 'Thank you, Martin. It certainly appears so. You know what to do. Please inform the others and see that Rebecca comes to my office immediately. Send a car for her without delay.'

As Pip sat in her office waiting for Rebecca, she considered the options that were now available to her. She wasn't sure whether this was the right time, but after everything that had happened and the future that was inevitable, she felt the urge to make her move. But she would wait until Rebecca arrived, until she made her decision.

To Be Continued.